T0354556

The Gift

REBECCA L. MASKER

Order this book online at www.trafford.com
or email orders@trafford.com

Most Trafford titles are also available at major online book retailers.

Printed in the United States of America.

ISBN: 978-1-4669-4724-5 (sc)
ISBN: 978-1-4669-4726-9 (hc)
ISBN: 978-1-4669-4725-2 (e)

Library of Congress Control Number: 2012912475

Trafford rev. 07/11/2012

 www.trafford.com

North America & international
toll-free: 1 888 232 4444 (USA & Canada)
phone: 250 383 6864 ♦ fax: 812 355 4082

PROLOGUE

August 1997

*J*ulie Forrester sighed heavily as she fastened the catch on her last suitcase. Her father was loading boxes into her battered Ford Escort while her mother spent a few last precious moments with Carly. Part of her was aching to run and tell her parents she had changed her mind, but she knew she had to be strong. Julie sighed again and sat down on her bed, stripped of all the bedding, and looked around the barren room.

This was the first time in her memory the room had been empty and the sight of it gave her a sharp pang of sadness deep inside. Julie hated this, hated it with everything she had, but she couldn't stay in this town any longer.

Rising from the bed Julie grabbed the handle of her suitcase and dragged it out of her bedroom and down to the front door. She considered taking one last look around the house she'd grown up in, but she knew that would be pressing her luck. Her emotions were already running on overdrive and she was determined to stay strong. Getting a good grip on her suitcase again she managed to heave it down the steps and out into the driveway. Her car was packed to its very limit and she had no idea how anything else would fit in it, but she would leave that to her father for the time being.

Her mother was holding Carly, cuddling her and talking softly to her. Julie knew how much her leaving was hurting her parents. They loved their only grandchild more than life itself and Julie felt terrible for what she was putting them through. They knew she had to try and make something of herself though; not for her, but for Carly. She might be only eighteen but she wasn't stupid. Being a single teenage mother in a strange place was going to be the hardest thing she'd ever done, but she was going to give it everything she had.

"Mama!"

Carly had caught sight of her mother and was now attempting to climb out of her grandmother's arms. When Julie saw the sad look on her mother's face as she took Carly from her it sent another horrible pang of guilt and sadness through her.

Julie opened the back door of the car and buckled Carly into her safety seat. The two year old cried as she was restrained but Julie merely kissed her cheek and closed the door, turning to her parents. Two years of parenting had taught her when to ignore the tears and tantrums and when not to. This was one good time to pretend Carly wasn't making a sound.

Jeremy Forrester had his arm wrapped around his wife, Elizabeth. Both of them looked sadder than Julie had ever seen them. For a long moment the three of them just stood there until, finally, her mother opened her arms and Julie went to her gratefully. Hugging her mother Julie felt the first of the tears prickling behind her eyelids and she blinked hard, forcing the tears back. She'd toughened up over the last two years. Raising a child as a single teenage mother without any contact from Carly's father had forced her to grow up and learn the hard way how tough life really could be. Tears were a luxury she rarely allowed herself anymore.

"Take care of yourself, little girl. You and Carly will always have a home here, no matter what."

Julie gave her mother one more hard, quick squeeze and then gently but firmly pushed her away, brushing angrily at the tears that had managed to escape and were trickling down her cheeks. She turned to her father almost reluctantly. She knew this would be her hardest goodbye and she wasn't sure just how to handle it.

Her father smiled at her and opened his arms. Julie stepped into them, resting her cheek against the softness of his flannel shirt, and inhaled deeply, breathing in the scent of his cologne and the pipe smoke that always lingered around him. They were the familiar smells of her childhood and she wanted to burn them into her memory to take with her to Arizona. Her father's embrace was warm and safe and a part of Julie longed to stay there forever and not worry about the future at all.

As though he could read her thoughts her father whispered in her ear, "You don't have to do this, baby. You and Carly can have a good life right here."

Julie felt the old doubts and fears gnawing at her insides for the umpteenth time, but she shoved them away and forced herself to smile up at her father.

"I do have to do this, Daddy. I have to try. If it doesn't work we'll come back and go from there. But I'm not giving up without a fight."

Her father brushed her hair back and cupped her face in his hands. "Make sure that when you stop for the night it's a well-lit area with good strong locks on the door. There are a few bucks under the ashtray in case you run short on cash."

Julie leaned up on her tiptoes to kiss her father's cheek. "You didn't have to do that, Daddy."

Jeremy Forrester smiled at her though he was unable to hide the sadness etched into his features. "Of course I did. You know very well I could never let you and Carly leave without giving you a little something."

Julie managed a small smile as she turned away from her parents and climbed behind the wheel of the car. She was buckling her seatbelt and half listening as her parents opened the door to say goodbye to Carly one last time.

"Be good, baby love. Grandma loves you so much."

An errant tear slipped down Julie's cheek and she tried desperately to steady her breathing as her mother kissed Carly's cheek and moved aside.

"Bye, honey pie. Be a good girl for Mommy."

Julie's father kissed Carly goodbye and shut the door. Carly was babbling happily in her seat and playing with one of her stuffed toys. Julie was relieved that her daughter was distracted enough not to notice her emotional upheaval.

Opening the passenger side window Julie looked over at her parents. "I love you guys. I'll call the first time we make a pit stop."

Without another word Julie rolled up the window and started the car. She avoided looking at her parents as she backed carefully out of the driveway and pulled out onto the road. Despite her determination not to cry the tears came anyway. When she reached the stop sign at the end of the street she'd grown up on Julie put the car in park and gave in to the wave of emotion threatening to overwhelm her.

Julie leaned her head against the steering wheel and cried for what felt like hours. When she was certain the tears had dried up she wiped her face on the sleeve of her shirt and put the car in gear again. She had a two day drive ahead of her and the old familiar determination was beginning to come back full force. She'd given in to her moment of weakness and now she was ready to move on.

"What do you think, baby girl? Are we ready for our big adventure?"

Julie smiled at Carly in the rearview mirror and was rewarded with a stream of happy babbling from her daughter. Carly's face gave her another burst of determination and she focused all of her attention on the trip that lay ahead of her. Arizona was waiting for her; her very first apartment, college and a new start away from all the bad memories of the last two years.

Turning on the radio Julie felt her spirits lift considerably as Carly began trying to sing along to what was playing. Peeking into the rearview mirror Julie saw Carly bouncing around in her safety seat, trying to dance, and she laughed out loud. As long as she had Carly she knew she'd be all right.

When Julie entered the on ramp to the highway for the first major stretch of the trip she began to feel the first twinges of excitement. She'd always been daring and adventurous and this was certainly the craziest thing she'd ever done. Julie was determined to make a better life for herself and for Carly and she was hell bent and determined to see it through to the very end.

Feeling her spirits begin to lift Julie began singing along to the music with Carly as they headed into the unknown towards their new future.

CHAPTER 1

March 2005

*J*ulie sat curled up in one of the patio chairs outside the townhouse she shared with her now ten year old daughter Carly. Carly was still asleep inside and the sun was just beginning to show itself. Even though it was only March the temperature was already well into the high sixties and Julie knew it was going to be another muggy Arizona day.

Taking a sip of her tea Julie leaned her head back against the chair and closed her eyes. She hadn't slept well the night before and she was fighting serious exhaustion. Carly had been a living nightmare the last few weeks. Almost every single morning before school she whined about not feeling well, pouting and even throwing a tantrum one morning when Julie insisted she attend school. Julie was rapidly growing tired of her daughter's attitude and was determined to find a way to nip it in the bud once and for all. How exactly she was going to accomplish that was as yet unknown, but she knew she'd figure something out.

Draining the last of her now cold tea Julie rose from the lawn chair and stretched, wincing as the bones in her back and neck crackled painfully. Entering the house she dropped her empty cup in the kitchen sink and, after peeking in to check on Carly, headed upstairs. Hopefully a hot shower would make her feel more human. She stripped out of her pajamas and tossed them in the general direction of the laundry basket. She kept her tired eyes closed as she turned the shower on and stepped under the spray. The hot water worked to loosen her sore muscles and as she reached for the bottles of shampoo and body wash on the shelf.

Julie cherished these little moments she had to herself in the morning. As dearly as she loved her daughter sometimes it felt good to be alone. Carly had been acting so strangely lately. Julie didn't know whether or not to be annoyed with Carly or worried about her. Lately she was leaning more towards being annoyed and she hated herself for feeling that way about the only truly good thing in her life.

For the last few years her life had taken on a rather monotonous routine and sometimes she longed for a change. Other times Julie welcomed the familiarity her routine offered her and she fought hard against change. Carly had been trying to convince her to get out more but Julie always found an excuse. She couldn't help but feel a tiny bit hurt that her daughter was trying so hard to get rid of her in the evenings when they spent quality time together.

Julie wasn't even able to really enjoy time with her best friends anymore. They were badgering her constantly about spending all her time either working or with Carly. Julie had been introduced to half a dozen eligible bachelors just in the last few weeks and she'd politely, but firmly, turned them all down and then turned her wrath on her friends who remained utterly unabashed. The last one they'd introduced her to appeared to be a little perverted and Julie had been scared that she'd find him waiting in her car when she left the clinic after work.

It was all too easy for Julie to remember with vivid detail how terrified she'd been when she first arrived in Arizona. Leaving home had seemed like a great adventure, something necessary that she'd done for the sake of her child, but suddenly finding herself in a strange place where she knew absolutely nobody had terrified her so badly she'd been half tempted to turn the car around and go back home to her parents.

Life these days was comfortable if not extravagant and that was just how Julie liked it. Growing up firmly set in the lower working class of a blue collar family she'd grown up understanding that things were tough and you had to work for what you got. She'd taken that attitude with her when she'd taken Carly across the country to Arizona to start a new life together and it had paid off in ways Julie had never dared to dream.

After leaving Maryland she and Carly had gotten settled in their new apartment with nothing but the bare necessities to get them through. The first few years in Arizona had been both incredibly difficult and, at times, utterly terrifying. More than once Julie had been faced with such exhaustion and anxiety that she'd seriously considered just saying the hell with it and moving back home where her parents could help take care of her and Carly. Those moments of self-pity were few and far between though, thank God, and the closer she got to finishing with medical school the less often they came to haunt her.

The landlady of the apartment where she and Carly lived, an older woman named Virginia, had been an absolute angel in disguise for Julie. Virginia had babysat Carly whenever Julie needed her and she hadn't charged an extraordinary amount of money. The thought of sending Carly to daycare had been horrifying, especially when Julie realized how much the average daycare charged. Working as a cashier in a local Wal*Mart had given her enough money to pay the bills, pay Virginia for babysitting Carly and put food on the table. Occasionally Julie would manage to save enough money to treat Carly to a movie or something but it was rare and Julie struggled with severe guilt for denying her daughter a better life.

Things had gradually gotten better once she finished medical school and got a job as an ER doctor at the local hospital. The hours were erratic at the beginning but it was worth it. She no longer had to worry so much about the bills and was able to do more fun things with Carly. Years of hardship had taught Julie a few lessons and she continued to put aside money for emergencies. The year before she had been able to put a down payment on the townhouse and she and Carly moved out of the apartment that had been their first home in Arizona.

Not living next door to Virginia had been hard, especially on Carly who looked at the woman as a surrogate grandmother, but Carly still went to Virginia's after school three days a week so at least they were still able to see each other.

Life was pretty damn good now and Julie was proud of herself for not giving up. She had a good job, she had an amazing kid and she had great friends that she knew could be trusted to be there for her and Carly no matter what. The only thing missing in her life was a man and it wasn't until quite recently that it really hit her that she might want a man in her life.

Julie had been at the bar with her friends having a few drinks, a ritual they had twice a month, and they had all been talking about Julie's lack of luck and experience with men. Her friend Sienna speculated out loud the possibility that Julie's working parts had probably shriveled up and fallen off from lack of use and Julie, who had just taken a sip of her drink, snorted laughter and sprayed the mouthful all over the table and her friends. All four of the girls had nearly fallen off their stools they were laughing so hard.

That night though the conversation had reentered Julie's mind and she wondered if Sienna might not be partially right at least. She hadn't been with a man since she'd gotten pregnant with Carly and that experience hadn't exactly made the Earth move or anything. Ten minutes with a boy she'd been desperately in love with and the next thing she knew her life was changed forever.

Kevin Meyers had been everything Julie had ever wanted and when he finally gave her the time of day Julie had been ecstatic. They'd known each other all their lives and had "dated" once before when they were in 1st grade. Julie hadn't been worried when she first found out she was pregnant with Kevin's child; at least not until Kevin disappeared. Less than a week after telling him she was pregnant Kevin and his family had left town and Julie hadn't heard from any of the Meyers since then.

When Carly was born perfectly healthy seven months later Julie had cried tears of relief and happiness. When she filled out the birth certificate she defiantly gave Carly her own last name, not wanting her little girl to be saddled with anything belonging to her so-called father. Though Carly had frequently asked about her father when she was younger she'd learned that the subject was better left untouched and had ceased asking questions about him.

Julie had been torn between guilt and sheer relief when the questions stopped. She was still bitter over Kevin's betrayal but that wasn't the real reason she didn't want to talk about the man. Ten years after she last saw the boy who fathered her child Julie still had feelings for him. She tried desperately not to think about Kevin because whenever she did the empty part of her that longed for a man seemed to throb and surge with almost painful intensity.

The water in the shower had gotten a little too cold for comfort and Julie stepped out, wrapping a towel around her quickly to keep from dripping water on her bedroom carpet. Opening the closet door she reached for her scrubs and laid them on the bed. Removing the towel and tossing it in the hamper she turned to the full length mirror that hung on the inside of the closet door and looked at herself critically.

At just twenty six years of age her body was still fit and firm. She was curvy without being plump and yet slim without being scrawny or looking undernourished. Her shoulder length brown hair was tinted with shades of blonde, one of the few luxuries she allowed herself, and her brown eyes were a soft coffee color. She supposed she was attractive in her own way. She had been told more than once that men had stopped to give her a second look but she was usually too busy to notice. It was rather depressing at times.

Sighing Julie forced herself to push the memories of her past behind her as she dressed for work, sitting on the bed to tie the laces on her comfortable sneakers. She pulled her hair back into a sensible ponytail and left the room, turning all the lights and the ceiling fan off before closing the door.

Julie heard Carly yawn and stretch before she even opened her daughter's bedroom. With her first real smile of the morning Julie knocked gently on Carly's bedroom door.

"Come in."

Carly still sounded half asleep, Julie thought to herself as she entered her daughter's room and perched on the edge of the bed. Carly was still buried under the covers with just her head poking out and, once her still sleep blurred eyes focused on her mother, she smiled.

"Morning, Mom." The words were barely coherent amid another jaw cracking yawn from Carly and Julie couldn't help but chuckle at how alike she and her daughter were.

Nothing had made Julie more grateful than to see Carly grow up to look so much like her. Julie had been terrified that Carly would favor her father and that she would be forced to reconcile her anger with Kevin each and every time she looked at Carly. Thankfully she was spared from having to deal with that and she thanked God for it every day.

Julie gently tucked an errant strand of Carly's dirty blonde hair behind her ear. "Morning, ladybug. You still feeling bad?"

Carly had been complaining of feeling ill the night before but now she shook her head. "No, I think I'm all right now. What time is it?"

"Not quite seven. You still have plenty of time to get ready for school."

Julie got up from her daughter's bed and started to leave the room. Turning back to Carly she said firmly, "Do not go back to sleep, young lady."

Carly flashed an overly innocent smile and Julie couldn't help but laugh. It felt good to laugh and it was Carly who made her laugh more than anyone else. Julie truly didn't know what she'd do without Carly.

In the kitchen Julie popped a couple of Toaster Strudels in the toaster and listened as the shower was turned on in the bathroom. Despite her determination not to think about the past Julie couldn't help it when her mind started to wander again.

Julie would never tell Carly this but she knew where Kevin was. He had come to her parent's house a few years after Julie left town. When Jeremy and Elizabeth Forrester refused to tell him where Julie and Carly had gone Kevin had left his card with all of his information on it and begged them to tell Julie he wanted to contact her. Julie had the card tucked in her wallet behind all the others but she'd never even attempted to call him or e-mail him.

Part of Julie hated herself for keeping the card; many times she ached to tear it into little pieces and sever all of her ties to Kevin Meyers. Another, more mature, part of her insisted that she keep it in case of an emergency. What sort of emergency would require her to contact Kevin she didn't know, but Julie felt a little bit safer knowing she could contact him if absolutely necessary.

Julie was again woken from her reverie, this time by the sound of Carly closing her bedroom door and bounding down the hallway into the kitchen. She was dressed for school in a pair of faded jean capris and a short sleeve t-shirt that would be relatively cool on such a stifling day.

"Do you want apple or cherry?" Julie asked as she put the Toaster Strudels on a small plate while Carly poured herself a glass of cranberry juice.

"Cherry," she said and sat down at the kitchen table. Julie joined her with their breakfast and a cup of coffee for herself. They ate in companionable silence and when the last bite was gone Julie rinsed the plate and her coffee cup.

"How would you like to go see a movie tomorrow night, Carly?" she asked

"Cool!" Carly exclaimed. "What movie?"

Julie put the dishes in the drain and sat back down again. "I was thinking about that new Disney movie; Ice Princess. I saw the preview last night and it looked cute. I thought maybe we could do a little shopping and get some lunch while we're at it. Maybe even get our nails done. We haven't had a girlie day in a while."

Carly's eyes lit up and the next thing Julie knew Carly had leaped from her chair and thrown her arms around her in a crushing hug.

"Thank you, Mommy!" Carly cried right in Julie's ear, nearly deafening her.

Julie laughed and hugged Carly tight, savoring the closeness she still shared with her daughter and knowing that the day would come, probably sooner rather than later, when Carly would have better things to do than spend the day with her mother.

Glancing at the clock on the stove Julie gently disentangled herself from Carly. "Go get your stuff, baby; the bus will be here any minute."

There was a new urgency in the way they bustled about the house. Julie rummaged in the depths of her purse for her car keys, cursing when she couldn't find them until she looked up and saw them hanging up on the hook by the front door. Carly had retrieved her backpack and was waiting outside. Julie closed the door and locked it, then walked Carly to the end of the townhome complex parking lot to wait for the bus.

They made it with just seconds to spare. They'd no sooner reached the entrance to the parking lot when the big yellow bus lumbered its way down the road and stopped with a screech of brakes to open the door for Carly.

"Morning, Dr. Forrester."

The bus driver, an elderly man named Hank, called down to Julie with a broad smile on his cracked and leathery looking old face.

Julie smiled up at the old man. "Good morning, Hank. How's Alma been feeling?"

Hank's wife had been ill off and on for several months and Julie had her doubts about whether or not the woman would survive to see the new year. She was quite surprised when Hank grinned at her and said, "She's feeling perkier than I've seen her in quite some time. Thanks for asking, Doc. You coming up there, Carly girl."

Julie hugged her daughter and gently shooed her onto the bus. Carly climbed the steps and took her seat next to her best friend Bree. Julie waved as the bus doors closed and all three of them; Carly, Bree and Hank waved back.

Julie watched the bus drive away until she could see it no longer and then went to her car. She was still driving the battered old Ford she'd come to Arizona with and was thoroughly convinced that the only thing keeping the piece of junk running was her own sheer force of will. Putting the key in the ignition Julie made the first of what would end up being several attempts to start the car, wincing slightly at the deafening rumble of the engine when it finally caught.

She put the car in gear and winced at the sudden loud backfire and resulting cloud of noxious fumes that poured from the muffler. The EPA would have a field day with her, Julie thought as she babied the car out of the complex and onto the main road. Even with the windows rolled all the way down the overpowering odor of exhaust permeated the interior of the car and she was soon feeling a bit lightheaded and dizzy.

As she navigated the familiar streets of Scottsdale Julie took a moment to appreciate the beauty of the area she now called home. Living in Scottsdale was a dream come true for Julie. After growing up in Baltimore, surrounded by good friends and good neighbors, she'd been determined to raise her daughter in a similar environment. Though downtown Scottsdale was often described as the desert version of Miami Beach it had character and was rich in history, something that was important to Julie.

Scottsdale had been inhabited, originally, by the Hohokam. The Hohokam was one of four major prehistoric archeological cultures in the part of the United States now known as the American Southwest. The first Anglo to stake a claim on Scottsdale was Jack Swilling in 1868. Swilling started the Swilling Irrigation Canal Company to improve the irrigation system originally constructed by the Hohokam, but it would be another twenty years before the population really began to boom.

The town was still known as Orangedale when George Washington Scott became the town's first resident. The land now known as Scottsdale had been purchased by George's brother Winfield in the 1880's. The Scott brothers were adept farmers and were known to have encouraged new settlers to create a desert farming community. The name of the town was changed to Scottsdale in 1894.

Scottsdale continued to thrive and was officially incorporated in 1951. Scottsdale is defined by its high quality of life and, in 1993, was named 'Most Livable City' by the United States Conference of Mayors. It was well known as being a good place to raise children and that had been important for Julie. The whole area was beautiful and after eight years she couldn't imagine ever living anywhere else.

Breathing deeply of the fresh air outside Julie slung her bag over her shoulder and headed into the building, waving to half a dozen people she recognized on the way. Julie specialized in pediatric medicine and opening her own clinic had been a dream come true. She had been overjoyed when the practice grew so big that she had to take on a second doctor as her partner.

Nancy, the clinic receptionist, was sitting in front of her computer drinking a Diet Coke. Julie figured that Nancy, who was kind but rather plump, was attempting to diet again for the umpteenth time since Julie met her and the thought brought a smile to her face.

Nancy looked up from the computer screen and smiled brightly at Julie. "Morning, Doc. Your 8:30 appointment had to cancel so you have some free time this morning."

Julie rolled her eyes in disgust as she sat in the chair beside Nancy to look over her shoulder at her appointment schedule.

"I'd be more surprised if Mrs. Dillard hadn't canceled. It's a good thing Cameron's only due for a check-up." Julie noted that her first appointment would now be at 9:30 which gave her about an hour to work on an article she was planning to submit to a local medical journal.

Entering her office Julie sat down behind the desk, locking her purse in the bottom drawer, and turned on her computer. It seemed to take forever for the system to load, but finally Julie was able to access her documents and open the article she had begun working on the day before.

For the last few years, actually ever since she finished medical school, Julie had been keeping up to date on innovations in pediatric medicine and was never hesitant to give her own opinion on often controversial topics. She'd been given a rather flattering award from a nationally recognized medical journal for being the youngest doctor to ever be published in that particular journal.

Julie was seated at her desk in front of the computer typing rapidly when someone knocked on the door and Nancy entered carrying a manila folder which she placed on Julie's desk. "Mr. Sharp and Lindsay are ready for you."

"Thanks Nancy," she said, saving her document as Nancy left the office, closing the door behind her. Julie draped her stethoscope around her neck, picked up the file folder and went from her office to the adjoining exam room.

"Hi, Lindsay. How are you this morning?" Julie smiled brightly at 6 year old Lindsay Sharp who gave her a dazzling smile in return. Mr. Sharp remained seated in his chair where Lindsay could see him but he, unlike many parents, gave Julie space in which to work. She greatly appreciated that respect from him.

"I'm good," Lindsay crowed as Julie gently began to examine the little girl.

"Anything in particular I should be looking for, Mr. Sharp?" Julie asked as she listened to Lindsay's heart (which was normal), checked her blood pressure (also normal) and examined her eyes, ears and nose.

"Not that I'm aware of, Doctor," he said. "As far as I know this is just supposed to be a routine check-up."

Julie nodded to show she had heard him as she checked Lindsay's pulse. Everything was perfectly normal so Julie next consulted the little girl's chart and noted that she was up to date with all of her shots and seemed perfectly good to go.

Turning to face him Julie smiled at Mr. Sharp. "Everything looks stellar; not a thing wrong with her."

"Excellent," Mr. Sharp responded and Julie lifted Lindsay off the table and set her on her feet.

"You can finish up with Nancy and I'll want to see Lindsay again in about three months for another check-up." Julie gave them one last parting smile and a wave before she returned to the computer in her office.

In between patients that morning Julie worked on her article and by lunchtime she was pleased with what she'd accomplished. She and Evelyn, the co-head of the clinic, had made plans to have lunch at the deli across the street from the clinic.

Julie arrived about ten minutes before Evelyn and was sipping a diet soda when Evelyn slid breathlessly into the seat across from her. Though Evelyn was older than Julie, in her early fifties, Julie liked and respected her a great deal and counted Evelyn as one of her closest friends. Now, when Julie looked up from her menu and took a good look at Evelyn's face, she saw that Evelyn looked more animated and excited than she'd ever seen her.

"What are you so excited about?" Julie asked curiously as Evelyn opened her menu and began scanning it.

Evelyn looked up at Julie, her eyes bright and her cheeks flushed, and gave her a beaming smile. "You'll never guess who showed up to surprise me this morning." When Julie shook her head, feeling a bit confused, Evelyn's smile widened. "Aaron."

Julie gasped in shock and had to clap a hand over her mouth to stifle a little cry of excitement. Evelyn's only child, son Aaron, lived in California and hadn't been to Arizona to see Evelyn since her husband died almost six months ago. Julie knew how hard it was for Evelyn being away from her son, especially since her husband's sudden death, and Julie totally understood now why Evelyn was so ecstatic.

"When did he get here, Evelyn?" Julie asked, but they were interrupted by the waiter. Julie and Evelyn quickly gave their orders and then turned back to each other.

Evelyn took a sip of her coffee, a grin still stretching across her face. Julie had never seen her look so happy and she was glad for her friend. "He showed up at the clinic just before you left to come over here. I was in my office working and the door opened. I assumed it was Nancy until I heard his voice and I almost couldn't believe it. I was afraid to look up because I was sure he wouldn't really be there, but he was."

"How long is he staying this time," Julie asked. She knew it had been hard for Evelyn to see Aaron leave after her husband's funeral and she hoped Aaron would be staying for a nice long visit.

Evelyn's smile widened to a degree that Julie believed impossible. "He's moving here. He says he's tired of California and that he misses Arizona too much to stay away any longer. He got a job transfer and he's going to start looking for a place to live tomorrow."

Julie was listening intently, her chin resting on her hand, and she couldn't help but smile at Evelyn's excitement. "I hope I get a chance to meet him. Everything was so crazy when Dan died that I didn't get that chance."

Evelyn's smile suddenly became a bit sheepish. "I was hoping you'd say that because I might have invited him to have lunch with us today. I'm sorry, Julie, I hope you don't mind."

Julie smirked at Evelyn who continued to look slightly abashed. "So you invited him to have lunch with us, did you?" When Evelyn nodded, looking a little worried, Julie just laughed and said, "I'm thrilled, Evelyn. I can't wait to meet him."

"Good, because he's here now. Aaron", she said loudly, "over here!" Evelyn waved at her son and Julie turned in her seat to see him approach.

Julie knew she would remember that moment for the rest of her life, the moment when she first saw Aaron Randall walking towards her with a smile on his face. He was wearing faded jeans that hung on his frame perfectly and a blue button down shirt open at the throat. As he got closer Julie was able to take in his dark hair, which was very nearly black, brown eyes and the growth of beard stubble on his chin. He was the handsomest man she'd ever seen and when he looked directly at her she felt like she might melt into a puddle. The part of her body that she usually managed to avoid, the part that ached for a man to fill it, was screaming at her not to let this one get away.

Julie was thoroughly relieved when Aaron greeted his mother first, giving her a chance to compose herself, so when he turned to smile brightly at her she was prepared and able to act more or less like her normal self.

"You must be Dr. Forrester," he said, holding out his hand to shake hers.

Julie hesitated for less than a second before she offered her own hand and they shook. She could feel calluses on his palms and when their fingers touched it sent little shocks all through her body.

"Call me Julie, please. It's a pleasure to finally meet you, Aaron. Evelyn talks about you all the time." Julie was quite proud of herself for sounding perfectly sane and normal. Yet she couldn't help but notice the sudden bereft way she felt when he released her hand.

"Should I be scared?" Aaron said jokingly as he sat down in the vacant seat beside his mother.

Both Julie and Evelyn laughed as Evelyn playfully swatted her son's arm. Their waiter approached then with a menu for Aaron and he scanned it quickly before ordering a tuna salad sandwich and a glass of iced tea. Julie couldn't help but feel somewhat mesmerized by this man that she'd only just met and she found herself wondering if she had ever felt these things for Kevin or if it had just been a cliché teenage crush that she blew out of proportion.

Confusion and doubts were clouding her mind and she nearly jumped out of her chair when Evelyn cleared her throat loudly. Forcing her mind to focus Julie looked at Aaron and realized he was watching her expectantly. Feeling thoroughly embarrassed Julie smiled apologetically at him and received a heart melting smile in return.

"I'm so sorry, Aaron, I must have been daydreaming. What did you say?"

"I asked how long you've had the clinic." Aaron took a bite of his sandwich and looked at Julie expectantly.

Willing herself to relax and not make a complete idiot of herself Julie said, "Almost a year. I worked at an Urgent Care facility before opening the clinic."

"Forgive me if this sounds rude, but you don't look old enough to even be a doctor, let alone have your own practice."

Julie laughed, feeling herself relaxing little by little. "It's never rude to make a woman feel younger than she is. I finished medical school in just five years."

"Wow. That's really impressive, Julie. Doesn't med school usually take eight years or longer?" Aaron took another bite of his sandwich and a swig of his iced tea, wiping his lips with a napkin.

"You might say I was driven to finish early. Having a daughter motivated me to work harder and get through quicker. I took a lot of extra classes that most med students tend to avoid. Suffice it to say I didn't get a lot of sleep those five years." Julie took a careful bite of her pasta, not wanting to make a mess and embarrass herself any more than she already had. She couldn't help but notice that Aaron looked impressed.

"That must have been so challenging. Raising a child and putting yourself through medical school. How did you balance everything? You must have worked to support yourself. How did you do it?"

Julie smiled at Aaron and was warmed when he smiled back at her, a private smile just for her. "It wasn't easy, Aaron. We were living in a small apartment at the time and the landlady watched my daughter for me when I was at school or work. I was a cashier at a Wal★Mart until I got the job at Urgent Care. I barely had time to brush my teeth, let alone do anything else."

"Things are better now, right?" Aaron took another bite of his sandwich and chewed as he gazed at her intently.

"So much better. The clinic closes at three o'clock three days a week so I can pick up my daughter at school and I never work past six on the other two days. Plus I have weekends off. It's more than I ever dreamed I'd have so soon after coming here."

"How old is your daughter?"

Julie smiled at him, feeling warmed by his obvious interest. She reached for her purse and pulled out her wallet, flipping it open to Carly's latest school photo. "Carly just turned ten a few days ago. This is her school photo from this year."

She handed the wallet to Aaron and he took it, sending hot sparks through her body when their fingers brushed briefly.

After studying the photo for a minute Aaron smiled warmly and handed the wallet back to Julie. "She's really beautiful, Julie. Thank you for showing me."

"She's the only real love of my life. I can't imagine life without her." Julie tucked her wallet back in her purse and zipped it up, allowing her mind to wander for just a second to relive the moment their fingers touched. She couldn't understand why something so innocent made her feel so strange.

"It can't be easy though; raising a child when you're still so young. How do you handle it?"

Julie thought about Aaron's question as she took a sip of her diet soda, wondering how she should answer and how much of herself to give away. Finally, choosing her words slowly and carefully, she said, "It is difficult, but it's also the most rewarding experience of my life. Being a single mother and having to be both mother and father to Carly has been a gift and nothing else matters to me more than being my child's mother."

Julie flushed when she noticed how intently Aaron was staring at her. His next words held a reverence that surprised and pleased her.

"That was really beautiful. It's truly magical to see someone who cares so much about their child. She must be a really special little girl."

"She is very special, thank you."

For a long moment Julie and Aaron held each other's gaze and both of them jumped in surprise when Evelyn cleared her throat loudly. Julie had completely forgotten Evelyn was there. Glancing at her watch Julie gasped when she realized they were almost ten minutes late getting back to the clinic for their afternoon appointments.

"Damn, Evelyn, we need to get going. I'm sorry Aaron, but we have to get back to work. We're already late. It was truly a pleasure to meet you."

When she offered her hand for Aaron to shake Julie tried to convince herself she was only being polite. It didn't work when she felt the electrical tingles all through her body at the touch of Aaron's warm fingers. She held Aaron's gaze for another second before Evelyn nudged her.

"We need to pay and get out of here, Jules," Evelyn said, adjusting her purse strap impatiently.

Aaron stood up and reached in his back pocket for his wallet. Julie blushed again when she caught herself staring at his rear end, admiring the way his jeans fit just tightly enough to be sexy without being gross.

"You two get going; this one's my treat." Aaron began shuffling some bills around in his wallet and Julie just stared at him, unsure how to respond. Finally she gently but firmly said, "Absolutely not, you don't have to do that."

Aaron grinned at her and Julie felt her knees weaken and begin trembling ever so slightly. "I know I don't have to, but I want to. Get going, both of you."

"Thanks, honey." Evelyn settled the matter, kissed her son on the cheek, and gripped Julie's arm to practically drag her out of the deli. Julie turned back once to wave at Aaron who waved back and winked, making Julie blush for a third time. She hadn't blushed this much since she was in high school.

Julie was totally distracted as Evelyn looped an arm through hers and it wasn't until she heard Evelyn chuckle softly that Julie was broken from her reverie.

"What are you laughing about?" Julie asked, curiously. She felt like she'd missed something.

Evelyn just raised an eyebrow and smirked at her. It took a few seconds before Julie got the point and she groaned aloud. "Don't even think about it, Evelyn. He's a nice guy and I like him but dating just isn't something I'm interested in."

Evelyn didn't say anything until they were back in the clinic. Julie was flipping through the file for her first post lunch appointment when Evelyn approached her with a very serious expression on her face.

"Jules, forgive me for being nosy, but I have to say this. You need to learn how to trust again. I know what you went through with Carly's father was a nightmare, but not all men are like that." When she saw Julie open her mouth to interrupt Evelyn held up a hand to stop her. "There are good men out there and Aaron is one of them. I'm being sincere about that and not just because I'm his mother. He was looking at you in the deli like he's never looked at any other girl I've ever seen him with. Give yourself a chance at some real happiness, Jules. You deserve it more than anyone I know and so does Carly."

"You make it sound so simple, Evelyn, but it's not. This whole situation is more complicated than you know and I'm already confused enough without adding a man to the big picture. Thank you for being so concerned though. You know how much I appreciate it."

Julie squeezed Evelyn's arm and smiled, rather sadly, Evelyn thought. Evelyn watched as Julie knocked on the door to her patient's room and then entered, smiling more brightly now. She was worried about Julie and she hoped that Aaron wouldn't give up on her too easily.

Kevin Meyers threw his pen down on the desk and, with a growl of frustration, loosened his tie and undid the top two buttons of his shirt. He felt like he was being choked and he cursed himself for getting into a profession that required a suit and tie every day. Work had been a nightmare all day and he couldn't wait to get home that evening and have a few ice cold beers.

Kevin groaned again when he realized that Marcie would be coming over to the house that night. He debated calling her and asking her if they could reschedule but he didn't feel like going through her guilt trip routine. He could still hear what she'd said the last time he'd asked to reschedule;

"Why don't you want to see me, Kevy? Don't you love me? I really miss you. Don't you miss me?"

He'd eventually gotten tired of her whining and changed his mind about rescheduling. She had pouted all through dinner, spent most of the evening winding him up until he felt like exploding, then decided that it was late and time for her to leave. He'd been forced to take care of himself in the shower that night and he was still feeling a little bitter about that.

Giving up the last of the paperwork as a bad job Kevin stood up and shoved manila folders haphazardly into his briefcase. Pulling on his blazer Kevin turned off the lights and grabbed his jacket on the way out of the office.

Kevin could feel the tension in his neck and shoulders increase when he pulled into the parking lot of the condo he called home and spotted Marcie's car. He hated it when she let herself into his apartment and he found himself seriously considering heading to a bar to get good and drunk before coming home.

Though it was a nice thought Kevin decided against it. He'd never been a big drinker and wasn't one to hold his liquor well. Having a few beers after a hard day at work was pretty much the extent of his drinking habits.

Heaving a deep sigh and bracing himself for the worst Kevin climbed out of his car with his briefcase in one hand and his coat draped over his other arm and headed into the building. Thankfully nobody was around to bother him and he was able to get into the elevator quickly. All too soon the elevator dinged as it reached the penthouse floor and Kevin, with another sigh, stepped out and opened the door to his apartment.

"Hi, honey!" Marcie cooed as she came bustling in from the kitchen. Despite feeling so bad Kevin couldn't deny that Marcie looked good in her skinny jeans and a tube top. He supposed he loved her in his own way but it would never be the earth shattering love that she wanted and expected from him.

Kevin had been introduced to Marcie at a party thrown by his father. Kevin hadn't been surprised when his father tried to push his son toward Marcie. She was just the type of woman Thomas Meyers wanted for his only son; attractive, young and more than content to be a wife, Thomas Meyers didn't believe women should work or have their own opinions. As far as he was concerned a woman's version of an opinion should be that of her husband's. His own wife Anne, Kevin's mother, had fit the bill perfectly for almost thirty years and Thomas had always ruled the household with an iron fist; sometimes literally.

Kevin could remember all too well the way his father had reacted when Kevin told him that his girlfriend, Julie Forrester, was pregnant with his child. Thomas was so used to getting his own way when he lay down the law that he was outraged that Kevin refused to remove himself from Julie's life and give up all parental rights to the child. Kevin loved Julie and he wanted to take responsibility for his own actions.

Thomas Meyers had never approved of Julie. She didn't come from the right side of the tracks for one thing and he frequently angered his son by calling the Forrester's 'trailer trash'. When Kevin refused to obey his father's orders Thomas Meyers made a drastic decision. As a politician in the city of Baltimore, Thomas held an enormous amount of power over people. Within a week after Kevin told him the news the Forrester's had changed their telephone number and Thomas was in the final stages of moving his family out of state.

Kevin felt the old bitterness and anger flood him as he remember walking to his car in the school parking lot one day and finding his father waiting for him. When his father told him that they were moving to Connecticut Kevin had a fit. He and his father had never argued like that before but in the end Kevin gave in as he usually did, hating himself for his weakness and for not being there for Julie or their child.

Kevin bided his time through his last two years of high school. Upon graduating he planned to find Julie and explain to her why he'd disappeared but his father had other plans. Thomas Meyers insisted on having his son go straight to work and college after graduation. When Kevin finally got out on his own and went back to Maryland to find Julie he discovered that she had moved out of state. Kevin had begged her parents to tell him where she was but they refused. He left them his business card out of sheer desperation and asked them to tell Julie he would always be available if she wanted to contact him.

Since then Kevin kept in frequent contact with Julie's mother, Elizabeth. Elizabeth had always liked him and felt sorry for him now, though she wouldn't go against her daughter's wishes and tell Kevin where they were located. Elizabeth provided Kevin with pictures of Carly throughout the years, including her school pictures once she started going to school. And Elizabeth Forrester is the only person who knows that every year Kevin buys his daughter a birthday card. He keeps them locked in a fireproof and watertight safe in his bedroom closet, waiting for the day when he can finally give them to her.

Marcie had been horrified to learn that Kevin had a daughter, but relieved when he told her that Carly wasn't in his life. Kevin had broken up with her over that but his father convinced him to make up with her. Actually, to be perfectly honest, Thomas Meyers had ordered his son to patch things up with Marcie. Kevin stood his ground until his father threatened to remove him from the will. Kevin had grown up living a privileged life and he still did thanks to his father's money. He wasn't sure if he would survive without his share of the family fortune and he always caved when his father threatened to cut him off. In those moments Kevin really hated himself.

Now, standing in the foyer of his condo with his fiancé before him, Kevin wondered how in the world he'd let himself get into such a horrible mess. He cared for Marcie, there was no denying that, but his heart had belonged to Julie since he was seventeen and it always would. Kevin would give up everything he'd ever had or ever would have just to have Julie and Carly in his life.

"You all right, honey? You look a little pale." Marcie's concerned voice brought Kevin back to reality and he forced himself to smile at Marcie.

"I'm just a little tired. Work was a real nightmare today." He opened his arms and Marcie hugged him, her arms tight around his back, and when Kevin leaned in for a kiss and felt Marcie's soft lips on his he felt the same twinge of guilt and betrayal he always did. He was betraying Julie by being with Marcie and he was betraying Marcie by being in love with Julie.

"Can I get you anything, baby? I can fix you a drink if you want."

Kevin smiled warmly at Marcie's concern and leaned down to kiss the tip of her nose. "All I want right now is a hot shower and a cold beer when I get out."

Marcie gave Kevin another little kiss and another squeeze. "I'll have dinner on the table by the time you come out."

With that Marcie made her way back to the kitchen and Kevin took a moment to admire the way her bottom looked in those tight jeans. He was certainly attracted to Marcie and he loved her as much as he could, but he knew it wasn't enough and that he should end things before she got hurt too badly. Kevin suspected it was too late for that. He was in too deep now and there was no getting out of this responsibility.

As he made his way down the hall to the master bedroom Kevin's thoughts began to wander again. He barely paid attention to what he was doing as he stripped out of his suit and padded naked into the bathroom. Adjusting the taps until the water was a comfortable temperature Kevin stepped under the spray and sighed contentedly as the hot water beat down on his sore muscles. He braced his hands on the shower wall and just stood there for a few seconds, savoring the peace and quiet and the feel of his muscles loosening.

Standing beneath the soothing spray, scrubbing away the tension of the day, Kevin thought about Julie again. He could remember her so vividly as she had been at the age of sixteen, but no matter how hard he tried he couldn't picture what she would look like now ten years later. He wondered if she had a man in her life and the thought sent an ache beyond his heart and into the depth of his soul.

Scrubbing himself with the sponge Kevin closed his eyes and conjured the memory of the night their daughter was conceived. It hadn't been easy for Kevin to get out of the house that night, but he remembered it like it had just happened yesterday.

Kevin lay on the bed in his dark bedroom, wondering if it would really be possible to pull this off. Taking a deep breath and steeling himself for the worst he opened the door and went downstairs to the sitting room where his mother was reading a magazine. Anne Meyers looked up when Kevin cleared his throat and she smiled at him.

"Hi, honey. Is everything all right?" she asked, closing the magazine and putting it on the coffee table in order to give Kevin her full attention.

"Would you mind if I went to a movie, Mom?" Kevin asked, mentally crossing his fingers that she wouldn't suspect anything.

His mother seemed to study him for a second before she asked, "Who with?"

"I was thinking about calling Jeff. I think everyone else is busy tonight." Kevin knew for a fact that all his friends were busy but he hoped his mother wouldn't call around to check up on him.

Kevin waited for an agonizing second until his mother finally smiled at him. "That's fine, honey. Just be home by midnight."

Kevin went to his mother and kissed her cheek. "Thanks, Mom."

Something in his mother's eyes made Kevin believe that she suspected the truth and he was relieved that she was allowing him to go out. It helped that his father was across the country on business. This never would have worked if his father had been home.

Kevin went back to his bedroom to change into clean jeans and a t-shirt. When he was dressed he sat at his desk, picked up the phone and dialed Julie's number, praying that she would be the one to answer and not one of her parents.

After half a dozen rings the sweetest voice Kevin had ever heard said, "Hello?"

Kevin had to force himself to breathe and remain calm as he said, "Hey, it's me. Can you meet me about a block from my house?"

There was silence on the other end for a long moment, long enough for Kevin to begin panicking, until finally Julie's soft voice said, "Are you serious? How are you getting away from your father?"

"He's out of town on business and Mom thinks I'm going to the movies with a friend. So, can you come pick me up?"

"I'll be two blocks from your house in about twenty minutes," she said and hung up before Kevin could say anything else.

Trying to conceal the goofy grin that had spread across his face Kevin went back downstairs and headed for the front door. Poking his head in the sitting room Kevin said to his mother, "I'm leaving, Mom. I'll see you later."

"Have fun, sweetie," his mother said without looking up from her magazine.

It was still muggy out as Kevin walked the two blocks to meet Julie. When he saw her father's beat up old pick-up truck parked near the stop sign he had to force himself not to increase his speed in his excitement and anticipation to see her. It seemed to take forever to reach the passenger door of *the truck and when he pulled it open and saw Julie for the first time in days he felt his heart speed up alarmingly. She looked almost unbearably sexy in a white sundress and cowboy boots with her light brown hair loose around her shoulders.*

"Hi there," Julie said, smiling at Kevin as he climbed into the truck. Kevin didn't answer, just reached out to cup the back of her neck in his hand and pull her close for a kiss. Julie wrapped her arms around the back of his neck and kissed him back with more passion than Kevin had ever experienced. Kevin could taste her raspberry lip gloss and when he felt the tentative touch of her tongue on his he felt an uncomfortable stirring and heaviness in his loins.

All too soon Julie pulled away and playfully stroked Kevin's nose before sliding back behind the wheel. Kevin was intensely aware of the new heat and electricity between them, but he was proud of himself for keeping the conversation normal as Julie wound her way confidently out of Kevin's neighborhood.

"Where exactly are we going?" Kevin asked, feeling a little confused when Julie made a turn on a dirt road that looked as though it hadn't been traveled in years.

"You'll see," she said, cryptically, and Kevin decided to just let go and trust her judgment.

They had gone about a mile down the road when Kevin felt Julie's hand on his leg, sliding closer and closer to his groin with each stroke. He gasped in shock when her hand rested on the bulge in his jeans and began to turn and press, her movements tentative and hesitant but no less enthusiastic. Kevin could feel himself nearing a climax and he fought as hard as he could to keep it from happening in his jeans. He was torn between relief and disappointment when she removed her hand in order to maneuver the truck to a stop. They were in a clearing with a gorgeous view of the sky twinkling with stars and Kevin was suddenly certain how the evening was going to end.

"Come on," Julie said, opening her door and jumping down from the cab. Kevin followed, wincing at the painful tightness of his jeans. He watched as Julie stepped nimbly on the back tire and swung herself up and over the side

of the truck to the bed. Kevin awkwardly scrambled after her and it was then that he noticed the sleeping bag spread out in the bed.

Kevin watched as Julie removed her boots and put them aside before crawling into the sleeping bag. "I'm lonely over here, Kevin," she whispered, her voice seductive, and Kevin removed his shoes and socks before crawling into the sleeping bag beside her.

They lay on their sides facing each other. Kevin rested a hand on her hip as he looked deep into her dark brown eyes, knowing he was in love with her and would always love her. "Did you plan this, Julie?" he asked, wondering how she'd managed to set everything up in such a short amount of time.

"I keep the sleeping bag in the truck so I can come here at night and watch the stars," she said.

There was silence for a long moment until Julie finally whispered to him, "I love you, Kevin. I want to make love with you tonight."

Kevin studied her for a moment, searching her face for any little hint of doubt, and when he couldn't find any he tightened his hand on her hip and pulled her body close to him. He heard Julie gasp as he crushed his mouth to hers in a passionate kiss. Kevin slid his hand beneath the hem of her dress and was shocked to discover that she was completely bare beneath it.

The feel of her bare skin beneath his fingers was more than Kevin could take. They clumsily tugged and pulled at clothing, trapped in the confines of the sleeping bag, but eventually managed to get the most cumbersome of their clothing off and tossed aside. Kevin's lips slid along Julie's cheek, down her neck and to her shoulder and she arched her back, pressing her body against him.

Without thinking about the fact that she was a virgin Kevin entered her, wincing at her cry of pain and the way her body stiffened. Only seconds passed though before Julie began moving with him, against him. They made love with an innocent passion, slightly clumsy and not exactly earth shattering, but sweet and beautiful. Kevin bit down on his arm to keep from screaming at the climax as Julie dug her fingernails into his shoulders.

Afterward they lay naked together wrapped in the sleeping bag, holding each other and talking softly. Kevin's fingers constantly moved across her skin and he savored Julie's little sighs of pleasure. They made love again before it was time to leave the clearing. Kevin watched as Julie put her dress and boots back on and attempted to fix her hair with her fingers. Unable to help himself Kevin reached for her, pulling her onto his lap and wrapping his arms around her body. Julie rested her forehead against his, her eyes closed, and Kevin kissed the tip of her nose.

"Thank you, Kevin. That was beautiful; just the way I always wanted my first time to be." The sincerity of Julie's words brought a lump to Kevin's throat, making it impossible to speak. Instead he kissed her tenderly before releasing her and climbing out of the bed and into the cab of the truck. They held hands on the way back to Kevin's neighborhood and parted with another soft kiss just before Kevin got out of the truck. He waved at Julie as she drove away until he couldn't see her anymore and then headed home, feeling strangely empty and depressed.

It was a few minutes to midnight when Kevin quietly let himself into the house, not sure if his mother had gone to bed or not. When he opened the front door though he could see light in the sitting room and knew she had waited up for him.

"I'm home, Mom," he said, peeking into the sitting room.

"How was the movie?" she asked and Kevin had to bite his lip to keep from grinning.

"It was excellent. I'd definitely see it again," he said. "Good night, Mom."

His mother smiled warmly at him. "Good night, sweetheart. Sleep tight."

Kevin entered his dark bedroom, closing the door behind him, and stripped out of his clothes. He crawled into bed naked and pulled the sheets up to his chest, reliving the evening in his mind. He knew it was a night he would never forget and he also knew that Julie owned him now; heart, body and soul.

Kevin was so engrossed in the memory of that perfect evening that it took him awhile to realize how cold the water had gotten. Shivering and feeling slightly shriveled he climbed out of the shower and wrapped a towel around his waist. He could smell dinner as he dressed in a pair of sweatpants and a t-shirt. He rolled his neck and shoulders experimentally, satisfied that most of the stiffness and tension had eased from his muscles.

Entering the dining room Kevin noticed that Marcie had placed two lighted candles in the center of the table and he couldn't help but smile at her thoughtfulness. He really did love her and it hurt him that he couldn't be the man she deserved. He couldn't help the way his heart felt though and for the last ten years his heart had ached for Julie.

"Feel better, babe?" Marcie's soft voice asked from behind him and Kevin nearly jumped out of his skin in surprise.

Regaining his composure Kevin turned to Marcie and smiled at her. "Yeah, much better."

"You were in there for quite a while. I was about to check on you to see if you'd fallen asleep."

Kevin watched as Marcie bustled about the dining room table, carrying in a platter of chicken parmigiana and stir fried potatoes and vegetables. The smell of her cooking was making Kevin's mouth water and he eagerly sat down at the table.

"Do you still want that beer, hon?" she asked.

"If you don't mind."

Marcie winked at him and went back to the kitchen, returning moments later with a bottle of beer, a bottle of wine and a wine glass. She sat down and handed Kevin the beer, then poured herself a glass of wine.

"I hope you're hungry; there's lots of food here," she said with a smile and Kevin chuckled warmly as he reached for the pan of chicken.

"I'm starving and this all smells delicious, sweetie."

There was silence as they filled their plates and dug into the food. At the first bite of the chicken Kevin sighed with pleasure which made Marcie giggle. They chatted easily as they ate and Kevin frequently touched Marcie's hand across the table, wishing he could love her more deeply.

After dinner Kevin insisted on doing the dishes for Marcie and he gently shooed her into the living room. When the last dish was rinsed and placed in the drain Kevin wiped his hands on a dish towel and went to the living room to join her. They sat together watching TV, Marcie tucked against his side with his arm firm around her, until after Jay Leno was over.

"I better be heading out. I didn't mean to stay so late," Marcie said and yawned widely.

Kevin hesitated for a second before tightening his arm around her and pulling her closer. "Why don't you stay here tonight. We have tomorrow off; it'll be nice having a relaxing morning together."

"Do you really want me to stay tonight, Kevin?" Marcie asked hesitantly.

Kevin felt a pang of sadness at the obvious doubt in her tone, knowing that he had nobody but himself to blame for it. Keeping his arm tight around her shoulders Kevin shifted his body, bringing her with him, and they both tumbled backward onto the couch. Marcie giggled as Kevin covered her body with his, pinning her playfully against the couch cushions, and teasingly licked the point of her chin with the tip of his tongue.

Kevin looked deep into Marcie's blue eyes and whispered, "Will you stay with me tonight, Marcie?"

Marcie smiled seductively up at him and threaded her fingers in Kevin's dark hair, drawing him down for a kiss. The feel of Marcie's mouth moving against his was intoxicating and Kevin felt himself relaxing even further. His hands skimmed her firm body and Marcie arched against him. When Kevin felt her reach for the hem of his shirt he shifted to give her better access. His sweatpants, her jeans and her tube top soon joined his shirt haphazardly on the floor of the living room and when their naked bodies came together Kevin groaned in pleasure.

They made love with a tenderness that Kevin found very profound. Marcie twined her legs around his waist and rained little kisses along his chest and neck as their bodies joined and they began to move as one. Afterward they lay on the couch catching their breath and then Kevin scooped Marcie into his arms and carried her into the bedroom. He crawled under the covers beside her and they lay facing each other.

"I love you, Kevin," Marcie said, her fingers splayed out against his chest.

Kevin took her hand and kissed each fingertip, his eyes never leaving hers. "I love you too, Marcie."

Marcie leaned forward for a light kiss and then tucked herself against Kevin with her cheek against his chest. Kevin combed his fingers through her blonde hair, listening to the steady rhythm of her breathing, and hated himself for wishing she were someone else.

CHAPTER 2

*J*ulie shifted the weight of the shopping bags she held in her hand to make her burden a bit more comfortable. "Where should we have lunch, baby?" she asked, turning to look inquiringly at her daughter.

Carly glanced around at the dining choices before turning back to her mother. "Can we go to McDonald's?" she asked and when her mother looked at her Carly offered her the most charming smile she could manage.

Julie tried to appear stern but failed dismally and finally, with a little chuckle, shifted her bags again and motioned for Carly to follow her. "Come on," she said, pretending to be exasperated, and then turned to give Carly a little wink.

With a little giggle Carly skipped along beside her mother as Julie crossed the street of the shopping center and opened the door to McDonald's. So far it had been a really good day. They'd eaten an early breakfast, got their nails done, Carly got her hair cut and they had done some serious shopping and after lunch they planned to see a movie.

Stepping up to the counter Julie scanned the menu, then turned to Carly. "What do you want, baby?"

"Chicken nuggets and french fries, please," Carly said and Julie turned to the girl at the counter who was waiting expectantly.

"I'd like a six piece chicken McNugget with a small fry, please." Julie turned back to Carly and asked, "Do you want a soda, Carly?" At Carly's affirmative nod Julie turned back to the counter girl. "I'd also like a bacon ranch salad with grilled chicken and two medium drinks."

"What drinks would you like, ma'am?" the girl asked, keying in the order on the register.

"Two Cokes, please."

The counter girl read Julie the total and Julie set her bags down to reach into her purse for her wallet. She paid the girl and a few moments later she and Carly carried their tray to a table that overlooked the crowded open air shopping center. Julie watched with a careful eye as Carly got them some napkins and straws, not relaxing until Carly was sitting at the table with her.

"Have you had fun today, honey?" Julie asked her daughter and was rewarded with a huge smile from Carly.

"So much fun, Mommy. Thank you so much."

Julie forked a mouthful of her salad and chewed thoughtfully. When she swallowed she asked Carly, "Has your teacher mentioned yet where you guys are going on your field trip?"

Carly shook her head as she swallowed a bite of chicken nugget and took a sip of soda. "Not yet. Mrs. Carter says we should find out soon if they have enough money in the budget for a field trip."

Julie looked at her daughter in surprise. "You mean you might not get a field trip this year?"

"That's what Principal Sheridan said at our last assembly," Carly said with a little shrug.

"It'll be a shame if you guys don't get a field trip this year," Julie said, taking a swig of her Coke.

Carly shrugged again as she munched on a french fry. "We still have the band and chorus concert and the fourth grade play before the end of the year."

"What play are they doing this year?"

Carly grinned excitedly at her mother. "Wizard of Oz!" she crowed excitedly and Julie smiled at her enthusiasm. The Wizard of Oz had been one of Carly's favorite stories growing up and she still read the book from time to time. Being part of the play that year would be a dream come true for Carly and Julie hoped her daughter would have a part in it.

"Julie?"

Julie nearly jumped out of her seat when she heard a man's voice behind her say her name a little uncertainly. She was thrilled though when she turned and saw who it was.

"Aaron! I didn't expect to see you here today. How are you?"

Julie couldn't help but notice how good Aaron looked in his cargo shorts and a polo shirt, His legs were incredibly muscular and dusted with a fine coating of dark hair, She forced herself not to blush as her mind wandered briefly to places better left unspoken and turned her attention back to Aaron.

"I'm good, thanks. Just picking up a few things for the condo." Julie noticed him glance in Carly's direction and then back at her, also noting the confusion and uncertainty in her daughter's face.

"I'm so sorry, Aaron. Carly, honey, this is my friend Mr. Randall. Aaron, this is my beautiful daughter, Carly."

Aaron held out his hand to Carly and said, "It's a pleasure to meet you, Carly."

"It's good to meet you too, Mr. Randall," Carly said politely, shaking Aaron's hand.

Aaron grinned at her and winked. "Please call me Aaron. Mr. Randall makes me feel so old."

Carly looked uncertainly at her mother. "Is that okay, Mommy?" she asked. She had always been taught to address her elders respectfully and the only adults she called by their first names were her mother's three best friends.

Julie smiled at her daughter and nodded. "It's fine with me if that's what Aaron wants."

Carly flashed Aaron her most dazzling smile and Julie had to stifle a laugh. Carly could be incredibly charming when she wanted to be and she could tell that her daughter liked Aaron.

"Would you like to join us, Aaron?" Julie asked and was torn between relief and disappointment when he shook his head.

"You enjoy your time with Carly; I don't want to interrupt that. I'm sure I'll see you around, Julie." He flashed another heart melting smile and then turned to Carly again. "I hope I see you again sometime too, Carly. It was really great to meet you."

He tipped Carly another little wink and waved on his way out the door. Julie was content to watch him go, admiring the way his rear looked in those cargo shorts, when Carly's voice startled her.

"Who was that, Mommy?" she asked, curiously.

"That's Dr. Randall's son. He's moving here from California."

"He's cool," Carly said, swallowing the last of her chicken nuggets and draining her Coke.

"I've only met him once, but he seems very nice," Julie agreed and then glanced at her watch. "We have to get going if we want to get good seats for the movie.

They dumped their tray into the garbage can and left McDonald's with their shopping bags. Ten minutes later, after a quick stop in the parking lot to load the bags in the car, they were seated in the theater with a bucket of popcorn between them, two more Cokes and a box of M&M's.

Julie tried to concentrate on the movie but all she could think about was Aaron and the very confused way she felt about him. By the time the lights came on in the theater Julie had just about driven herself crazy trying to convince herself that Aaron really wasn't all that special. She had no idea what the movie had been about and just tried to keep up as Carly prattled on about it.

Both of them were exhausted when they got in the car to head home and Julie wasn't surprised when Carly dozed off in the passenger seat. When they got home Carly headed straight to her room to take a nap before dinner and Julie followed suit. Laying fully clothed on her bed Julie laced her fingers behind her head and stared contemplatively up at the ceiling, wondering what it was about Aaron that had her so lost and confused. She didn't know but she hoped that whatever it was would fix itself sooner rather than later.

Carefully sliding out of bed Kevin tiptoed out of the room and into the kitchen. Marcie was still fast asleep, her short blond hair tangled and beautiful against the black pillowcase, and he wanted to have a little surprise ready for her when she woke up.

In the kitchen Kevin put together a lovely Spanish omelet and a fruit salad. Putting the omelet on a tray along with the salad he also added two glasses, a pitcher of orange juice, a pot of herbal tea and two teacups.

Returning to the bedroom Kevin saw that Marcie was still asleep and he smiled softly. Removing his robe Kevin slipped naked into the bed beside her with the tray balanced over his lap and leaned over to brush a gently kiss against her cheek.

"Wake up, sleeping beauty," he whispered in her ear and Marcie stirred slowly awake. When she saw the breakfast tray her eyes lit up and Kevin was glad he'd made the effort for her.

"Wow! I'm starting to feel a little spoiled," she said, sitting up in bed holding the sheet over her breasts.

Leaning over Kevin kissed her gently and together they devoured the omelet and the fruit salad. When the food was gone Marcie sighed and stretched. "I should get going. I promised my mother I'd have lunch with her today and you know how she gets if I cancel."

Kevin lay in bed with his head propped up on one hand watching appreciatively as Marcie got dressed. She felt his eyes on her and turned to him. "This isn't fair you know," she said, pretending to be stern.

Kevin smirked at her and stretched luxuriously. "What isn't fair?" he asked innocently

"You shouldn't be allowed to look so rumpled and sexy when I have to leave," she said, sounding thoroughly disappointed.

Kevin just laughed and sat up in the bed as Marcie came over to give him a kiss goodbye. "I'll call you later," he said after the kiss ended.

Marcie sauntered out of the room, knowing just how good she looked in her jeans, and turned back to give him a wink before closing the bedroom door behind her. Kevin couldn't help breathing a sigh of relief when he heard the front door of the condo close. Marcie was great and he loved her, but no matter what they were doing his thoughts always strayed to Julie.

Kevin lay back against the pillows and sighed again. Even after ten years apart thoughts of Julie made his heart pound in a way that Marcie just wasn't able to. He wished he had the nerve to break things off with Marcie for good. It wasn't fair to keep pretending to be something for her that he wasn't and would never be. Marcie deserved better and she should be set free to find a man who could love her the way she deserved to be loved.

Kevin knew that he wouldn't do anything that might affect the comfortable and luxurious lifestyle he'd been accustomed to since childhood. The problem was that Marcie would be the one hurt the most by his weakness and selfishness and Kevin hated himself for that.

With another deep sigh Kevin rolled over onto his belly and yawned widely, his jaw cracking painfully. He'd like to get a few more hours of sleep, if only to keep from having to think about the horrible situation he was trapped in. He had to do something or a woman he genuinely loved and cared about was going to be badly hurt and Kevin didn't think he would be able to live with himself if that happened.

It was just after seven that night when Julie finished with supper. She'd made beef stroganoff from a meal kit, which was a lifesaver for any working single mother, steamed broccoli and carrots and brown rice. After everything was on the table Julie wiped her hands on a dish towel and went to get Carly, feeling a little concerned that her daughter had slept for so long.

"Carly? Honey, it's time for dinner. Wake up, baby."

Carly stirred, groaning weakly, and Julie was suddenly on the alert for something seriously wrong. Carly seemed lethargic and weak, unlike her normal self, and Julie couldn't deny that she was worried at that moment.

"Carly, honey, are you ok?" Julie asked, gently cupping her daughter's cheek. Carly was cool to the touch so there was no fever and she was beginning to wake up a little bit more.

"I'm fine, Mommy. Still a little tired though. What's for dinner?"

Julie's fears abated when she heard Carly's voice sounding perfectly normal and some of the color returning to her pale cheeks.

"Stroganoff, veggies and rice. Come on, baby, before it all gets cold." Julie got up from the bed and offered Carly her hand. Carly took it and, on impulse, Julie turned and pulled her daughter into a tight hug.

Carly looked up in surprise when her mother released her. "What was that for, Mommy?" she asked, wondering if something might be wrong with her mother.

Julie gave Carly another brief squeeze. "I just love you, my little ladybug."

Carly smiled up at her mother and squeezed her hand tightly. "I love you too, Mommy."

Julie kissed the top of Carly's head and then, still holding hands, they made their way to the kitchen to eat supper. Julie poured each of them a glass of ice cold milk and she watched carefully to make sure Carly ate a good meal. She was relieved when Carly had a second helping of the veggies and rice; if she'd been seriously ill her appetite wouldn't have been that good.

Julie and Carly chatted all through supper and afterward Carly washed the dishes while her mother rinsed them and put them in the dish drain. They spent the rest of the evening sitting together in the living room, Julie watching television and Carly curled up on the chair engrossed in a book.

While the credits of the show she had been watching rolled Julie looked at her watch, sighed and stretched. "It's almost ten, honey. Time for bed."

Carly finished what she was reading and closed her book, marking the page carefully. "OK, Mommy."

Julie watched as Carly bustled off down the hall and then returned about ten minutes later in her pajamas. Julie opened her arms and Carly went to her. After a hug and a kiss on the cheek Julie playfully swatted her daughter's bottom. "Go to bed, ladybug. I'll see you in the morning."

"Good night, Mommy."

"Good night, honey."

When Carly was out of sight and Julie heard her bedroom door close she sighed heavily, feeling drained and praying she'd be able to sleep that night. Getting up from the couch Julie turned off the TV and all the lights downstairs, checked the front and back door to make sure they were locked and then went upstairs to bed. She changed into a pair of light pajamas that would be cool in the sticky heat and crawled under the sheets, pulling them up to her chest.

Lacing her hands behind her head Julie thought about the great day she and Carly had shared and the memory brought a smile to her face. It was what she was thinking about when she rolled over onto her side and almost immediately fell into a deep and untroubled sleep.

Aaron Randall lay on the narrow single bed in the guest room at his mother's place. His condo wouldn't be ready to move into for a few days, but he didn't mind staying at the home place. The only problem was that it held too many memories of his father and Aaron missed the old man like crazy.

Despite his painful memories of his father Aaron was happy to be home. He'd liked California but Arizona would always be home and he'd been anxious to move back for quite a while. Now that his mother was alone it gave Aaron even more of an incentive to move back and now he'd finally done it.

Lacing his fingers behind his head Aaron heaved a deep sigh. If he were totally honest with himself he could admit that part of the reason he'd been anxious to leave California had been Abbie, his girlfriend of almost ten years. Aaron had been furious, with Abbie and with himself, when he found out that Abbie had been cheating on him for the last three years of their relationship. When he confronted her she blamed it on him because he wouldn't marry her,

Thinking back to the last time he'd spoken to her Aaron couldn't deny that Abbie had had a point when it came to the discussion of marriage. Aaron wanted to be certain that he loved the woman he married and, despite the fact that he had deep feelings for Abbie, he wasn't as in love with her as he thought he should be in order to make that ultimate commitment.

That had been almost a year ago and Aaron still felt sick at the thought that Abbie had cheated on him for so long instead of just breaking up with him and moving on with her life. It hurt too that less than a month after they split up Aaron found out that she'd run off to Las Vegas to elope with the man involved in the affair. Aaron was slowly recovering from the horrible betrayal, but up until now he'd been convinced that he wasn't ready for another steady relationship.

All that changed the instant he laid eyes on Julie Forrester. The woman was beautiful, there was no question about that, but even more than beauty Aaron could see kindness, strength and tenacity as well. Those were things he found undeniably sexy and his feelings grew even more powerful when he heard the way she spoke about her daughter.

Aaron had to smile at the memory of meeting Julie's daughter that day. Carly was the mirror image of her mother, destined to be a truly beautiful woman, and Aaron could tell that Julie was doing an amazing job raising her. He knew from what his mother had told him that Carly's father wasn't in the picture and Aaron couldn't help but feel a bit sorry for the man. He obviously had no idea what he was missing out on when it came to being part of Carly's life.

Reaching over to the bedside table Aaron retrieved his MP3 player, placing the ear buds in his ears and turning the player on. Music always helped him focus when he was confused about something and his taste in music ran the gamut from country to jazz to rock to whatever was playing on the Top 40 that had a good beat and good lyrics.

Closing his eyes as the guitar riffs of classic Aerosmith filled his ears Aaron's thoughts returned to Julie. He could sense that she was uncertain about a relationship with anyone and that her daughter took precedence over everything else. He was determined to find a way to convince her to give him a chance. Aaron wasn't sure what it was about Julie that had him so unnerved but he felt it in his heart that they had the potential to be something really special.

It was after midnight and Kevin was still awake, drinking his fourth can of beer and feeling an almost unpleasant buzz beginning to take shape. He had been sitting at the desk in his little home office area of the kitchen trying to draft a letter and unsure how to do it.

Kevin had struggled with his torn feelings all day and had finally decided to write those feelings down in a letter to Marcie in the hopes that reading them might make them easier to deal with. He also hoped that it might convince her to end things with him, thus letting him off the hook with his father's edict. Finally, after crumpling up about a dozen sheets of paper filled with lines of scribbled out words. Kevin put pen to paper and began to write.

Marcie,

I know that what you read when I give this to you will hurt you and I'd like to apologize in advance for that. Please understand that I love you dearly though not as deeply as I know you would like me to. There is a reason for this, one I don't expect you to understand, but I have to tell you the truth. I can't live this way anymore, feeling torn between loving you and wishing you were someone else.

Marcie, my true heart belongs to another woman and I know that sounds cruel given how long you and I have been together, but it's the truth and it's well past time I told you everything about my past.

At the age of seventeen I fell in love with a girl I had known since we were very small children. We had been friends once when we were young until the difference in our lifestyles and the way we grew up became too much to overcome. Her name is Julie Forrester and she is the woman who, to this day, owns my heart and soul.

We dated for almost a month when my father found out about us. He knew the Forrester's and didn't believe that Julie was good enough for his only son. I was forbidden to ever see or speak to Julie again. One night, about three weeks after my father laid down that edict, he was away on business and I managed to get past my mother by lying about going to a movie with some friends. In reality I was meeting Julie and we drove to a little clearing near where she lived.

Julie and I were both virgins until that night and that was the night she got pregnant with our daughter. You've seen the photo of Carly and not a day goes by when I don't regret not being there for her the way a father should. It's one of the three things I'm least proud of.

When Julie came to me and told me she was pregnant with our child I was scared at first, but soon I became excited at the prospect of being a father. I knew it would be difficult, but with both of our families supporting us I knew nothing could go wrong. I assumed that the idea of a grandchild would soften my father towards Julie. I had never been more wrong about anything in my life.

I told him and my mother at the same time and my father became so enraged that I was actually frightened of him for a moment. He seemed completely beside himself as he stormed and raged at me about being a failure and ruining the future he'd planned so carefully for me. I let him have his say and, when he was done ranting, I told him that I was sorry he felt that way but I was going to take responsibility for my role in getting Julie pregnant.

My father didn't speak to me for several days and I tried to convince myself that he would get used to the idea. Imagine my surprise when I let school one afternoon about a week after I told my parents the news and saw my father leaning against my car in the parking lot. When I asked him why he was there he took my arm and led me to his car. He told me to get in but I refused until he told me what was going on.

In one week my powerful politician father managed to move our whole lives to Connecticut. When I opened my mouth to protest my father took me by the shoulders and said that he was sure I'd understand someday that he was doing this for me and that it was the right thing to do. I almost hit him when he said that people like us were too good to be 'breeding' with people like Julie Forrester.

I threatened to run away but my father just chuckled and told me it wouldn't be worth it because he could have me found within minutes. I felt betrayed and defeated, but I *got into the car and let him drive away. I never even had a chance to tell Julie why I was leaving and I know she believes that I abandoned her.*

You have to understand that my father is domineering and a control freak. He has to have things his way and he'll use very unscrupulous methods to get what he wants. Whenever we had a major problem he would always threaten to cut me off financially and that's the one thing that has always terrified me. Since birth I've lived a privileged life and I'm afraid to try living any other way. That is probably me greatest shame and the one thing about myself I wish I could change.

We moved to Connecticut and I finished high school. I tried to call Julie when my father wasn't home but they had changed their telephone number and I suspected that my father had coerced them into doing that so I couldn't contact them. I believe he thought he was doing what was best for me but I will never forgive him for the position I am in now.

After high school I fully intended to go back to Baltimore and explain things to Julie. By the time I was able to get away from my father I was too late. Her parents told me she had moved and no matter how much I begged and pleaded they refused to tell me where she and our child had gone. Her mother must have taken pity on me because she gave me one of Carly's baby pictures to have and that is my most prized and cherished possession. I could lose everything else and not care, but if I lost my daughter's photograph I would be inconsolable. Before leaving the Forrester's home I left my business card and asked them to tell Julie I had been looking for her. This was about eight years ago and I have yet to hear from her. I don't expect to anytime soon either, though it's the one thing I wish for every time the clock reads 11:11.

I'm sorry that I can't explain all this to you face to face, but I promise that after you read this letter I will tell you why I had to do it this way. Please believe that I do love you, but not the way you deserve to be loved and that isn't fair to either of us.

I'm so very sorry, Marcie.

Kevin

When he signed his name to the bottom of the page Kevin was surprised to see a tear drop fall onto the paper. He hadn't realized that he'd begun to cry, but now that he'd started he found he couldn't stop. Tears slipped unheeded down his cheeks as he folded the letter and sealed it in an envelope. His hand shook as he wrote Marcie's name on the front of the envelope and set it aside.

For a long moment Kevin simply sat in his chair without moving until he finally put his face in his hands and gave in to the tears. His body shook with gut wrenching sobs but Kevin couldn't find the strength to stop them from coming. With the letter to Marcie next to his elbow on the desk Kevin let his heart break in two as he cried and cried and cried well into the night.

CHAPTER 3

*J*ulie pressed a hand to her forehead, fighting back tears and trying to regain some composure. It was one of her days to pick up Carly from school and the entire day had been a nightmare to begin with. Now, as if she weren't stressed enough, Julie had left the clinic only to find that her piece of junk car had a flat tire. She had attempted to call AAA for help but her phone wasn't getting any service. That was when the frustrated tears first began threatening to fall.

Forcing herself to take a deep breath Julie had gone inside the clinic to call AAA from the clinic phone only to discover that they wouldn't be able to make it for at least forty five minutes and, according to her watch, she was already ten minutes late picking up Carly.

Using the clinic phone again Julie called the school to tell them that she would be late picking up Carly. It hurt her to know that Carly would be waiting for her, possibly worrying. Julie had never been late picking up her daughter and this was hurting her terribly.

Julie left the clinic, knowing there was nothing she could do but wait, and on impulse crouched down beside the car to examine the tire. She was just wondering if she might be able to figure out how to fix it when she heard a voice behind her.

"Julie? Is something wrong?"

Julie was so startled by Aaron's voice that she lost her balance, toppling over and landing hard on her bottom. Well, Julie thought, now I can add humiliation to the list of things that went wrong today. She was about to pull herself up when Aaron offered his hand. Julie hesitated for the barest instant before grasping his hand and letting him pull her up. Despite how awful she felt Julie was still glad to see him and there was no denying the tingle of electricity she felt when he took her hand.

"Thanks," Julie said when she was upright, brushing off the seat of her pants. "And in answer to your question everything is wrong."

Julie fought for control but she was unable to stop a single tear from slipping down her cheek. She closed her eyes, pinching the bridge of her nose, and nearly jumped out of her skin when she felt Aaron gently brush the stray tear with his thumb.

Looking up at him Julie was flabbergasted at the concern in Aaron's eyes and, despite her misgivings about the way he made her feel, she found herself wanting to tell him what was wrong.

"This whole day has just been horrible from the beginning. It's one of my days to pick up Carly at school, I'm almost twenty minutes late, my car has a flat tire and the tow truck won't be able to make it here for at least another half hour."

Julie sniffled, feeling more tears begin to slide down her cheeks, and she ran a hand through her hair before crossing her arms tightly over her chest. When Aaron gently put his hands on her shoulders she was compelled to look up at him.

"Julie, can you trust me to help you?" he asked and, after hesitating for a brief second, Julie nodded. "I want you to take my car and go pick up your daughter. I'll stay here and change your tire. You have a spare, right?"

Julie's mouth had dropped open in shock and at first she didn't have a clue what to say. "Yeah, it's in the trunk," she finally managed to stammer. "Aaron, I can't take your car."

"Yes you can. You have to get your daughter. I don't want her to worry about you."

Julie felt a sense of déjà vu when he said those words. It was as though he could see inside her and read her thoughts. Julie hesitated for a second while Aaron reached in his jeans pocket for his keys. He tried to hand them to her but Julie was still reticent. So, taking her hand in his, he gently placed the keys in her open palm and then closed her fingers around them.

"My car is the blue Ford Focus parked over there," he said, pointing out his car. "Go get Carly. I should have the tire done by the time you get back."

Without waiting for her to say anything Aaron popped the trunk and dragged out the tire and the jack. Julie just stood there watching him for the longest moment and finally she whispered, "Thank you, so much, Aaron."

Aaron didn't answer, just winked at her and waved. Julie couldn't help but smile as she made her way to Aaron's car and climbed in behind the wheel. As she started the car and backed out of the space she still couldn't believe that there could actually be anyone as good and kind as Aaron and that was the moment when she first began to really wonder if maybe she should give him more of a chance.

Carly bounced up and down on the tips of her toes, feeling more and more nervous and angry with each passing moment. She'd gotten tired of having her backpack slung over her back and it now lay on the sidewalk at her feet.

"Mrs. Riley, what if something happened to my mom?" Carly asked for perhaps the hundredth time.

Mrs. Riley, one of the office assistants, had agreed to stand outside with Carly after her mother called to say she'd be late. She had sounded fine on the phone and Mrs. Riley had told Carly this numerous times, but she still said it again.

"Carly, your mom is fine. She's just had a little car trouble and she'll be here as soon as she can. Now please settle down and quit bouncing around."

Carly glared at Mrs. Riley and plopped down on the sidewalk with her legs crossed Indian style. Like her mother Carly had had a very bad day and she wasn't in the mood for something like this to happen. She wanted to go home and be alone and she was suddenly very angry at her mother for letting this happen.

She'd be here already if she had a decent car, Carly grumbled to herself. Carly continued to think unkind thoughts about her mother until she saw an unfamiliar blue car pull into the parking lot with her mother behind the wheel.

Carly watched indifferently as her mother climbed out of the car, waving at her and Mrs. Riley as though nothing had happened.

"Hi, Mrs. Riley. I'm so sorry about this. Thank you for keeping an eye on Carly."

"It was no trouble at all, Dr. Forrester. What happened anyway?"

Carly's mother heaved a deep sigh and rolled her eyes in exasperation. "When I left the clinic I noticed my car had a flat tire. Luckily though a friend of mine showed up and let me borrow his car while he changed my tire."

Mrs. Riley looked shocked and then she smiled broadly. "Wow! Talk about knight in shining armor."

Carly's mother laughed which angered Carly even further. "You're telling me." She then turned to Carly and Carly knew that her mother was expecting a hug or something but Carly wasn't in the mood.

Before her mother could say anything Carly stood and slung her backpack over one shoulder, glaring at her mother. "Can we go now, Mom? I've been here forever."

Without another word Carly marched to the blue car and climbed into the passenger seat, folding her arms across her chest. She knew she'd be in trouble for having a bad attitude and a smart mouth but after the day she'd had she found she didn't really care. Carly sat fuming in the car while her mother and Mrs. Riley talked. When she caught sight of the look on her mother's face as she came back to the car and climbed in behind the wheel Carly knew she was going to be in for a really long night.

Julie started Aaron's car and put it in gear, backing out of the parking space. Shifting gears again she pulled forward, waving to Mrs. Riley on the way out. When they were clear of the school Julie turned to her daughter.

"What's with the bad attitude, Carly? You know how I feel about that."

Carly ignored her, just continued to stare out the window with her arms folded tightly across her chest. Julie fought to control her temper as she asked, "Are you mad at me for being late? You know it wasn't my fault. Things like this happen sometimes."

Again Carly refused to answer her but Julie was sure she heard her daughter give a derisive little snort. That is it, Julie thought as she felt the anger that had building all day suddenly rise to the surface. Julie found a place to pull over and put the car in park. Reaching over to her daughter she grasped Carly's chin and turned her face so they were eye to eye.

"You listen to me, Carly Nicole. I will not tolerate this attitude of yours. Now what's going on? If this is all because I had an emergency then I am very disappointed in you. It's very disrespectful to act this way just because something happened that's out of our control. Now tell me what's going on?"

Carly wrenched her face away from her mother, but not before Julie saw a few tears begin to slide down her cheeks. Julie felt bad for having to speak sternly to Carly but that was the way things happened sometimes. She put the car back in gear and pulled out onto the road again.

"Fine, if that's the way you want to play the game. But understand this, little girl. You're grounded until you tell me what brought on this attitude problem of yours."

That got Carly's attention and she turned to stare at Julie in disbelief. "What!?! You can't do that."

Julie shot a dangerous look at her daughter. "Oh, you bet I can. That's what make me the parent and you the child, little girl."

Carly leaned back in her seat again with her arms folded across her chest. She shot a malevolent look at her mother before saying in a scathing tone, "I hate you, Mom."

Julie couldn't deny that hearing those words hurt deeply, but she forced herself to remember that Carly didn't mean it and that she had done the right thing. "Well, I'll just have to live with that, won't I."

Neither of them spoke another word until they reached the parking lot of the clinic. Julie was thrilled to see Aaron leaning against the driver's side door of the car and she could already tell that the tire was fixed. She watched with regret as Carly got out of the car and slammed the door, stalking away from her mother towards their beat up old car.

"Hi there, Carly. How are you?" Aaron asked and Julie could see he was surprised at the angry look on her face.

"Carly, say thank you to Aaron for his help and then get in the car," Julie said sternly and for a second she was sure that Carly was going to ignore her.

Finally, after a few seconds of silence. Carly spit out the words, "Thanks, Aaron." Without another sound she got into the passenger seat of her mother's car and resumed her earlier position with her arms folded across her chest.

Aaron looked questioningly at Julie but she just shook her head. "Don't ask because I have no idea. Listen, Aaron, thank you so much for your help. It really meant a lot to me."

Aaron grinned at her and shrugged. "Don't thank me. I was happy to help."

They stood facing each other for a moment before Julie suddenly remembered something. "Oh my, God! I almost forgot to give you back your keys." She dug them out of her purse and handed them back to Aaron.

He laughed and said, "I wouldn't have minded if you'd forgotten. Then I would have had an excuse to see you again."

Julie didn't have a clue how to respond to that and they stood there studying each other for another minute. Finally she said, "Well, I'm sorry to cut this short but I better get the Empress home and try to figure out what's bothering her."

"Of course. I hope it's nothing serious," Aaron said and Julie smiled warmly at him.

"I'm sure it's nothing. She's probably just mad because I was late."

Aaron opened the door for Julie and as she got in he bent over to see Carly and said, "See you later, Carly."

To Julie's relief Aaron seemed neither surprised or upset by Carly's continued silence. He just grinned and winked at Julie as he closed her car door. She started the car and rolled down the driver's side window. "Thanks again for your help, Aaron. Hopefully I'll see you around."

With another smile she put the car in gear and was about to pull out of the parking lot when Aaron said, "Wait a minute, Julie. I was wondering, would you like to have dinner with me this Friday night?"

Julie knew he would ask eventually but she was still caught off guard. This could be the one that would change her life, she thought to herself, but how do I trust a man again after what Kevin did to me. This thought ran through her head in about half a second as Julie looked up at Kevin's expectant face. Finally, knowing that she was putting herself in danger of being hurt again, she smiled a little more flirtatiously at him and said, "I'd love that."

Julie found Aaron's surprised expression both amusing and very cute as she rummaged in her purse for her business card holder. Removing one of the cards and her pen she flipped the card over and scribbled on the back. Handing the card to Aaron she said, "My home number is on the back. Give me a call and we'll make arrangements. See you later, Aaron."

Feeling ridiculously proud of herself Julie drove away from the clinic, waving one last time at Aaron and honking the horn, but her good mood faded a little bit when she saw how truly awful Carly looked. Julie sighed, knowing that it was going to be a long night and she better be prepared for a fight if she wanted to get Carly to tell her what was bothering her.

Kevin sat on the couch after work that afternoon with a cold beer open on the coffee table before him. He had called Marcie on the way home and asked her to come over and she should be on her way at that very moment.

Kevin nearly jumped out of his skin when he heard the front door of the condo open and Marcie's sweet, lilting voice say, "Is anybody home?"

Taking a deep breath and steeling himself for what he was about to do Kevin called out, "I'm in here, Marcie."

Marcie came around the corner to the living room and when Kevin saw her he almost lost his nerve. He knew deep down that this had to be done and it would be better to get it out on the table and over with.

Marcie must have sensed something was wrong because her smile faded and she gingerly approached Kevin on the couch. "Sweetie, is something wrong? You look really down"

"Marcie, I need you to do something for me and not ask any questions," Kevin said. He picked up the envelope that was laying on the coffee table beside his beer and, standing up to face her, he handed the envelope to her. "I want you to go in the bedroom and read this. I'll explain everything when you come back out."

Kevin flinched at the look of fear in Marcie's eyes but it was too late to back out now. "Kevin, what's going on?" she whispered and the sound ripped a hole in what was left of Kevin's heart.

Reaching out to take her shoulders in his hands Kevin looked deep into her eyes. "Please do this for me, Marcie. It's important and I promise I'll explain everything after you read it."

Still looking uncertain Marcie nodded and Kevin squeezed her shoulders, then watched her walk towards the bedroom. He heard the bedroom door close and then sat back down on the couch, his head in his hands and waited for the end.

For fifteen agonizing minutes Kevin sat on the couch and waited. When he heard the bedroom door open and Marcie's approaching footsteps he had to remind himself to keep breathing. Daring to look up Kevin flinched at the sight of Marcie's face, pale and streaked with tears. Her eyes were red and puffy and she looked angrier than he'd ever seen her.

"You couldn't tell me this to my face like a man, Kevin?" she asked, holding up the crumpled pages.

Kevin slowly shook his head. He wanted to turn away from her but he knew he deserved to see this pain he'd caused her. "No, Marcie, I couldn't and if you'll let me explain I will."

Marcie sat down in the chair across from him, crossed one leg over the other, and said, "This I have to hear. Go ahead and see if you can explain this, Kevin."

"I could blame all of this on my father and all the power he holds over me. But the reality of the situation is that I'm a coward. I'm too afraid of being cast out on my own with no support from my family that I was willing to let my father control my life. Part of that control was dating you. You're the type of woman Dad wanted me to be with, someone who would look good on my arm without asking too many questions."

At those last few words Marcie flinched and the tears began to fall again. "Wow, Kevin. You really know how to flatter a girl. Do you have any idea how humiliating and degrading this whole thing is? For five years I've nurtured this relationship and this is what I get in return. You're right; you really are a coward."

Kevin reached out to touch her hand and she drew back sharply, hissing at him. "Don't you dare touch me! You do this and then you think you have the right to touch me? Those days are over Kevin. That is what you wanted, right? That's why the song and dance. You wanted me to break up with you so your Daddy couldn't blame it on you and cut you off." Marcie got up from the chair and threw the crumpled letter at Kevin. "You're pathetic and I'm glad that we're over. I feel sorry for the next poor girl that gets sucked into your miserable little life."

Kevin didn't say a single word as Marcie picked up her purse and stalked out of the condo, slamming the front door behind him. Despite feeling horrible for the hurt he'd caused her Kevin couldn't stop a grin from slowly spreading across his face. He was finally free! Now all he had to do was find a way to get in touch with Julie and try to explain things to her. That would be a challenge but it was one that he'd spent the last ten years preparing for and, now that Marcie was out of his life, he was ready for anything.

Julie finished washing the last of the dishes and wiped her hands on a dish towel. She'd eaten supper alone since Carly refused to come out of her room, insisting that she wasn't hungry, and Julie was now debating whether or not to try and talk to Carly again. She knew something serious was bothering her daughter but she couldn't even begin to figure out what.

As if that wasn't enough on her plate she also had an upcoming date with Aaron to think about. Julie was still surprised that she'd accepted Aaron's invitation but she was also quite pleased. He certainly made her feel something she'd never felt before and she just hoped he wouldn't be turned off by her pathetic lack of dating experience.

Straightening up the last of the mess in the kitchen Julie steeled herself for another angry outburst from Carly as she knocked on her daughter's door. When she didn't get a response Julie gently pushed open the door to find Carly lying in bed reading a book.

"I have nothing to talk about, Mom," Carly said, not taking her nose out of the book, but Julie was finished playing games with her daughter.

Sitting on the edge of the bed Julie reached out and took the book out of Carly's hand, marking her page and set it on the bedside table. "I need to know what's bothering you, Carly. Is this because I have a date with Aaron?"

Carly sighed heavily and finally shook her head. "No, it has nothing to do with Aaron. I'm actually really glad you're going out with him, Mom. He seems really cool."

"Then what's the problem, ladybug? I thought we didn't keep secrets from each other. You've always been able to tell me what's bothering you." Julie reached out and tucked a strand of hair behind Carly's ear and she was heartened to see her daughter's face grow a bit softer and less hostile.

"Fine, I'll tell you," Carly said with a sigh. Julie stretched out sideways across the bed with her head resting on her hand, her eyes never leaving her daughter's face.

"In social studies we're working on culture and families and Mrs. Carter assigned us a family tree to make. I was able to do your side of the tree, Mommy, but I don't know anything about my father's family so I had to leave it blank. When I handed it to Mrs. Carter she looked at it and asked why it wasn't finished." Carly stopped there and took a big breath. Julie could see she was fighting tears and her protective mothering instincts had suddenly kicked into high gear.

"She said this in front of all the other kids, Carly?" Julie asked her daughter and Carly nodded, looking miserable.

"Everybody heard her say that I was going to get a zero for not finishing my work. I told her that I didn't know my father and all the other kids laughed at me. Then this one girl, Brittany, she said that I shouldn't get special treatment just because my mother didn't know my father. And then Mrs. Carter said to Brittany, 'It's not Carly's fault that her mother is trailer trash'.

Carly was crying openly now but Julie barely recognized it as she put her arms around her daughter and held her close. She hadn't been called trailer trash in almost eleven years but she could still hear Thomas Meyers saying the words to Kevin while Julie stood there beside him. He'd said it as though Julie had been stupid or something and couldn't understand what he was saying. That brought back bad memories and Julie vowed to herself that Mrs. Carter would pay for what she'd done to Carly.

When the tears abated slightly Carly pulled back and looked up at her mother. "I'm sorry, Mommy," she said when she saw the angry expression on Julie's face.

Julie cupped Carly's face in her hands and looked into her eyes. "You have nothing to be sorry for, Carly Nicole. I will take care of this. That's a promise."

Julie hugged her daughter again, squeezing her tight, and she didn't notice Carly's little wince of pain. Missing that would soon change their lives in the most unimaginable ways. When she released her Julie looked at Carly and gently brushed her hair back from her sweaty face.

"Thank you for telling me this, ladybug. Why don't you come out and have something to eat. I fixed you a plate in case you got hungry sometime tonight."

Carly nodded, wiping the last few remaining tears from her face. "I am pretty hungry," she said and Julie got up from the bed and offered Carly her hand. Carly took it and, before they left Carly's bedroom Julie pulled her daughter into her arms for a tight hug.

"I promise you I will fix this, ladybug," Julie said when she pulled back, framing Carly's face between her hands.

Carly smiled a little weakly and said, "I know you will, Mommy."

Holding Carly's hand Julie led the way to the kitchen and heated up a plate of chicken rigatoni while Carly sat down at the table. Julie sat with Carly while she ate and the two talked easily as they always did. Julie could tell that Carly was still upset though. She was quite subdued and it made Julie horribly angry to think of someone, anyone, treating her daughter in such a disrespectful way.

At times like this, when her daughter was hurting, Julie felt like a mother bear defending her cub and she was determined to see two things happen. Number one, Mrs. Carter and that little brat Brittany would be apologizing to her daughter, and number two, Mrs. Carter would be kissing her teaching career goodbye. Julie was going to have to rearrange tomorrow's schedule. Taking care of this problem was her number one priority right now.

After dinner Carly washed and dried her dishes and put them in the drain. After the kitchen was clean she and Julie sat in the living room to watch TV. Julie noticed that Carly was clingier than normal, staying tucked against Julie's side until Julie told her it was time for bed.

Julie turned everything off downstairs about half an hour after Carly went to bed and, on her way upstairs to her own room, she peeked her head in to check on Carly. To Julie's relief Carly was sound asleep. She had been worried that Carly would have trouble sleeping that night and it made her smile to hear her daughter snoring softly.

In her own bedroom Julie's thoughts were torn between dealing with Carly's school problem and her upcoming date as she undressed for bed. Julie couldn't ignore the little tug deep in her belly whenever she thought of Aaron and, as she was drifting off to sleep, she realized how happy she was that she'd accepted Aaron's invitation.

The next morning Julie sat at the table drinking her second cup of coffee and watching Carly torturing her cereal with the spoon. Julie couldn't help but feel concerned as she studied Carly's pale little face and the deep purple shadows beneath her eyes.

"Honey, why don't you eat that cereal instead of trying to kill it," Julie said in an attempt at some humor.

Carly just shook her head and Julie noticed a thin sheen of sweat standing out on Carly's forehead. Reaching across the table Julie laid a gentle hand on Carly's forehead and could detect a bit of heat. Carly's fever was low grade but it was still a fever and Julie always worried when Carly was ill.

Julie was just about to ask her daughter if she was feeling all right when Carly moaned, "Mommy, I don't feel so good," and dashed from the table into the bathroom with her hands pressed to her stomach.

Julie followed her, wincing at the retching sounds coming from the bathroom, and waited until Carly was finished. She wet a rag and filled a small cup with water before kneeling on the floor beside her daughter. Gently cupping Carly's chin Julie lifted her face so she could wipe it with the cool rag.

"Here, ladybug, swish some of this and spit," Julie said holding the cup of water to Carly's lips. Carly took a tiny sip, swilled it in her mouth, and then spat it into the toilet. Julie hit the lever to flush the toilet and then offered the cup to Carly again. "Take another sip. You can swallow this time."

Carly obeyed wordlessly and when her mother opened her arms Carly went to her gratefully. Julie held her daughter, noting that Carly was shivering, and gently stroked her light brown hair. When she pulled back Julie tucked some hair behind Carly's ears as she said, "I'm keeping you home from school today. Hopefully it's just a twenty four hour bug, but I'd rather be safe than sorry."

Rising from the bathroom floor Julie winced as her knees popped painfully. She reached out a hand to Carly and helped her up, then gave her another little hug. "Brush your teeth and gargle, honey, and then then I want you to get back into bed. I'm going to call Virginia and see if she can come here to babysit. I want you in bed today until that fever goes down."

Julie left the bathroom after gently touching Carly's nose and went back to the kitchen where the phone hung on the wall. Julie dialed Virginia's number, all the while listening to the sounds of Carly brushing and gargling in the bathroom.

The phone rang once, twice, three times and Julie was beginning to get discouraged when Virginia's voice finally came on the line and said, "Hello?"

"Hey, Virginia, it's Julie."

"Hi, Julie. How are you?"

Julie twisted the cord of the phone around her finger and paced back and forth. "Actually I have a little problem. Carly's sick and I was wondering if you could come watch her for the day. I'll pay extra for having you come here instead of taking Carly over to your place."

"I can be there in about half an hour. How sick is she, Julie?" Virginia asked and Julie said a silent prayer of thanks that Virginia had been available.

"Thanks so much Virginia. I'm pretty certain it's just a little bug but I still want to keep her home from school, She feels warm, like she has just a touch of a low grade fever, and she just threw up so maybe that got the worst of it out of her system." Julie said, leaning against the counter.

"Well, like I said before, I can be there in about thirty minutes. And don't worry about paying me extra. You just pay what you usually do, it's not a problem."

Julie felt tears prick her eyes. Virginia's kind voice telling her it wasn't a problem brought back so many memories of her college days when Carly was a baby and Virginia was her babysitter. "Are you sure, Virginia?" she finally asked, fighting to keep her roiling emotions from the surface.

"Of course I'm sure. I'll see you in a little bit," Virginia said and hung up before Julie could say another word. Hanging up the phone Julie stood leaning against the wall for a long moment, feeling suddenly weak and drained, but she managed to pull herself together to check on Carly.

On the way to her daughter's room Julie detoured to the bathroom and searched in the medicine cabinet until she found the thermometer. Knocking on Carly's door Julie waited until her daughter said, weakly, "Come in," and then gently pushed the door open. Carly had changed back into her pajamas and was curled up beneath the covers.

"Hi, ladybug. Are you feeling any better?" Julie asked, crossing the room to sit on the side of Carly's bed.

Carly shook her head apathetically and Julie gently rested a hand on her daughter's forehead. She still felt warm to the touch so Julie said, "Can you sit up just a little bit, honey?"

Carly obeyed, groaning and holding her stomach, but nothing happened after a few seconds passed and Julie was able to put the thermometer under Carly's tongue. They waited until it beeped and Julie felt a bit better when she saw that it only read 100.2 meaning it was a very low grade fever.

"I think it's just a bug, sweetie, but I still want you to rest today. That means staying in bed. You can sit up and read if you want but I don't want you doing anything strenuous, OK."

Carly nodded, laying back against the pillows again, still looking too pale and used for Julie's taste. "I have Virginia coming to stay with you while I'm at work and you can always call me if you need me." Julie kissed her daughter's forehead and said, "I'll be back with some Tylenol and a glass of Pedialyte before I leave for work, ladybug."

Carly just nodded apathetically as Julie left the room, leaving Carly's door open so she could hear her if she called. Julie cleaned up the bathroom and sprayed it with Lysol to freshen the air after Carly's bout of vomiting. When the bathroom was clean Julie went to the kitchen and filled a glass with strawberry flavored Pedialyte. On her way back to Carly's bedroom Julie stopped in the bathroom to retrieve the children's Tylenol from the medicine cabinet.

"Can you sit up again for me, honey?" Julie asked her daughter and watched as Carly very slowly moved to a sitting position. Julie perched on the edge of Carly's bed and poured the proper dosage of medicine in the plastic measuring cup, then handed it to Carly. Carly made a face, but she swallowed the medicine with a little wince of disgust.

"Here, baby, take a sip of this to get rid of the medicine taste." Julie handed Carly the glass of chilled Pedialyte and Carly took a small sip. She handed the glass back to Julie and Julie put it on the nightstand where it would be within easy reach for Carly when she needed it.

"I'll be back to see you before I leave, baby," Julie said and went back to the bathroom to rinse the measuring cup and replace it and the bottle of Tylenol in the medicine cabinet. She was in the kitchen rummaging through her purse to make sure she had everything she needed for the day when someone knocked on the front door.

"The door's open, Virginia," Julie called from the kitchen and she listened as the front door opened and then closed. Virginia appeared a second later and Julie smiled at her gratefully. "Thank you so much for doing this," she said.

Virginia waved an airy hand and said, "It's not a problem. Is there anything special I should know?"

"She's strictly Pedialyte when it comes to liquids today. If her fever goes down she can come out and lay on the couch to watch TV but I want her to stay calm and quiet. If she's hungry and she feels like she can eat try to find something light to give her for lunch and there are also Pedialyte ice pops in the freezer if she wants one. Other than that you already know the drill."

Virginia smiled and nodded. "Sounds good, Jules. You better get going or you'll be late for work."

"I'm going as soon as I say goodbye to Carly," Julie said and headed down the hall to her daughter's room. Carly was still sitting up in bed and Julie, surprised, asked, "What are you still doing up, ladybug?"

"I was waiting for you so I could say goodbye," Carly said and the sweet innocence in the words brought a little lump to Julie's throat. She crossed the room and bent down to give her daughter a hug.

"Virginia's here and you can call me if you need anything. I love you, ladybug," Julie said, giving her daughter one final squeeze.

"I love you too, Mommy," Carly said and she blew her mother a kiss which Julie returned as she left the room.

Grabbing her purse off the table and her keys off the peg next to the back door Julie called over her shoulder, "Thanks again, Virginia. I'll see you later."

"Bye, Jules. Don't work too hard."

About ten minutes after Julie left Virginia went to check on Carly and found her already sound asleep with the covers pulled up to her chin. Not wanting to wake her up Virginia tiptoed out of the room, leaving the door partly open behind her, and settled on the couch in the living room with a novel she'd brought to keep herself occupied. Virginia had a feeling this was going to be an easy babysitting job as she opened her book and began to read.

Julie was distracted at work all morning; partly out of worry for Carly and partly because she was concentrating so hard on what she planned to do and say when she went to Carly's school that afternoon. She'd gotten Nancy to juggle her schedule a bit and Evelyn had helped by agreeing to take some of her patients for an hour so she could go to Carly's school and deal with Mrs. Carter.

Julie arrived at the school around one o'clock that afternoon and pulled her car into the same space she'd used the day before with Aaron's car. Turning off the engine Julie tucked her purse underneath the passenger seat, climbed out of the car and closed the door, locking all four doors before crossing the parking lot and pulling open the front door. She turned left and entered the main office, approaching the front desk where the receptionist was seated before a computer.

"Hello, Dr. Forrester," the receptionist said, her tone surprised. "What can I do for you today?"

"I need to see Principal Sheridan. It's very important."

The receptionist looked a bit flustered as she picked up the phone and dialed the principal's office. Julie listened with half an ear as the receptionist murmured into the telephone and when she hung up Julie turned her full attention on her. "I'm afraid the principal is busy, Dr. Forrester. Would you like to leave a message or set up a meeting perhaps."

"You get him back on the phone and tell him he has two options; he can come out and invite me into his office himself or I'll invite myself in. Either way I fully intend to see him today."

Julie felt bad when she saw the expression on the receptionist's face as she picked up the phone again but Julie pushed that aside as she remembered Carly's tears the night before and her own anger at the way her child had been treated. Julie waited patiently as the receptionist spoke into the receiver again and she was soon rewarded by the door to the principal's office banging open and Principal Sheridan himself striding out with a disgruntled look on his face.

"What is so important, Dr. Forrest. Believe it or not I am a very busy man. Not all of us have leisure time to waste."

Julie's expression didn't waver as she said evenly, "Most people would at least exchange pleasantries before diving right into being rude and impolite, Principal Sheridan. But I'm willing to overlook that and assume that you've kindly invited me into your office to chat. Shall we?"

With that Julie strode around the desk and into the principal's open office door, leaving the man gaping behind her for several seconds before he followed her. Julie sat in the visitor's chair while Principal Sheridan sat down in his own executive chair.

Julie waited until she had the principal's full attention before saying, "My daughter, Carly, told me a very interesting story last night, Principal Sheridan."

She repeated what Carly had told her and watched with growing satisfaction as the principal's expression grew more and more angry and unbelieving. When she was finished telling the story Julie said, "I trust that this matter will be dealt with exactly as I've requested. Am I right, Principal Sheridan."

The principal hesitated for a moment before he punched a button on the telephone and said to the receptionist, "Margaret, I need you to get me the class attendance list for Mrs. Carter."

Turning back to Julie he said, "I hope you understand that this has to be approved by the superintendent before I do anything about Mrs. Carter. But I don't believe it will be a problem, not after what you've told me. And I'd like to apologize. I'm ashamed that someone who works for me and my school would treat a student in such a way."

"Your apology isn't necessary, Principal Sheridan. You didn't do anything wrong. I'd like to speak to Mrs. Carter before I leave. Could you tell me what room she's in?" Julie said, pleasantly, knowing that she might have to fight to get that information.

Principal Sheridan hesitated for a second before shaking his head. "I'm sorry, Dr. Forrester, but I can't let you do that."

Julie smiled and said, "I'd like to see you try and stop me, Principal Sheridan."

The principal glared at her across the desk for a long moment but when Julie continued to smile pleasantly at him he sighed heavily and said, "She's in room twenty two. Please don't do anything that *I'll* end up regretting.

Julie stood and started to leave the office, but turned at the door to face the principal and said, "Thank you for your time and cooperation Principal Sheridan."

Leaving the office Julie strode down the hallway, making turns when she had to, until she reached room twenty two. Taking a deep breath she knocked on the open door and then stepped halfway inside. The look on Mrs. Carter's face made Julie see red and she had to fight to keep control of her temper and her emotions.

"I'd be grateful if I could speak to you outside for a moment, Mrs. Carter," Julie said, feeling quite proud of herself for sounding so composed.

Mrs. Carter gave her a big fake smile and simpered, "I'm sorry Ms. Forrester but I'm quite busy right now. I'm afraid not all of us have leisure time during the day."

Julie's pleasant attitude faded right there and then as she stepped into the classroom and faced Mrs. Carter. "It's Dr. Forrester," she corrected. "Doctor, as in MD. I'm a doctor, Mrs. Carter. So much for trailer trash. And I have no problem dealing with this issue right here, right now."

Mrs. Carter had turned a little pale when Julie uttered the phrase 'trailer trash' and Julie was quite pleased at the effect she'd had on the teacher.

Julie regained her pleasant and conversational tone as she said, "I just wanted to be the one to let you know that I've already discussed the issue of what happened yesterday with Principal Sheridan and he intends to speak to the superintendent about your termination. I hope you know how to say, 'do you want fries with that', because I'm going to do whatever it takes to make sure you never teach a class in this city again. You have a nice day now, Mrs. Carter."

Without another word Julie turned and strode back out of the classroom, savoring the dumbfounded look on Mrs. Carter's face, and felt quite proud of herself for the way she'd handled everything and the fact that she'd be back to work with time to spare. This had turned out to be a good day and she couldn't wait to get home and tell Carly all about it.

Carly was curled up on the couch with a blanket wrapped around her watching television when Julie arrived home that evening shortly after five o'clock. Virginia was seated in a chair working on a crossword puzzle book and they both looked up and smiled when they saw her.

"Hi, Mommy!" Carly said and Julie was thrilled to see that she had a bit more color in her cheeks compared to that morning.

"Hi, ladybug," Julie said, sitting down next to Carly and hugging her tight. "Hey, Virginia. I take it you didn't have any trouble."

Virginia smiled and shook her head. "Not a bit. Carly's fever went down to almost normal and she was able to eat a bowl of tomato soup and a toasted cheese sandwich for lunch."

"That's my girl," Julie said and gave her daughter another little squeeze.

Virginia closed her puzzle book and tucked it back into her purse along with her ink pen. Standing up and stretching she said, "Well, now that you're home I better get going. I'll see you later, Carly." She bent down to give Carly a hug.

"I'll walk you out, Virginia. Be right back, baby." Julie patted Carly's knee and rose from the couch. She walked Virginia out to her car and when Virginia started the engine and rolled the window down Julie leaned in. "Thanks again, Virginia. You're a lifesaver."

Virginia smiled and said, "I was happy to do it. Carly's such a great kid and I miss getting to spend time with her."

"You know you're welcome here anytime," Julie said.

"I know, but you need your private time with her. You missed out on so much when she was little. I don't want to intrude now when you have more free time to spend with her." Virginia's tone became teasing as she said, "So, Carly tells me you have a date. That's very interesting. Holding out on me are you, Jules?"

Julie laughed ruefully and rolled her eyes. "Yes I have a date and no I'm not holding out on anybody. It's just a date, not a royal wedding."

Virginia patted Julie's hand and smiled warmly at her. "You know I'm just teasing. I'm happy for you, hon. This is well overdue and I hope it works out well."

Julie smiled, thinking about Aaron, and said, "I hope so too."

Virginia put the car into gear and waved at Julie as she pulled out of the parking lot. Julie waved back until Virginia was out of sight and then headed back inside to start dinner. Carly sat at the table with a sweatshirt on over her pajamas while Julie fixed them some vegetable soup and roast beef sandwiches.

When the food was done and Julie sat down at the table she looked at Carly and said, "So, I talked to your principal today about what happened in class yesterday and he's going to take care of it."

"What's he gonna do, Mommy?" Carly asked, taking a small bite of her sandwich and washing it down with a sip of her water. Julie had agreed that since she wasn't vomiting anymore and didn't have diarrhea she could stop the Pedialyte.

"I'm not sure yet. He has to meet with the superintendent but I'm sure he's going to do something. I don't want you to behave any differently in school because of this, Carly. You let me and your principal deal with this, ok."

Carly nodded as she chewed a mouthful of vegetables. "I will, Mommy," she said finally to satisfy her mother.

After dinner they cleaned up the dishes and the kitchen before returning to the living room to watch TV. Carly went to bed early, complaining that she still felt a little weak and drained, but Julie was certain that she'd be able to go to school the following day.

Shortly after eleven Julie turned in herself after checking on Carly. Her daughter was fast asleep and snoring softly. Julie tiptoed gingerly into the room to feel her forehead and was pleased that Carly felt perfectly cool to the touch. Putting on her pajamas Julie slipped beneath the sheets and turned over onto her side. As always her thoughts turned to Aaron and she fell asleep with a smile on her face as she thought about their upcoming date.

CHAPTER 4

ulie watched in the mirror as Carly lay sprawled on her belly across the bed with her feet in the air. Carly had been so excited when Julie asked her to help her get ready for her date and Julie was grateful for the company. There was no denying she was nervous and it helped having Carly there with her for support.

Aaron had called her the day before and told her he'd made reservations at Donovan's Steak and Chophouse in Phoenix. It was about a twenty five minute drive from Scottsdale and he'd asked her to be ready by six o'clock so they'd have plenty of time to get there.

Julie had left work a little before three and picked up Carly. As soon as they got home she'd stripped out of her scrubs and climbed into a hot shower. After climbing out of the shower and drying off she'd rubbed moisturizing cream into her skin and slipped into her bra and panties. As soon as she was decent she'd asked Carly if she'd like to help her finish getting ready and Carly had jumped at the invitation.

Julie put on her one good dress and Carly zipped it up for her. It was a simple, sleeveless black dress that dipped in the front and showed off just enough cleavage for Julie to feel comfortable. The soft fabric clung to her curves in all the right places and fell perfectly to mid-thigh. She added a pair of pearl drop earrings and a matching necklace as well as a pair of dress sandals with a low heel.

"You look so beautiful, Mommy," Carly said softly, almost reverently, and the words warmed Julie all the way down to her toes.

"Thank you, ladybug," Julie said, giving her daughter a hug and a kiss on the forehead.

Carly followed Julie as she went to the bathroom to put on her make-up. Julie concentrated as she carefully applied mascara and eyeliner, then a touch of lip gloss. She hated lipstick and never wore it but she liked the way the gloss made her mouth look and feel. When her make-up was done she brushed out her hair and let it fall naturally to her shoulders.

As Julie was fixing her hair someone knocked on the front door. Checking her watch she saw it was too early to be Aaron which meant it must be Virginia.

"Can you get the door for me, please, Carly."

"Sure, Mommy." Carly skipped off down the stairs and Julie heard her a moment later chattering to Virginia. After one last look in the mirror Julie decided she didn't look half bad and, after taking a steadying breath, she grabbed her purse and made her way downstairs.

"Wow! You look amazing, Jules!" Virginia cried when she got a look at Julie. "Turn around, let me see you."

Feeling a little silly, but with a smile on her face at the same time, Julie spun around slowly and laughed when Virginia whistled.

"I don't know who this guy is but I do know he's gonna like what he sees tonight."

Julie shook her head, still laughing, and said, "Thanks, I think." Just as she opened her mouth to say something else someone knocked on the door again and Julie felt the bottom fall out of her stomach.

"I don't know if I can do this," she moaned, feeling suddenly terrified instead of just a little nervous.

Virginia gave her a gentle push towards the door. "You can do this and you will. Now go on."

Taking another deep breath and willing herself to relax Julie made her way to the front door, hesitated for just a moment, and then pulled it open. She gasped audibly when she saw Aaron standing there looking utterly dashing in a dark suit and tie.

"You look amazing, Julie," Aaron said to Julie at the exact same time she said to him, "You look fantastic, Aaron."

They both laughed and Aaron handed her one of the two yellow roses he held in his hand. "This one's for you," he said and Julie took it, feeling more and more like a princess with every passing moment.

"Thank you very much. Who's the other one for?" she asked.

"The other one's for Carly. Where is she?" Aaron said and for a long moment Julie was too tongue tied to say anything. Nobody had ever shown such an interest in her daughter and it warmed her right down to her soul to see how thoughtful Aaron was when it came to Carly.

"She's in the living room, probably eavesdropping on us. Carly, honey, Aaron has something for you!" she called and Carly poked her head around the corner.

"Hi, Carly," Aaron said brightly.

Carly smiled a little bashfully and said, "Hi, Aaron."

Aaron held out the yellow rose to her and said, "This is for you. I got one for your mom and I didn't want you to be left out. Do you like it?"

Carly took the single flower and sniffed it gingerly. "It's really pretty. Thank you, Aaron."

"You're very welcome," he said to Carly with a smile. Then, turning to Julie, he asked, "Are you ready to go?"

"As ready as I'll ever be," she said and Aaron laughed. Julie gave her daughter a quick hug and kissed her cheek. "Be good for Virginia, sweetheart."

"I will, Mommy. Have a good time."

Julie waved and closed the front door. Now that she was actually in Aaron's presence she felt more confident and less nervous. She could smell the heady aroma of his cologne and the scent caused something to tighten deep in her belly.

Julie was pleased and flatter when Aaron opened the car door for her before climbing in behind the wheel. They were silent as he started the car and pulled out of the parking lot. Once they were on the road though he glanced at her and said, "So, have you ever been to Donovan's before?"

"No, but I've heard a lot about it. It gets really rave reviews from what I've heard. Have you been there before?"

"No, but my parents went there a few times for anniversaries when I was little and I know my mom always really liked it there."

Julie leaned back in her seat as the two of them chatted easily during the thirty minute drive to Phoenix. She found herself quite amazed at how easy it was to talk to Aaron and she found herself wondering why she'd been nervous about this date in the first place.

They arrived at the restaurant ten minutes before the time of their reservation and were able to be seated immediately. Julie was quite impressed when she saw the waiters all dressed up in formal wear and how romantic everything looked with candles flickering gently on the tables. They were given a cozy corner booth and right away Aaron requested a bottle of wine for their table.

Before they could really begin talking their waiter appeared. "Good evening. Can I start you off with an appetizer?"

Both Aaron and Julie scanned their menus. "What do you think, Julie?" Aaron asked and Julie hesitated for a moment.

"How about the fried calamari?" she asked Aaron and he nodded. The waiter wrote it down on his pad and disappeared.

Julie sipped at the glass of sparkling water the waiter had brought out with him. "This place is really amazing, Aaron. Thank you for bringing me here."

Aaron smiled at her and drank some water. "You're very welcome. And it is a nice place. I have to say I wasn't expecting it to be quite this fancy."

"I feel a little spoiled tonight," Julie said, with a wink, and Aaron laughed.

"I'm glad," he responded,

Aaron reached across the table and, after a moment's hesitation, Julie took his hand. Immediately she felt his thumb begin caressing her skin. It had been a long time since she'd been touched, really touched, by someone and she hadn't realized just how touch starved she really was.

The waiter arrived just then with their appetizer and they were forced to let go of each other's hands so they could scan their menus again and decided what they wanted. Finally they both decided on the filet minion medallion with grilled portabella mushrooms and au gratin potatoes.

After the waiter left to put in their order Aaron reached again for Julie's hand and this time she took it with no hesitation, tracing his skin with her thumb. Noticing a small scar on the back of his hand Julie asked, "How did you get that," rubbing the area of skin she was referring to.

"My dad and I used to build models, airplanes and cars and stuff like that, really nice ones. When I was about twelve my parents bought me this really intricate and detailed model of the Titanic to build. We were in the den putting some of the last pieces on it when my dad accidentally grazed the back of my hand with the sharp point of one of the pieces."

Aaron was silent for a minute, watching Julie's thumb rubbing against the scar, as though lost in the memory. Julie waited patiently until Aaron snapped out of his reverie and said, with a small smile, "That's one of the things I miss most about my dad. Putting together those models. We must have built at least fifty of them from the time I was old enough to help until I went away to college."

Julie squeezed Aaron's hand, aching at the sadness in his voice, and said softly, "Your dad was a really good man. I'm honored to have been able to know him."

"Thank you for saying that, Julie," Aaron said softly and she could tell he had been touched by her words.

Aaron was silent for another long moment and they both took sips from their wine glasses. "So, what do you like to do for fun?" Aaron asked her finally.

Julie snorted laughter a bit inelegantly and said, "Fun? I don't have time for fun. Most of my time is spent working and being a single mother."

"Well you must do something for yourself," Aaron pressed.

Julie thought about it for a second before she answered. "I do go out with my girlfriends twice a month to have a few drinks and dance. There's a night club we go to called Axis/Radius that has great music and really great mixed drinks. It's nice to go out with the girls and just let loose for a little while."

"Sounds like you have good friends," Aaron said. At that moment their waiter arrived with their meals and they were forced to let go of each other's hands again.

"They're the best. I don't know what I'd do without my girls." Julie smiled and took another sip of her wine, savoring the taste and the simple joy of being out with a man she really liked.

They dug into their entrees and at the first bite Julie let out a little sigh of pleasure. "This is fantastic," she said and Aaron laughed.

"This place definitely deserves its reputation."

Julie took another bite and chewed slowly, rolling the food around on her tongue to really savor it, and said, "This is really a far cry from the boxed meal kits I usually make for me and Carly."

"You don't cook?" Aaron asked, curiously.

"I don't have time to cook. And I'll admit that I'm not exactly Paula Dean when it comes to the kitchen. Do you know how to cook, Aaron?"

Aaron nodded as he chewed a mouthful of potato. When he swallowed he wiped his lips with a napkin and said, "My mom insisted I learn how to cook so I wouldn't starve once I was on my own. At the time I hated it but now I love to cook. It's very soothing and relaxing, especially after a rough day."

They continued to chat as they ate their meals and Julie realized she was growing more and more attracted to Aaron as the evening progressed. She found herself wondering if he was going to kiss her goodnight when he took her home and hoped that he would.

After dinner they split a piece of Dutch apple pie and when that was gone Julie felt as though she might explode. She couldn't remember ever eating quite that good. After the pie was gone Aaron pushed his chair back and stood up, offering Julie his hand. She took it and was pleased when Aaron held it until they reached the counter to pay their bill. Ever the true gentleman Aaron opened the door of the restaurant for her and when they were out in the warm evening air he looked over at her with an inquiring look on his face.

"Do you like surprises?" he asked, mysteriously.

Julie grinned widely and said, "I love surprises."

"Then you'll love this," he said and opened the car door for her.

Julie's curiosity was starting to get unbearable when Aaron said, twenty minutes after they left the restaurant, "Look over there, to your right."

Julie looked and gasped at the sight before her. She'd heard of the Phoenix Civic Space Park and had always wanted to go there but never had the time. Now Aaron had taken her to see it and she thought once again how it seemed he could read her mind sometimes.

"Oh, Aaron, it's so beautiful. How did you know I've been wanting to see this for ages?"

Aaron just laughed and said, "Intuition I guess. Either that or just plain luck. Come on, let's take a walk around."

Opening the car door for her he offered his hand which she took and their fingers laced together almost automatically as they began to stroll through the park. They kept up a constant stream of chatter and made two turns around the park before Julie glanced at her watch and said, regretfully, "It's getting late. I better get home and relieve Virginia."

Still hand in hand they strolled back to the car and Aaron opened her door for her. They were a bit quiet on the ride home but it was a comfortable silence and Julie savored it. After pulling into a parking space in front of Julie's townhouse Aaron walked Julie to her door. For a long moment they just looked at each other until Julie finally said, "Thank you, Aaron. Tonight was really wonderful."

Aaron smiled down at her and said, "You're welcome. I'm glad you had fun."

They stood there for another long second, both of them shifting uncertainly from one foot to the other, until finally Aaron sighed softly and reached out to lightly cup Julie's cheek. Julie trembled slightly as she leaned into the touch, closing her eyes as Aaron's thumb began moving lightly against her skin. She could feel him moving closer to her and she reached out to rest her hands on his shoulders, Julie could feel his soft breath on her face just seconds before their lips met in a tentative, hesitant first kiss.

Julie knew she would remember that moment for the rest of her life. It had been so long since she'd been kissed that she'd been afraid of forgetting the mechanics. The moment their lips touched instinct flooded her and she drew strength and comfort from that as she returned the kiss with an innocent eagerness. Her body felt flushed and oddly heavy as they kissed beneath the porch light.

All too soon it ended as Aaron gently pulled away from her. Looking a bit sheepish, like a little boy caught with his hand in the cookie jar, he said, "I hope that wasn't too forward, this being our first date."

Julie smiled coyly up at him. "Do you hear me complaining?"

Aaron laughed at that and Julie could tell he was relieved to hear her say that. Leaning against him Julie sighed as Aaron put his arms around her and held her. She wrapped her arms tightly around his back and rested her cheek against his shoulder. They held each other like that for a long moment before Julie regretfully pulled away.

"I really have to get inside," she said, fishing in her purse for her keys.

Aaron unlocked her door for her and, with a quick kiss on the cheek, Julie slipped through the door and slowly closed it, wanting to memorize the way Aaron looked with the porch light glowing above him.

Julie quietly moved through the house until she reached the living room where she found Virginia seated in the chair reading a magazine.

"Hey, there. How was the date?" Virginia asked, looking up at Julie with a sly smile on her face.

Julie smiled back, feeling warm and tingly all over, and said, "It was wonderful. Better than I imagined it would be."

"You're glowing," Virginia said teasingly. Julie just rolled her eyes and Virginia laughed. "I guess I better get going. Carly's asleep; she complained of feeling weak and tired so I told her to go to bed early. There was no fever and she ate dinner so I don't think it's anything to worry about."

"I'll try and keep her quiet this weekend and hopefully she'll be all right by Monday. She gave me a hard time about going to school all week last week. I wish I knew why she's been trying to get out of school all the time lately."

"I don't know," Virginia said as she slung her purse over one shoulder. "Give me a call if you need anything. I'm really glad you had fun, Jules. Nobody deserves it more than you." Virginia squeezed Julie's shoulder on the way out.

As soon as the front door was closed Julie locked it, then went around to the back door to make sure that was locked too. Slipping off her shoes and carrying them with her Julie checked on Carly briefly before heading upstairs to her own room. Julie's mind was entirely focused on Aaron and the kiss they shared as she undressed and crawled into bed. Normally Julie would have been turned off by a man who wanted to kiss on the first date, but with Aaron it was different. It felt like she'd known him her entire life, like he was meant to be a part of her life, and the intensity of her feelings frightened her a little.

Rolling over onto her side Julie forced herself to stop the psycho-analyzing and just think about the date. It had been truly wonderful and she found herself certain that it was just the beginning of something special between her and Aaron.

Aaron entered his new apartment after dropping Julie off, shutting and locking the front door behind him. He immediately headed for the kitchen where he poured himself a glass of water and drained it in one gulp. Heading into his bedroom he began to undress, feeling a little suffocated by the suit, but ultimately glad he'd worn it when he remembered the look on Julie's face at her first sight of him.

Crawling into bed Aaron set the alarm on his bedside table. Getting up early was a habit for him and he hated the way he felt when he slept too late. As he laced his hands behind his head his thoughts turned again to Julie and he found himself wondering when and where he would see her again. He knew that something special had happened between them that night and that she had felt it too. He was crazy about her and he wasn't about to let her slip away from him.

Closing his eyes and rolling over onto his side Aaron recalled the details of their kiss on the front porch of her condo and fell asleep with a slightly goofy grin on his face.

Julie was simultaneously woken by two things the following morning; the phone on her nightstand ringing and Carly diving into her bed and bouncing up and down.

With a little groan Julie reached for the phone and said, "Hello?" She still felt half asleep until she heard the voice on the other end of the line.

"Up and at 'em, kiddo!" Aaron's bright and cheerful voice said and Julie immediately sat up straight, wide awake now.

"Hi, Aaron! Why are you calling me at seven in the morning?" Julie tried to keep her voice neutral as she tried to wake up a little more.

"I've been up for over an hour. I just couldn't wait any longer to hear your voice. I figured you got up early because of Carly," he said and she could tell he felt bad.

Julie leaned against the pillows and Carly snuggled into her side. Stroking her daughter's hair Julie said, "We usually try and sleep in on the weekends. She was up early this morning though, jumping up and down on my bed." At that Julie playfully tickled Carly, making her giggle and try to twist out of her mother's hands.

"She's awake now?" Aaron asked.

"Yeah, she's right here. Do you want to talk to her?"

"Sure, I'd love to talk to her," Aaron agreed and Julie held the phone out to Carly.

"Aaron wants to talk to you. I'll be right back." When Carly took the phone Julie made a mad dash to the bathroom to take care of some early morning business. She could hear Carly chattering and giggling into the phone. Again Julie thought of how lucky she was to have a man in her life that cared about Carly.

When Julie returned from the bathroom and sat down on the bed again Carly handed her the phone with an excited expression on her face. "Here, Mommy, he says he needs to talk to you."

Julie took the phone and put it back to her ear. "What's going on? Why's Carly so excited?"

She heard Aaron's husky chuckle and the sound sent shivers down her spine, "I told her I might have a surprise for her today. How would you and Carly like to go out for breakfast with me this morning?"

Julie closed her eyes and fought back tears of pure joy and gratitude. For the first time in her life someone wanted to include Carly in their plans and it warmed Julie from head to toe in a way she'd never expected. Finally, after taking a moment to compose herself, Julie said, "I'd like that."

"Great! I'll be there around eight," Aaron said.

"That sounds perfect, Aaron. I'll see you soon." Julie hung up the phone and turned to Carly who was practically wriggling with excitement.

"What's going on, Mommy?" she asked excitedly and Julie grinned at her.

"Go get dressed," she said, giving Carly a gentle push towards her room.

"Why?"

"Because Aaron is taking us out for breakfast this morning. He'll be here in about an hour."

Carly let out a little squeal and jumped up and down. "I get to go too?" she asked and Julie couldn't help but laugh at the surprised look on her face.

"Only if you're dressed by the time he gets here," Julie said and Carly dashed off to get ready.

After a quick shower to help her wake up Julie went to her closet to get ready. She skimmed through her clothing, wanting to look pretty but casual. Finally, after agonizing over several options, she chose a pair of white cotton capri pants and a mint green blouse made out of gauzy material that clung invitingly to her curves and made her look both sexy and casual. She brushed her hair and applied some light make-up before slipping her feet into a pair of comfortable flip-flops, then went to check on Carly.

She found her daughter sitting on the bed in her room already dressed in a pair of purple plaid bermuda shorts and a purple t-shirt. Julie leaned against the doorframe and watched as Carly laced up her sneakers, feeling a peacefulness she couldn't ever remember feeling before.

"I'm ready, Mommy," Carly crowed, jumping up from the bed.

Since Carly was such a bundle of excited energy Julie agreed that they could wait for Aaron outside and she sat on her lawn chair while Carly played with a jump rope. Julie watched with a smile on her lips as Carly went through a series of jump rope tricks that Julie couldn't even imagine doing. She was also singing little jump rope rhymes to herself and Julie was reminded with a pang of nostalgia her own childhood when she used to love playing with a jump rope.

Before she could get too caught up in old memories, some of them more painful than others, Aaron's car pulled into the parking lot with Aaron behind the wheel and honking the horn. Carly immediately abandoned her jump rope and ran to greet Aaron as he climbed out of the car.

Julie followed at a more sedate pace, a little unsure how to greet Aaron in front of her daughter, but she was spared the worry when Aaron simply smiled warmly at her and said, "Hi, Julie. You look beautiful today." Then, turning to Carly, he added, "You both look beautiful. I'm the luckiest man on the planet today."

That was nice, Julie thought, as she watched Carly's grin grow even wider. Aaron clapped his hands together then and said, "So, is everyone ready to go?"

"Ready whenever you are," Julie answered and Aaron opened the doors for both her and Carly before climbing back in behind the wheel.

As he was pulling out into traffic Julie and Carly buckled their seatbelts. "Where are we eating, Aaron?" Carly asked from the backseat.

"I was thinking about IHOP. They have a really good variety of pancakes and french toast. Is that good for you, Carly?"

Carly nodded vigorously and Aaron smiled at her once before turning his attention to the road. Julie had her sunglasses pushed back on her head and was simply enjoying the ride and the feeling of being a family. She knew they weren't yet, but it was nice to be with a man who included Carly in his life. That was something she hadn't expected to ever find and now that she had she wanted to savor every single second of it.

Carly kept up a constant stream of chatter from the backseat; talking about school, her friends, what she liked to do for fun. Aaron asked her a lot of questions and Julie was relieved that he wasn't irritated by Carly's endless supply of energy. Aaron told Julie a little more about his job as a sales and operations manager for a major retail company.

They were all still chattering when Aaron pulled the car into a parking space at IHOP. Carly insisted on walking between them as they entered the building. Julie was a little frustrated by that; she would have liked to hold Aaron's hand. But it felt good to see how well Aaron and her daughter were getting along. Still, Julie thought, only time would really tell if he would be able to handle having Carly around full time.

They were seated in a booth after entering the building. Julie and Carly sat across from Aaron and a waitress soon appeared to take their drink orders. Both Julie and Aaron ordered coffee and small glasses of orange juice. Carly tried to talk her mother into letting her have a soda but Julie remained firm and Carly eventually gave in and settled for grapefruit juice.

They were still perusing their menus when a young waitress appeared at their table, smiling cheerfully with her pad and pen ready to take their order.

"Ladies first," Aaron said, waving a hand at Julie and Carly.

Trying to hide her broad smile Julie took one last quick glance at her menu. "I think I'll have the spinach and mushroom omelet with a side of fresh fruit."

The waitress jotted down her order and looked expectantly at Carly. Carly hesitated for a brief second; she was always shy about talking to strangers but Julie always encouraged her to do things like give her own order at restaurants. Finally she said, "I want the strawberry banana pancakes, please."

Aaron ordered the stuffed french toast combo with eggs, hash browns and bacon. After their waitress left to put their order into the computer Julie gave Carly a squeeze and a kiss on the cheek. "You did a good job, baby. I'm very proud of you."

They chattered all through breakfast, Aaron and Julie both going through two cups of coffee, and Julie couldn't remember ever feeling quite so happy or content. After they finished eating Aaron paid the bill while Julie and Carly waited on a bench outside in the warm sunshine.

"Hey, how would you guys like to do something fun today?" Aaron said as he came out of the restaurant to join them.

Carly was immediately alert and curious. "Like what, Aaron?"

Aaron thought about it for a second and finally said, "How about spending the day at Crackerjax?"

Carly's eyes lit up and even Julie couldn't help but feel a little excited. Crackerjax was a very popular family fun and sports park in Scottsdale. Julie had always wanted to take Carly there but for one reason or another their plans always fell through. She couldn't believe that Aaron had suggested it. Sometimes it really seemed like he could see inside her and know just what to do and say.

"Mommy, can we go!?!" Carly asked excitedly, looking from Julie to Aaron and back again.

"It sounds good to me," Julie said and laughed as Carly began squealing and jumping up and down. She was pleased and surprised when her daughter suddenly threw her arms around Aaron's middle and squeezed tightly.

"Thank you, thank you, thank you!!" she cried and Aaron hugged her back, laughing a little. Julie could see in his eyes that he was pleased his suggestion had gotten such rave reviews and even more pleased at Carly's hug.

They piled back into the car and began the drive to the fun park. Carly was fidgety the whole way and Julie had all she could do to contain her own building excitement. Crackerjax had everything from batting cages to arcade games to miniature golf and bumper boats. She couldn't help feeling a little bit like a kid again.

The three of them spent the rest of the morning and a good part of the early afternoon at Crackerjax. They played two rounds of miniature golf, much to Carly's delight and endless games of skee ball in the arcade. Aaron hit the batting cages and taught Carly how to hit a ball in one of the slow pitch cages. Julie watched with a lump in her throat as Aaron patiently guided Carly in the right way to hold the bat and how to position her feet to keep her balance. Nothing had prepared her for this; finding a man who cared about her little girl almost as much as she did.

As they enjoyed the attractions of the park they ate an almost never ending supply of Crackerjacks and went through half a dozen bottles of water. They were all slightly burnt from the sun by the time they climbed back into the car and Julie wasn't surprised when Carly fell asleep in the backseat. When they got to Julie's place Aaron carried Carly inside and put her to bed. She didn't even stir except to roll over and clutch at her old stuffed dog that she'd had for years.

"She's out like a light," he said softly when he left her room. Julie was sitting in the chair she kept outside the front door of her condo. Aaron hesitated slightly, shifting anxiously from foot to foot, and finally said, "I should get going."

Julie stood up as he started down the walk and caught his wrist in her hand. He turned to face her and Julie, after a moment's hesitation, leaned up on tiptoes and brushed his mouth with a light kiss. "This has been one of the best days I've ever had, Aaron. Thank you, for everything."

Aaron cupped her face gently in his hands. He kissed her forehead, the tip of her nose, both cheeks and her chin before finally bringing his lips to hers. They kissed softly, tenderly, and Julie could feel herself falling even deeper for him than she already had.

"I'll call you later, Julie," Aaron whispered when they finally parted and Julie simply nodded, not trusting her own voice. She watched as Aaron climbed into his car and pulled out of the parking lot, waving until she could see him no longer.

It wasn't until Aaron left that Julie really noticed how exhausted she was. She entered the condo and, after peeking on Carly to make sure she was all right, went up the stairs to her own room and collapsed still fully dressed on top of the covers. Despite her exhaustion Julie lay awake for several minutes, replaying every detail of the day they had spent together, and fell asleep with a small smile playing at the corners of her mouth.

Looking back months later Julie would find herself wondering how she'd missed so many obvious signs. It was as if the events to come had been flashing in great big neon letters and she was just ignoring it. She tried to tell herself that it was easy enough to overlook, but in reality she simply hadn't wanted to see it. After all, who wants to know beforehand when their seemingly perfect world will suddenly be shattered?

CHAPTER 5

*A*s Julie stood in front of the mirror getting ready she couldn't keep her thoughts from straying to the last few weeks of her life. Since Aaron came into her life Julie was happier than she ever remembered being. Not only had they gone on some really spectacular dates they'd also spent a lot of time with Carly doing family activities. Seeing Aaron take such an interest in her daughter was profound for Julie and she thanked God for bringing him into their lives.

As much as she enjoyed them being all together as a family she couldn't deny that she was anxious to have some real private time with Aaron. So when Carly was invited to a friend's house for a three day weekend sleepover party Julie agreed immediately. The first thing she did after making all the arrangements for Carly's party Julie called Aaron and invited him to her place for dinner.

Julie's knowledge of cooking was limited but she was determined to make a special meal for the two of them. After getting out of work a little early Julie went home that Friday night, feeling a little twinge of sadness knowing that Carly wouldn't be home until Sunday, and stripped out of her scrubs for a shower. Now, twenty minutes later, she was still standing in front of the mirror trying to figure out what to wear.

Finally, after choosing and then discarding several options, Julie finally dressed in a pair of faded jeans and a very sheer black chiffon blouse. She normally wouldn't have worn anything that revealing but she was hoping that this might encourage Aaron to take things between them to the next step in their relationship.

Julie couldn't deny she was nervous about that step. She'd only ever slept with one person before and that had been over ten years ago when she got pregnant with Carly. She hoped that she wouldn't embarrass herself or be so bad at sex that Aaron didn't want to see her anymore.

Running her hands through her hair Julie sighed, wondering if she would really be able to go through with this. When she heard a knock at the front door the butterflies in her stomach kicked into high gear, but Julie forced herself to remain calm and collected as she opened the door with what she hoped was a seductive smile on her lips.

"Hi there, handsome," she said, holding the door open. She was quite pleased to see Aaron's gaze taking in her appearance appreciatively.

"You look gorgeous, baby," he said, pulling her into his arms. Julie went willingly and when their lips met in a tender kiss she melted against him, her knees trembling slightly.

When the kiss broke Aaron playfully rubbed his nose against hers in an Eskimo kiss, making Julie giggle. Closing the door behind him Aaron stepped into the condo and followed Julie into the kitchen. "So, Carly's already at her sleepover, right?" he asked.

"Yeah, her friend's mom picked up the girls at school this afternoon. I miss her already."

Julie was standing at the counter when she felt Aaron's strong arms around her waist and she leaned back against him. His lips were against her ear as he whispered, "But it gives us a chance to be alone. I love Carly, but I also love having you all to myself once in a while." He nipped at her earlobe with his teeth and nuzzled her neck, his beard stubble scratching against her skin in an almost unbearably erotic way.

Julie was trying to get dinner out of the slow cooker where it had been simmering all day, but she was finding it increasingly difficult to concentrate on the task at hand. Aaron's hands were warm and firm against her belly through the thin fabric of her shirt. His lips were constantly moving against her neck, her cheek, her ear, and she could feel what little self-control she had at that point rapidly slipping away.

Turning gently in Aaron's arms Julie leaned slightly away from him against the counter so she could look up into his face. Aaron's eyes were dark and hooded with obvious passion and arousal and the sight made Julie gasp. Forcing herself to breathe properly she said, "I made beef stroganoff for dinner. Are you hungry, honey?"

Aaron didn't say anything, just bent his head and brushed a kiss against the line of her jaw. His mouth moved to her neck, hot and moist against her skin, and when she felt his teeth lightly nip the pulse point at the base of her throat she gasped in surprise. Wrapping her arms around Aaron's back she clung to him, feeling nervous anticipation building to a crescendo inside her, and she knew that the moment had finally arrived.

Julie had her eyes closed and her head back when she felt Aaron's lips against her ear. "I was thinking we could skip dinner for now and just go straight for dessert," he whispered seductively.

His words fueled something in Julie she didn't even realize had existed and she crushed her mouth to Aaron's in a fierce, passionate kiss. Aaron responded eagerly, swept Julie into his arms, and carried her to the bedroom. He set her gently on her feet and when the kiss broke Julie went to her bathroom and returned with two candles which she set on her dresser and lit. While she was doing that Aaron had turned the covers down on the bed and now they stood facing each other.

Slowly Aaron reached for her and pulled her close, his fingers going to the buttons of her shirt as he kissed her again. Julie sighed with pleasure when she first felt Aaron's touch on her bare skin and she leaned in to rain kisses on his neck. Her fingers trembled slightly as she unbuttoned his shirt but finally she got it open and slid her hands inside, running her fingertips almost reverently over his chest and belly.

Winding a hand in her hair Aaron gently tugged her up to face him and kissed her again, the passion intensifying with every passing second between them. Julie pushed the open shirt off Aaron's shoulders and then reached for the snap on his jeans, hesitating just slightly before undoing them and sliding her fingertips along his belly and past his navel until she reached the trail of hair that disappeared beneath his pants and shorts.

Barely stifling a groan of longing Aaron unsnapped Julie's jeans and tugged until they pooled around her feet. She stepped out of them and Aaron pulled her into his arms again for another kiss, slowly steering them both towards the bed until Julie tumbled backward and immediately scooted back against the pillows. Aaron stepped out of his own jeans and then his boxers and joined Julie on the bed. She lifted her hips to allow Aaron to slide her panties off and when their naked bodies came together they both sighed with pleasure.

Their lovemaking was in turns tender and intense, passionate and gentle, and afterward Julie lay cradled in Aaron's arms with her head on his chest and his hand in her hair.

"Are you all right, honey?" Aaron asked, concern in his soft voice.

Julie lifted her head and rested her chin on his chest so she could look into his eyes. "I've never been better," she said and at that moment her stomach gave a rather ungainly rumble of hunger. They both laughed and Julie added, "Except for the fact that I'm starved. For some reason I missed dinner tonight."

"Let me go fix us a few plates and we can eat in here," Aaron said, sliding out of bed.

Julie felt her cheeks turn slightly pink as she watched Aaron leave the bedroom naked and then return ten minutes later with two plates of the stroganoff she'd made. She tucked the sheet around her bare breasts as Aaron crawled back into bed and they ate in the candlelight. The act of eating in bed, naked beneath the covers, felt oddly sensual to Julie and she welcomed the feeling with open arms.

In between eating they talked softly, their conversation interspersed with little kisses, and when the food was gone they lost themselves in each other again, making love with a fiery passion that left Julie feeling breathless, She fell asleep afterward with her head pillowed on Aaron's chest while Aaron lay awake for a few minutes, stroking her bare shoulder and arm with his fingertips.

Listening to the comforting sound of Julie's soft, even breaths felt like Heaven to Aaron. He loved her, there was no doubt about that, and their lovemaking had only amplified his feelings for her. Even more than that though he also loved what they were as a family with her daughter and Aaron often found himself imagining what their own children might look like someday.

Sighing Aaron tightened his arm around Julie and pressed a kiss to her forehead before settling back against the pillows. He knew it was too soon to really consider making things between them permanent, but he truly hoped with all his heart that their relationship was destined to last forever.

Kevin Meyers had been more than a little lost after Marcie left. He'd gotten into several arguments with his father about their break-up, but when his father confronted Marcie about him and she refused to take Kevin back he relented and Kevin found himself able to dream about Julie and Carly in peace.

Using his considerable deductive skills and his ability to spot details most people overlooked Kevin attempted to locate Julie and Carly using the Internet. He quickly became frustrated when he was unable to find anything and he began seriously contemplating going to her parents again and begging them to tell him where his family was.

Kevin might have gone down that road, despite knowing deep down that they wouldn't tell him anything, if it hadn't been for the unexpected phone call he received late one warm summer evening that would change the course of his life forever.

It was early on Sunday morning when Julie received the horrible phone call; the kind of phone call every parent dreads. She and Aaron had made breakfast together and were eating at the kitchen table, naked beneath their bathrobes, and Julie was feeling content all the way down to her toes when the phone rang.

"Hello?" Julie said, picking up the receiver and holding it to her ear.

Aaron watched in growing alarm as Julie's face turned paper white and he was immediately on his feet, his hand on her waist and his expression concerned.

"Where are they taking her, Dana!?!" Julie asked, her voice an octave higher than normal. After listening for a second Julie slammed the phone down and took off up the stairs to her bedroom with Aaron hot on her trail.

"Baby, what happened to Carly?" he asked, already getting dressed without even waiting for an answer. He watched her in her underwear as she struggled to pull on a pair of cotton pants and a t-shirt. She had tears in her eyes and was still ghostly pale when she turned to look at him.

"Carly fainted at her friend's house this morning. Dana said that Carly had been in the kitchen and had complained of feeling funny just before she hit the floor. Oh my God, Aaron, what if something's seriously wrong with her!?!"

Julie gave in to the tears then, collapsing in Aaron's arms and sobbing against his chest, and Aaron wrapped his arms around her back and held her tight, whispering soothingly in her ear. When the sobs tapered to sniffles and hiccups Aaron gently cupped her face in his hands. "Worrying now isn't going to help. We're going to go the hospital and check on her and then when we find out why this happened we'll go from there. OK?"

With one little hitching sniffle Julie nodded, wiping her eyes with the palm of her hand, and Aaron could see her trying to forcibly pull herself together. They finished dressing in silence and left the condo. Julie had never been more grateful for Aaron's presence than she was then as she slid into the passenger seat of his car. She was still fighting tears and she had a feeling she wouldn't have been able to drive very well given her present condition.

Aaron broke more than a few traffic laws getting to the hospital and when they reached the emergency room parking lot and climbed out of the car he took Julie's hand and they jogged into the building and up to the receptionist's desk. Aaron let Julie take over then for which Julie was again grateful. She needed some control over the situation and this was a setting that was familiar and almost comforting to her.

"Excuse me, I'm Dr. Forrester. My daughter Carly was brought here by ambulance a little while ago. Where is she? Can I see her?"

The receptionist typed something into the computer and waited for it to load. Finally, after several agonizing seconds, the receptionist looked up and said, "She's in the ER; just go through the double doors and you'll be able to speak to a nurse or a physician about her condition."

Julie thanked the woman and, reaching back to capture Aaron's hand in hers, made her way through the swinging doors into the hustle and bustle of the hospital emergency room. Approaching the nurse's station Julie said anxiously, "Excuse me. I'm Dr. Forrester; my daughter Carly was brought here by ambulance a little while ago. Can you tell me what room she's in?"

Julie's grip on Aaron's hand was almost painfully tight as they waited for the nurse to search for Carly's file. After what felt like forever but was really only a few seconds the nurse said, "She's in room fourteen. The doctor should be in to see her shortly."

Without another word Julie strode down the hall with Aaron right at her heels until they reached the door to room fourteen. Taking a deep breath to try and compose herself Julie pushed open the door and stepped inside. Carly was sitting up in bed wearing a hospital gown and watching television. When she saw Julie she smiled but they could tell she was scared and still didn't feel well.

"Hi, Mommy. Hi, Aaron."

"How are you feeling, ladybug?" Julie asked, going to perch on the edge of Carly's bed and gently smoothing her hair back off her forehead. Aaron took note of Carly's too pale face and the dark circles under her eyes and felt the first twinge of fear that this might be something serious.

Carly yawned widely and Julie shifted position so she could put her arm around Carly and let her daughter snuggle against her. "I'm really tired, Mommy," she said with another wide yawn.

"I'm sorry, baby. As soon as we talk to the doctor we'll go home and you can go to bed."

Julie caught Aaron's eye and he could see she was very concerned. He was about to go out to the nurse's station to find out when the doctor would be arriving when an older man wearing dark green scrubs entered the room. He smiled warmly at Julie and Aaron could tell from the warm look Julie gave him that they knew each other.

"Dr. Benton!?! It's so good to see you again," Julie said. She and the doctor shook hands and then exchanged a quick hug. Julie turned to Aaron and said, "Aaron, this is Dr. Benton. He was one of my professors in medical school."

"Julie was one of my best students," Dr. Benton said with an air of obvious pride in his voice. Julie beamed with pleasure and Aaron could sense that she had a lot of respect for this doctor.

Approaching the bed where Carly lay the doctor sat down in a chair facing her and said, "Hi, Carly. I know you're not feeling well so we'll make this as brief as possible. I need to ask you some questions so we can try and figure out why you fainted, OK?" When Carly nodded the doctor continued. "Have you been feeling sick at all the last few weeks, Carly?"

"Some mornings when I first get up I feel really sick. And at night before I go to bed I feel bad sometimes too," Carly answered.

"How about any dizziness or feeling really weak and tired?"

"I feel like that a lot. Sometimes I'm so tired in the afternoon after school that I go to bed really early."

Dr. Benton scratched a few notes on his chart. "Have you been having any pain in your joints; your knees, your elbows, anything like that?"

"Sometimes after gym class my knees hurt really bad, but it usually goes away after a while."

The doctor scribbled for a moment before looking up and smiling brightly at Carly. "Thank you, Carly. We'll just get a nurse in here to draw some blood and then you should be good to go home."

Standing he shook Carly's hand and as he was releasing it he gently turned her hand so he could see the underside of her wrist. "Carly, where did you get that bruise?"

Carly looked at it and shrugged her shoulders. "I don't know."

The doctor didn't say anything, just smiled at her again as he squeezed her hand and turned to Julie and Aaron. He shook Aaron's hand and then Julie's. As he was leaving the room he turned back to Julie and said, "Julie, could I speak to you in the hall for a moment?"

Julie turned to Aaron, fear still etched deep into her features. "Can you stay with Carly, hon?"

When Aaron nodded Julie followed Dr. Benton out to the hall. "What do you think is wrong with her?"

"Right now I'd rather not say. She could have mono or she could be anemic. Those are the two obvious possibilities, but you know as well as I do that only the blood tests will tell us what we need to know."

Dr. Benton patted Julie on the shoulder and, with a sigh, Julie went back to the room to sit with Carly. Less than five minutes later a nurse came to draw blood which made Carly cry. Julie soothed her as best she could but Carly was weepy all the way home after she was discharged. Julie sat in the backseat of Aaron's car cradling her daughter on the drive home.

When they reached the condo Aaron carried Carly inside and tucked her into bed with a kiss on the cheek. He couldn't help but feel worried when he saw how pale and lifeless she was and he was beginning to wonder if maybe she was more seriously ill than any of them realized.

"Is she still asleep?" Julie asked from the kitchen where she was nursing a bottle of beer.

Aaron sat down across from her and took a swig out of her bottle. "Yeah. Hopefully some sleep will help. I don't like how pale and drawn she looks, Julie."

Julie didn't say anything right away. Finally with a sniffle she looked up and Aaron was surprised to see tears in her eyes. "I'm scared, Aaron. What if it's something serious?"

Aaron opened his arms and Julie came to him and sat on his lap, burying her face in the hollow between his neck and shoulder.

"We'll worry about that when we have to. The blood tests should come back in a few days and then we'll know exactly what we're up against. Until then I think the best thing to do is keep things as normal as possible for Carly's sake."

Julie sniffled again and wiped her eyes with the back of her hand. She attempted a smile but it didn't quite reach her eyes the way her smiles usually did. Aaron gently caught her chin between his thumb and forefinger and brought her face to his for a light kiss.

"No matter what happens, Julie, I'll be here. For you and for Carly. If either of you need me I don't care what time of the day or night you call. You and Carly come first for me, sweetheart and I promise that you won't have to deal with any of this alone."

He looked deep into her eyes as he said the words and Julie put her arms around his neck, hugging him tight. Aaron wrapped his arms around her back, their bodies molding together, and they held each other like that for a long while there in the kitchen. Neither of them knew exactly what was going to happen next, but at least they could be sure of having each other to help get them through.

Aaron was sitting at the desk in his office going through some paperwork when the phone rang. Picking it up he uttered a distracted, "Hello?" He was instantly alert when he heard Julie's frightened voice on the other end of the line.

"Aaron, please tell me you have some free time you can use. Dr. Benton just called about the test results and he wants to see both of us in his office this afternoon."

"He wants to see me, too?" Aaron asked, feeling a little surprised.

Julie's breathing was shallow and he could tell she was fighting for control of her emotions.

"He said he feels it's important for both of us to be there. Carly had a low grade fever this morning so I kept her out of school. She's at home with Virginia right now. Can you meet me at the clinic, Aaron? Please?"

Though he knew he was going to get behind in his work he didn't care at that point. All that mattered to him in that moment was Julie and Carly. For the doctor to want to speak to them in person it must mean something bad and Aaron was suddenly terrified.

"I can be there in fifteen minutes. Wait for me out front."

He heard Julie sigh with relief. "Thank you, Aaron. I love you."

"I love you too, baby. I'll see you in a few minutes."

Forcing himself to shove his growing panic down deep inside Aaron rushed out of his office, telling his secretary on the way out that he had an emergency to deal with, and out to the parking lot. Climbing into his car he put the key in the ignition, revved the motor and peeled out of the lot. Aaron drove far more aggressively than he normally did and made it to the clinic five minutes sooner than he'd anticipated. He didn't even park the car, just let it idle as Julie came bounding out to the lot.

"Get in and tighten your seatbelt, babe." Julie had barely gotten the car door closed when Aaron roared out of the lot and back into traffic. "Where's Dr. Benton's office located, Julie?"

"Children's hospital in Phoenix." Julie's voice was tight and clipped with worry. Aaron reached across the seat and grasped her hand, holding it tightly. "Thank you for being here with me, Aaron. I don't think I could handle any of this alone."

Aaron ached to hear the tears in her voice and he brought her hand to his lips, lightly kissing the back of it. "You won't have to go through any of this alone, Julie. I'm going to be with you and Carly every step of the way, no matter what."

With a watery smile Julie leaned over to give Aaron a brief kiss on the cheek, then settled back in her own seat. Aaron held her hand as they navigated their way to Phoenix, neither of them saying much. As terrified as Aaron was he couldn't even begin to imagine how frightened Julie must be. Carly had been all she had for most of the last ten years and Aaron knew that the thought of anything happening to Carly was devastating and terrifying for Julie.

It took a few wrong turns when they arrived in Phoenix before they were able to find their way into the parking lot of the children's hospital. Aaron opened Julie's door for her after locating a parking space and they walked hand in hand into the building.

"Excuse me, I'm supposed to have an appointment with Dr. Benton," Julie said as when she reached the welcome desk.

The receptionist smiled warmly which made Aaron feel immediately at ease, at least with the staff anyway. "Of course. Take the elevator to the second floor and there will be a color coded chart of all the doctor's offices and locations. Just follow the chart."

"Thank you very much."

Aaron stepped aside to let Julie get on the elevator first then stepped in behind her, pressing the button for the second floor. Julie was leaning against the wall, her eyes closed and her arms folded tightly across her chest and Aaron could see her shivering slightly as though she were chilled. When the elevator opened for them they studied the chart and located the appropriate entrance for Dr. Benton's office.

Pulling open the door Julie approached the desk and waited impatiently as the receptionist, who was on the phone, signaled her to wait. Finally the receptionist hung up the phone and opened the sliding window. "Can I help you?"

"We're here for a meeting with Dr. Benton. I'm Dr. Forrester. He called and said it was important."

"Come on back; the doctor left a note asking that you be escorted to his office as soon as you arrive."

Julie gripped Aaron's hand tightly and they followed the receptionist to Dr. Benton's office. The receptionist closed the door behind her without another word as Julie and Aaron sat down in the visitor chairs across from the doctor's desk. They waited for an agonizing fifteen minutes and both of them nearly jumped out of their chairs when the office door finally opened.

"Julie, I'm so glad you were able to get here so soon. Aaron, a pleasure to see you again." The doctor shook both their hands and then went around the other side of the desk to sit in his own chair. Aaron noticed that he had a file with Carly's name and birthdate on it and he felt something tighten painfully in his stomach.

The doctor hesitated for the briefest second before looking at Julie with the saddest expression Aaron had ever seen. "I'm so sorry to have to be the one to tell you this, Julie. Your daughter's blood test results have come back. Carly has Acute Lymphoblastic Leukemia; ALL. From the looks of her test results I'm willing to bet that this isn't her first blast crisis. She needs to be admitted as soon as possible for testing and treatment. I'm so sorry, Julie."

Aaron could feel tears stinging his eyes, but he forced himself to remain in control. Julie's reaction was frightening him a little bit. She hadn't said a single word; just stood up from her chair and began pacing the room with her hands buried in her hair. Aaron could hear her mumbling to herself and it took him awhile to figure out what she was saying. Just one word over and over again, "No."

Julie stopped pacing and stood facing one of the office walls. Aaron nearly jumped in shock when she slammed her fists against the wall as hard as she could. Then, out of nowhere, a primal sounding scream filled the room and it took Aaron half a second to realize the sound had come from Julie.

"No, no, no, no, no!!" she screamed, pounding the wall with each word she uttered. "Oh, God, my baby!"

Aaron managed to shake himself loose from whatever daze he'd been in and he went to her, wrapping his arms around her. She leaned into him willingly, sagging limply in his arms, and began to sob against his chest. He'd heard people cry before but never these painful, gut wrenching sobs that he feared would shake her body apart. As he stroked her hair Aaron gave in to his own tears and they stood there like that for a long time, crying in each other's arms.

When the worst of the tears subsided Julie lifted her head from Aaron's chest and looked up at him with such anguish in her face that it almost broke Aaron's heart.

"How do I tell her she's sick? God, she's just a little girl."

"Julie?"

The sound of Dr. Benton's words seemed to bring both Julie and Aaron back to reality. Moving in a daze they returned to their seats, Julie gripping Aaron's hand painfully tight, and tried to focus all their attention on Dr. Benton.

"I've already called in a pediatric oncologist to take over as Carly's primary care doctor while we deal with this crisis. Her name is Rebecca Marsden and I personally recommend her over any other oncologist in the area. Dr. Marsden and I both feel that it's imperative that Carly be admitted either tomorrow or the day after at the very latest."

Tears began slipping down Julie's cheeks again and Aaron could see her struggling to keep her composure. Despite everything he couldn't help but feel a bit sorry for Dr. Benton. He imagined it wasn't easy to give parents news like this; especially a parent he knew and respected.

"I'll talk to her tonight and we'll admit her tomorrow. I want to start treating this as soon as possible." Julie sounded much more in control and Aaron suspected that she was trying to look at the situation from the perspective of a doctor rather than a mother.

Julie and Aaron stood and they both shook hands with Dr. Benton again. "I'll set up Carly's check-in time and call you later today. I'm so sorry Julie, but I want you to know that we're going to do everything we can to beat this thing."

Julie offered a shaky smile and then, on impulse, gave Dr. Benton a quick hug. "I know you will. All I care about right now is being strong for my girl." Taking Aaron's hand she squeezed it hard and Aaron returned the pressure. "We'll see you tomorrow, Dr. Benton."

Aaron watched Julie closely as they made their way back down to the car and he wasn't surprised when she broke down again as soon as she slid into the passenger seat and shut the door behind her. Aaron held her while she cried, unable to stop a few tears of his own from slipping down his face. After what seemed like forever Julie's sobs tapered and she pulled away from Aaron, wiping her eyes with the back of her hand.

"I think I ruined your shirt, honey," she said, plucking at the various wet spots on Aaron's shirt.

Aaron covered her hand with his and then brought it to his lips to kiss her fingers. "It's OK, baby. it's just a shirt." Putting his hand on the back of her neck Aaron drew her close for a gentle kiss.

"Can we stop at Starbucks before we head home? I need some coffee and a chance to compose myself before I can face Carly." Julie leaned back in her seat and Aaron started the car, putting it in gear and maneuvering his way out of the lot and into traffic.

"Sure, baby. I could use some coffee myself."

Julie reached over and gently touched Aaron's face with the back of her hand. "Thank you for being there with me. I couldn't have handled it without you."

Aaron took her hand and pressed a kiss to her palm. "I told you I'd be there for you and Carly no matter what. There's no way you're getting rid of me now, Julie."

"I don't ever want to get rid of you, Aaron."

The way she said the words gave Aaron a tingly feeling from head to toe. They'd danced around the subject of their future as a couple but this crisis would be the ultimate test of the strength of their relationship. Hearing Julie say out loud that she wanted him in her life was like music to Aaron's ears.

When they finally found a Starbuck's Aaron went to the counter to order for them while Julie ducked into the ladies room to freshen up. He noticed that she still looked pale when she finally joined him at a table but she seemed more in control of herself than she had been at the doctor's office.

Aaron reached for Julie's hand across the table and she took it, squeezing it with a grateful smile. Neither of them spoke very much as they sipped their coffee. Aaron was lost in thought when Julie's voice brought him back to reality.

"How am I supposed to tell my baby she's sick? Aaron, she's just a little girl. This is so unfair."

"I don't know, honey. But I do know that if we stay together and stay strong we can get through this."

Julie squeezed his hand again but Aaron could tell she was distracted. Finally, after waiting patiently for a minute, he asked, "Honey, are you okay?"

"If I ask you to do something really important for me do you promise not to let it hurt your feelings?"

Feeling a little startled Aaron thought about her words for a second. "I don't know if I can promise that, but I can certainly try," he finally said, slowly and carefully.

Julie looked across the table and deep into Aaron's eyes. "I want you to be there when I tell Carly. Actually, no, I *need* you to be there. But I also need to be the one to tell her. For ten years it was just me and Carly and I feel like it's something I have to do myself. Please tell me you understand, Aaron."

Julie's pleading voice almost broke Aaron's heart. "Of course I understand, Julie. And I will be there when you tell her, but I promise I won't say a word unless you ask me to."

Julie brought Aaron's hand to her lips and kissed it, then pressed his hand against her cheek. "Thank you, Aaron."

"You're welcome, baby."

They tossed the remains of their now cold coffee into the trash and left the coffee shop. After climbing back into the car they began the drive home to Scottsdale, both of them pondering to themselves how in the world they were supposed to tell a ten year old child that she had a terrible disease and could die.

All too soon Julie's condo complex came into view and, with a deep sigh, Aaron pulled into his usual space outside Julie's unit. He opened the passenger door for Julie and together they walked to the front door of the condo. As Aaron was getting ready to unlock and open the door Julie stopped him, putting her arms tightly around him and crushing her mouth to his. Aaron was startled at first but he quickly responded, lifting her clear off her feet in his eagerness.

When they pulled apart Julie lightly brushed her lips against his one more time in a feather light kiss. Looking deep into his eyes Julie whispered, "I love you so much."

With a soft smile Aaron gently cupped her face in his hands and kissed the tip of her nose, then both cheeks. "I love you too, my baby love. I love you and Carly more than anything else in the world."

"Aaron!"

Carly's squeal startled Aaron and he wasn't prepared for Carly's assault as she threw herself into his arms. He couldn't help but notice, as he hugged her, how young she looked in her pink Snoopy pajamas. Forcing himself to remain calm and in control Aaron crouched down so he was at Carly's level and could look her in the eye.

"How you feeling, Carly girl?"

"Tired and my stomach still feels a little funny. Are you staying for a while, Aaron?" she asked, excitedly, her small hands resting on his shoulders.

Aaron grinned at her and leaned close to rub his nose against hers in an Eskimo kiss. "I'll stay until your mother kicks me out, sweets."

"You know that'll never happen," Julie's voice said from behind him and he turned to see her walking arm in arm with Virginia.

They all laughed and Aaron watched as Virginia gave Carly a hug and said goodbye to her. Aaron took Carly's hand and led her back to the living room where he sat on the couch. Carly sat down beside him and immediately snuggled into his side with her head on his chest. They sat like that watching television for a few minutes while Julie walked Virginia to her car and said goodbye.

When Julie came into the living room the first thing she did was turn the television off. "Mommy!" Carly whined and Aaron couldn't help but smirk at the tone of her voice. "Why'd you turn it off?"

Julie didn't answer right away; instead she came and sat next to Carly, putting an arm around her shoulders and hugging her tightly. Aaron, recognizing what Julie was about to do, stood and moved to the chair where he could be present but not in the way.

"I turned it off because we need to talk, ladybug," Julie said and Aaron heard the slight tremor in her voice.

"Talk about what, Mommy?"

Julie gently tucked a loose piece of hair behind Carly's ear. "Sweetie, Aaron and I had a meeting with Dr. Benton today. He got the results of your blood tests back." At that point Julie's voice became decidedly shakier and Aaron could tell she was about to break down. Finally, after taking a deep breath, Julie looked back at Carly who stared at her mother with a baffled expression on her face. "Baby, you have leukemia."

Carly's pale face turned even whiter and her bottom lip began to quiver a bit. "Isn't that really bad, Mommy?"

"It means you have cancer, sweetheart. You're being admitted to the hospital tomorrow for tests and treatment. You'll probably be there for a few weeks at least."

Tears began to slip down Carly's cheeks and Aaron ached to hold her and comfort her, but he forced himself to remain where he was.

"Am I gonna die, Mommy?" Carly pleaded, her voice suddenly choked with tears.

Julie looked completely helpless and finally turned to Aaron, a pleading expression in her eyes. Aaron sat down next to Carly and hugged her tightly, wanting to hold her and protect her forever.

"Your mother and I and the doctors are going to do everything we can to keep that from happening, Carly. You'll be under the best care possible and we're not going to give up or give in. Do you understand me?"

Carly nodded and wiped some tears off her face. "I'm scared, Aaron." With those words Carly finally broke down and cried. Aaron hugged her tight and Julie wrapped her arms around them both, capturing them in a three way hug with Carly tucked safely in the middle.

"We're scared too, ladybug," Julie said softly. "But you have to remember that you won't be alone. Aaron and I will be with you every step of the way. I promise."

Carly sniffled and looked up at Aaron with such innocence in her big eyes that it nearly shattered what was left of Aaron's heart. "Do you promise too, Aaron?"

Aaron cupped Carly's face in his hands and looked her straight in the eye. "I promise with all my heart, Carly. I will be there with you and your mother through all of this."

The three of them sat on the couch like that for a long time, holding each other tight and trying to offer each other silent strength to deal with what was to come. Aaron stayed for dinner, which none of them ate much of, and at bedtime Carly begged Aaron to stay so they could all sleep together in the big bed. Aaron knew Julie was hesitant about him staying, but in the end Carly's pleading and tears and her own need to have Aaron around made her give in. They all slept fitfully that night, Aaron and Julie on either side of Carly, all of them painfully aware of what the next day would bring and none of them ready to face it.

Breakfast the following morning was another silent affair. They all picked at the bacon and eggs that Aaron had made and eventually most of it went in the garbage disposal. Dr. Benton had called the day before asking them to be at the hospital for admission by nine and they wanted to get there early so that Carly could be given a tour of the hospital and some idea of what to expect.

After realizing that none of them were going to be able to eat Julie went with Carly to her bedroom to help her pack for the hospital stay. Aaron sat at the table making a list of people they needed to call that day about Carly's condition; namely Carly's school, Julie's parents, Aaron's mother, Virginia, and the families of Carly and Julie's close friends.

Aaron looked up from his list when he heard Carly come back to the kitchen and he was struck again by how young and innocent she looked in her sweatpants and t-shirt. Julie was right behind her carrying a small overnight bag that looked packed so tight it might bust a zipper. Carly was clutching her old stuffed dog, her face too pale with nervousness.

Opening his arms to her Carly went and sat on his lap, burying her face against his shoulder. "We're going to get through this, sweetheart."

Aaron held Carly for a long time, until Julie cleared her throat to get their attention. "We have to go, guys," she said, her voice shaky with unshed tears.

Holding Carly's hand Aaron led the way out of the condo with Julie bringing up the rear so she could lock the door. Aaron opened Carly's door for her and then Julie's before he got in behind the wheel. They tried to keep up a stream of casual chit-chat on the way to Phoenix but it was tinged with strain and tension.

Carly was trembling with fear as Julie and Aaron escorted her to the welcome desk. They waited until the receptionist behind the desk looked up and smiled warmly at them.

"How can I help you this morning?"

"I'm checking in my daughter, Carly Forrester."

The receptionist punched something into the computer, waited a few seconds, then looked back at Julie. "Take the elevator to the seventh floor, that's the oncology unit, and the receptionist up there will get you set up with your pre-admission tour."

Julie thanked the woman and together she and Aaron led Carly to the elevator. Carly pushed the button, something she always liked to do when they had to use the elevator, and they rode in silence to the seventh floor. Julie had to admit that the hospital was impressive and didn't even really look like a hospital. It was the perfect environment for children and she felt a tiny bit better about Carly being there.

When they reached the seventh floor Julie spoke to another receptionist. The receptionist asked Julie a number of questions about Carly and then wrapped a bright purple hospital bracelet around Carly's left wrist. They were told to take a seat in the waiting area and that a nurse would be out shortly for the pre-admission tour. Julie was also given a clipboard and a large packet of paperwork to fill out. The forms took about ten minutes to finish and after Julie gave them back to the receptionist there was nothing left to do but wait.

"Carly Forrester?"

All three of them started at the sound of Carly's name and they turned to see a dark haired woman in scrubs approaching them.

Sitting down on the table so she could speak to all three of them the woman held out her hand to Carly first.

"Hi, you must be Carly." They shook hands and the woman's bright nature and obvious rapport with Carly served to put both Aaron and Julie at ease. "My name is Shannon; I'll be one of your nurses today. Are these your parents?" Shannon turned to smile warmly at Julie and Aaron was pleased to see her relax a fraction.

"That's my mom, Julie, and that's her boyfriend, Aaron."

Shannon shook hands with both Aaron and Julie and, after exchanging pleasantries, she turned back to Carly with a broad smile that Carly returned, surprising both Aaron and Julie. "How are you feeling this morning, Carly?"

Carly's smile immediately faded as she said, "Really scared."

"I bet. Hospitals aren't very fun, are they?" Carly shook her head and Shannon smiled encouragingly at her. "But we're gonna take really good care of you and your mom and Aaron are welcome to be here as much as they like. Now, are you ready to take a little tour of where you'll be staying?"

Carly nodded and they both stood up. "Wait, can my mom and Aaron come too?"

"Of course they can," Shannon said with a smile and a nod.

Carly stuck close by Julie's side as Shannon guided them through the seventh floor unit. The first thing Shannon did was show them Carly's private room so they could drop off her overnight bag. Then they were shown the garden area, the playground and the playroom. They were also shown the classroom and introduced to one of the hospital teaching staff who would help Carly keep up with her schoolwork. When they returned to the room Shannon explained that there was room for one adult family member to stay with Carly overnight. She also told Carly to feel free to bring movies and things from home to make her stay a little less frightening as well as a little less boring.

"Why don't you make yourself comfortable, Carly. You'll be getting a surprise visitor in just a little while."

"Who's the visitor, Shannon?" Carly asked, intrigued despite herself.

Shannon winked at her and smiled. "If I told it wouldn't be a surprise."

Carly turned to look curiously at her mother and Aaron. "Do you know what the surprise is, Mommy?"

Julie shook her head, feeling as mystified as her daughter. "I have no idea. What do you think it might be, Aaron?" she asked, feeling rather unsettled by the information overload of the last hour or so.

They were all startled by a sudden knock at the door. When the door opened a very heavyset girl with a pretty face stepped in. Her friendly smile and obvious confidence put Julie instantly at ease and she found herself liking this girl without having even met her.

"Hi, are you Carly Forrester?" the girl asked and when Carly nodded she stepped all the way in. Offering her hand to Carly the girl said, "My name is Leighton and I'm one of the Hospital Friends."

Carly shook the girls hand, obviously intrigued and curious. "What's a hospital friend?"

Leighton didn't answer right away as she was introducing herself to Julie and Aaron. Finally, turning back to Carly, she said, "A hospital friend is someone who helps make staying at the hospital a little less lonely. We make rounds to see the patients and play games with them or just talk, especially if the parents have to step out for something. You're my newest patient, Carly. I really look forward to getting to know you."

"How many of you are there Leighton?" Julie asked. She was liking this surprise more and more with each passing moment.

"It usually depends on the number of patients staying on each floor. Right now, on this floor, it's myself and two other people and we each have four patients we're assigned to."

Julie smiled brightly, feeling more relaxed and at ease than she had since before Carly's fainting spell. "That is such a great idea. It's really honorable of you to devote your own free time to helping sick kids, Leighton."

"I actually specifically requested this floor after my brother was diagnosed with cancer. He's in remission now, but after seeing what he went through I was really inspired to help other kids with the disease."

"Are you a student, Leighton?" Aaron chimed in, also looking quite a bit more relaxed than he had been earlier.

"I'm in my first year of college. I'm hoping to get a teaching degree someday."

Julie stole a glance at Carly and brightened when she saw the broad smile on her daughter's face. "Well, Leighton, it was truly a pleasure meeting you. I don't suppose you have a few minutes to visit with Carly while Aaron and I make some important phone calls?"

Leighton pulled up a chair by Carly's bedside. "Absolutely. Go do what you need to do and take your time. Carly and I can get acquainted for a little while."

Going to Carly's bedside Julie smoothed her hair back and kissed her forehead. "Would you mind if Leighton stays and visits while Aaron and I make some phone calls?"

Carly shook her head and smiled at her mother. "It's okay, Mommy. Just don't stay away too long, please."

Julie kissed her daughter's forehead again and then gave her a little Eskimo kiss. "I promise we'll be back soon. I love you, baby." Julie turned to Leighton and smiled warmly at her. "Leighton, I can't tell you how much better I feel knowing that there will be someone around to keep Carly company if I have to step out. We'll try not to be too long so you can visit your other charges."

Julie patted Leighton's shoulder on the way out of Carly's room. When she and Aaron reached the rooftop garden Aaron turned to Julie with a slightly guilty expression on his face. "Honey, would you be all right if I went into work for a few hours? I promise I'll be back no later than two. It's just I have a ton of paperwork that needs to be done and I'm going to have to figure out some arrangements for taking time off."

Julie hated the idea of being left alone. Aaron's quiet strength seemed to help her stay calm and collected, but she knew Aaron's job was important also and she didn't want to see him lose it on account of her or Carly. Forcing herself to smile Julie said, "Of course it's okay. Just make sure you come back."

Aaron cupped her chin in his palm and brought her face close to his for a tender kiss. "You know I'll be back." He gave her another kiss and then wrapped his arms around her, holding her tight. Julie clung to him, her face against his chest. "I love you, Julie."

"I love you too, Aaron." Julie pulled away from him, angrily wiping away a tear that had slipped down her cheek. When he started to reach for her, concern on his face, Julie gently pushed him away. "Just go before I change my mind. I'll see you in a few hours."

Julie sat down at one of the round tables and put her face in her hands, giving in to the tears for a few moments. When she felt a little better she pulled her cell phone out of her purse and scanned her address book in search of the speed dial number she was looking for. When she found the right one Julie took a steadying breath and pushed the button, holding the phone to her ear.

After three rings Julie heard her mother's voice at the other end say, "Hello?"

"Mom, it's Julie."

Julie's mother, Elizabeth, was instantly alert to the sound of something wrong in Julie's voice. "Honey, what's the matter?"

The sound of her mother's concern was making Julie cry again, but she tried to keep her voice as steady as possible as she said, "Mom, I know it's a lot to ask but can you and Daddy come out here for a few days if I buy you the plane tickets?"

"Baby, what's wrong?" Elizabeth Forrester could tell her daughter was crying and she suddenly felt frantically worried.

"Carly's really sick, Mommy. She has leukemia." Saying the word out loud made it sound so horribly real that Julie broke down crying again. In between sobs she could hear her mother crying on the other end of the phone.

"Oh, God, baby. How serious is it?"

Julie swallowed hard and forced herself to stop crying. "They're not sure yet. I checked her into the hospital this morning and they're going to start running tests and stuff tomorrow. I know it'll be hard for you and Daddy to get away, but I need you here with me, Mommy."

"Let me talk to your father and we'll figure something out. Give Carly a big kiss from Gramma and Grampa, okay."

Julie smiled through a film of tears. "I will, Mom. I love you. Tell Daddy I love him too."

"I will, baby, and I'll call you later to let you know what the plan is."

"Bye, Mom."

"Bye, Jules."

Julie closed the phone and, after another bout of crying, made the rest of the phone calls she had on her list. Calling the school wasn't too bad and she was relieved when they agreed to transfer all of the necessary paperwork and lesson plans to the hospital school. Calling her friends and the parents of Carly's friends was hard. But it was Virginia and Evelyn that sent Julie into fits of sobbing yet again.

After all the calls were made Julie just sat out there in the garden trying to collect her thoughts. There was one person she hadn't called yet, one person she wasn't sure if she should call, and the confusion she was feeling was tearing her apart. Part of her believed that Kevin had a right to know and the other part of her insisted that since he hadn't been around for the last ten years of Carly's life it was none of his business. For the time being, Julie decided as she got up from the table and headed back into the hospital, she wasn't going to tell him but the option was going to stay open until she got some advice; from Aaron and from her mother.

When Julie returned to Carly's room she leaned against the door frame for a moment watching as Carly and Leighton chatted animatedly. Carly caught sight of her mother in mid-sentence and her smile brightened even further.

"Hi, Mommy! Where's Aaron?"

"He had to go in to work for a few hours. He'll be back this afternoon." Julie sat down in the chair across from Carly's bed and Leighton, after a moment's hesitation, rose from her own chair.

"I'd better get going, Carly. It was really great visiting with you. I'm sure I'll be seeing you again. Bye, Dr. Forrester."

"Please, call me Julie, Leighton," Julie corrected gently, with a smile.

Leighton smiled back and, with a wave to both of them, she left, closing the door softly behind her. Julie came over to sit at the foot of Carly's bed and said, "I talked to Gramma and she wanted me to tell you she loves you. And I also called your school and they're going to arrange for you to keep up with your classes right here at the hospital."

At that moment there was a knock at the door and a woman wearing a white lab coat entered the room. "Hello there, ladies. I'm Dr. Marsden and I'll be Carly's oncologist while she's staying with us here."

Dr. Marsden shook hands with Carly first and then with Julie. After exchanging pleasantries the doctor sat down in one of the chairs beside Carly's bed and smiled at her.

"I know this is really scary, Carly. But we're going to take very good care of you, okay?" Carly nodded and the doctor continued. "Now, we've scheduled you for a series of tests starting tomorrow morning and I want to go over them with you and your mom so you know exactly what's going to happen."

When Carly nodded that she understood the doctor continued. "The first two tests we'll be doing are called a bone marrow aspirate and a bone marrow biopsy. Do you know what bone marrow is, Carly?"

Carly shook her head and Dr. Marsden smiled at her. "Bone marrow is a spongy liquid inside the bone where the blood cells are made. For both of these tests what we'll be doing is inserting a needle into your hip bone and we'll be drawing out both a little bit of your bone marrow and also a small piece of your hip bone. We need to do that so we can test both the marrow and the bone for cancer cells."

"Will it hurt?" Carly asked in a small voice and Julie flinched a little. She knew what the answer to that question would be.

Dr. Marsden smiled gently at Carly. "Some pain where the needle goes in is normal, Carly. But I promise we'll try to be as gentle as possible."

"Can my mom come with me when you're doing it?"

"Of course she can be there."

Carly relaxed a fraction at that and Dr. Marsden returned to her list of tests they would be performing. "We'll also be doing something called a bone scan. What that means is a machine will scan your body looking for anything about your bones that isn't normal. We'll inject a bit of dye into your vein and the dye will immediately travel to any parts of your bone that are different from the others."

"Does the bone scan hurt, Dr. Marsden?"

"Not even a tiny little bit. But you might feel a little closed in and nervous so try to keep your eyes closed and think about a happy memory or sing a song to yourself. Anything that will help you relax."

"Will Mom be able to come with me for this too?"

Carly looked panic stricken as the doctor slowly shook her head. "I'm afraid not, Carly. But she'll be out in the waiting room and you can see her the minute you're done."

"Another test we'll be doing is called a creatinine clearance which will tell us how well your kidneys are functioning. Creatinine is a protein moved through the blood by your kidneys. For twenty four hours we'll be collecting your urine and after that we'll perform the test. And it won't hurt a bit," Dr. Marsden added, anticipating Carly's question.

"The CT scan, which stands for Computerized Axial Tomography Scan, is a special X-ray that takes three dimensional pictures of the inside of your body. All you have to do is lie really still on the table for about an hour while the machine takes pictures of your insides.

Unfortunately, this is another test that your mom can't come in with you."

"The echocardiogram is a test to help us determine the strength and function of your heart. Jelly will be spread over the skin on your chest and the person doing the test will move a small, round disk around on your chest. Sound waves will travel through your heart and make a picture on the screen. It may be a little bit uncomfortable, but your mom can sit with you for this one."

"The lumbar puncture, or spinal tap, is done to check for cancer cells or infections around the brain or the spinal cord. You'll have to lay on your side with your legs curled up so your back is curved. I'll be placing a needle in between the bones of your spine and collecting fluid from your spinal canal."

Julie spoke up then, her voice hoarse with emotion. "Is the spinal tap really necessary at this point, Dr. Marsden."

"I'm afraid so. We need to know exactly how far this has gone if we're going to be able to treat it correctly."

Julie sat back in her chair, her hand over her eyes, and the doctor continued. "You'll probably feel some pain or have a headache after the spinal tap, but that's perfectly normal and we'll be able to give you pain medicine to help with the discomfort."

Dr. Marsden paused for a moment, studying Carly's pale and watchful face, before continuing. "The MRI, or Magnetic Resonance Imaging, is a scanner that will take pictures of your body while you lie flat on a table. Your mom can't come in with you but she'll be able to see you from the control room and talk to you through a microphone."

The doctor shuffled some papers before she continued, giving Carly and Julie a few seconds to process all the information they'd received so far. "The pulmonary function test will determine how well you're able to breathe. You'll be inside an enclosed area with clear walls and a seat. The nurse will place a nose clamp on you and you'll be asked to breathe into the plastic mouthpiece attached to the machine. You may have to do it a couple of times to get an accurate reading."

Carly looked terrified and Julie was positively stricken. The thought of all that being done to her baby was horrifying. But as she locked eyes with Dr. Marsden she felt an immediate rapport with the woman and knew that the tests and procedures were in Carly's best interest.

"That'll be the last of the tests, Carly. There might be a few more down the road when we're more certain of exactly what we're dealing with, but for now the ones I've explained will be it. Now, if you and your mom want to take a tour of the equipment and everything just let your nurse know and she'll set something up for you so you have some idea what to expect."

Dr. Marsden stood and shook hands with both Carly and Julie again. Holding Carly's hand for a second longer than necessary the doctor said gently, "I understand you're scared, Carly. But we have excellent people here who will take good care of you and your mom. I promise you that."

As soon as Dr. Marsden left the room Julie came to sit at the foot of Carly's bed again. Carly looked far too pale and used and it broke Julie's heart to see her daughter in such a state.

"Do you want to take a tour of the places you'll go to be tested, ladybug?" Julie asked.

Carly considered it for a moment and then nodded slowly. Julie pushed the nurse call button and a few seconds later Shannon came striding into the room.

"What can I do for you?"

"We'd like to set up a tour of the procedure rooms for Carly to get an idea of what to expect when the tests start tomorrow."

Shannon smiled brightly at Carly. "Of course. Let me just tell the doctor you want the tour and we'll figure out a time. It should be sometime late this afternoon so feel free to relax and maybe catch a little nap. You both look exhausted."

Julie thanked the nurse and when Shannon left she reached out to gently touch Carly's cheek. "Do you feel like taking a nap, honey?"

she asked her daughter and Carly yawned widely in response, making Julie laugh.

"I am a little sleepy, Mommy."

Julie rose from the bed and helped pull down the sheet and blanket so she could tuck them around Carly. When she kissed Carly's cheek a wave of emotion came over her and she swayed slightly where she stood.

"Are you gonna take a nap too, Mommy?" Carly asked and Julie, after yawning hugely, nodded.

Julie sat down in the sleeper chair and tilted it back so she could attempt to get comfortable. She winced as her back began to ache right away, but there was no way she was leaving Carly's side unless she absolutely had to.

"Mommy?"

Carly's soft voice made Julie forget all about the rack of torture that the hospital called a sleeper chair. "What is it, ladybug?"

"Can we get one of my blankets from home and my pillow?"

Julie pondered Carly's request, wondering why she hadn't thought about it before. "Of course we can, baby. I'll ask Aaron to pick them up on his way back from work."

"Thank you, Mommy."

"You're welcome, Carly."

Carly turned over on her side, her arms wrapped tightly around her stuffed dog, and Julie noticed that she fell asleep almost immediately. None of them had gotten any sleep and she couldn't help but feel concerned about the idea of Aaron driving when he was so tired. Waiting to make sure that Carly was really asleep Julie slipped out of the room and went in search of Leighton.

"Leighton, could you just sit with Carly for a few minutes while I make a phone call. She's asleep but if she wakes up I don't want her to be alone," Julie said when she finally found Leighton organizing toys in the children's playroom.

"Sure, Julie. I'll head that way now. Take your time."

Julie watched as Leighton headed down the hall to Carly's room, not wanting to leave the building until she was certain that someone was with her daughter. When Leighton entered Carly's room Julie made her way back down to the garden and sat at the same small table, pulling out her cell phone and punching the button to speed dial Aaron.

"Hello?" Aaron's voice sounded harried and exhausted and Julie immediately felt bad for bothering him at work again.

"Hi, honey, it's me."

Aaron was suddenly alert and frantic. "Is something wrong? Is Carly okay?"

"She's fine, honey, calm down. I was wondering if you could stop by the condo and pick up her patchwork quilt and a pillow from her bed. She just asked for them a few minutes ago and I want to make her as comfortable as possible while she's staying here."

"Sure, I can do that. I'll be leaving here around two, maybe a little after." Aaron suddenly yawned loudly and Julie felt another little pang of concern about him driving while so tired.

"Aaron, if I ask you to do something would you?"

She could tell he was smirking by the tone of his voice when he replied, "It depends on what you want me to do."

"Stay in Scottsdale tonight. Go home or crash at my place and get some sleep. I'm worried about you driving all the way back to Phoenix on what little bit of sleep you got last night."

Aaron was silent for a moment and Julie waited patiently. "But I miss you, Julie. And I don't want to be away from Carly."

"I know, Aaron, but we both need you to stay alive and driving while you're so sleepy is really dangerous. Please, it's just for one night."

Again there was silence on the other end of the phone as Aaron considered Julie's request. Finally he said, "All right, if you're sure that's what you want."

Julie breathed a sigh of relief; at least that was one less thing she would have to worry about for the time being. "I'm sure, baby. Get some rest and we'll see you tomorrow."

"Thanks, Julie. I love you, baby."

"I love you too, Aaron."

"Give Carly a hug and a kiss for me and tell her I love her too."

"I will. Bye, honey. I'll see tomorrow."

"Bright and early tomorrow. Bye, baby."

Julie closed her phone after hearing the click that told her Aaron had ended the call. She was exhausted and she wanted nothing more than to curl up in a real bed and sleep. But the chair upstairs would have to suffice for the time being at least. Trudging back inside Julie took the elevator to the seventh floor and made her way to Carly's room. Leighton was sitting on the chair reading a book and when she heard Julie enter she looked up and smiled brightly.

"She's still sound asleep."

Julie smiled and turned her attention to Carly's sleeping figure. It looked as though she hadn't moved an inch since falling asleep and Julie was glad her daughter was getting some proper sleep. "Thanks again, Leighton. I can take it from here."

Leighton said goodbye and left the room, closing the door behind her. Julie opened one of the closet doors and found an extra blanket which she took back to the sleeper chair. Curling up under the blanket Julie rested her head on the back of the chair, trying to ignore the ache in her back, and eventually fell into a restless and uncomfortable sleep.

Julie woke to a soft voice beside her and when she opened her eyes the nurse, Shannon, was crouching beside her chair.

"What's wrong? Is Carly okay?" Julie's voice was slurred with sleep as she struggled to untangle herself from the blanket and sit up in her chair.

"She's fine, Julie, relax. I just came to tell you that it's a little after four and you and Carly have a tour of the procedure rooms scheduled for five. I wanted to give you time to wake Carly and get your composure together beforehand."

Julie pinched the bridge of her nose hard, trying to stave off the headache that was forming behind her eyes. She was still tired and having difficulty focusing, but she managed to smile shakily at Shannon who returned the smile.

"Thanks, Shannon. I'll wake Carly up in a few minutes."

Shannon patted her arm softly and straightened up. "Remember, the tour starts at five and I'll be the one escorting you so be ready."

After Shannon left the room Julie stood up, swaying slightly on the spot, and when she was sure she wouldn't fall over she made her way over to Carly's bed and sat down at the foot.

"Carly, honey, it's time to wake up." Julie's soft voice was barely more than a whisper, but it woke Carly almost instantly.

Carly sat up in the bed, rubbing her eyes tiredly, and smiled up at her mother. "Hi, Mommy. What time is it?"

"Just a few minutes after four. Shannon was just here, she wanted me to tell you we're going to take a quick tour of the procedure rooms so you know what to expect tomorrow."

Carly looked scared again and Julie hated herself for having to give her daughter any more bad and frightening news. "Where's Aaron, Mommy? Isn't he coming with us?"

Julie pushed a lock of hair behind Carly's ear. "Aaron's spending the night home in Scottsdale. I didn't want him driving all the way back here as sleepy as he was. He'll be here first thing tomorrow and he's bringing a surprise for you."

Carly brightened fractionally at that which eased Julie's mind. They chatted until Shannon returned at five to ask Carly if she was ready for her tour. Carly practically bounded out of bed and, after capturing her mother's hand, eagerly followed Shannon out into the hall.

"The first tests the doctor will be doing tomorrow, the bone marrow tests, will be done right from your own hospital bed," Shannon said as she led Carly and Julie down the hall to the elevator. Once they were all inside Shannon let Carly push the button to take them to the first floor.

"Most of the procedures will be done by the Radiology department, Carly," Shannon said as they stepped off the elevator and made their way toward the appropriate location. Shannon pushed open the door and then stood aside to let Carly and Julie enter before her.

As they walked through the radiology department Shannon pointed out various pieces of equipment to Carly. "That's the table for your bone scan and this one down here is where you'll have your CT scan." Shannon continued to walk down the hall as she added, "The creatinine test, the ECHO and the spinal tap will also be done in your room so there's nothing to see there for the time being."

Pointing through another window Shannon said to Carly, "This is where you'll have the MRI done, Carly." The last thing on the tour was to show Carly where she'd have the pulmonary function test. After the tour was finished, which took about twenty minutes, Shannon escorted them both back to Carly's room and told them she'd be back shortly with a menu so they could pick something for dinner.

Carly and Julie resumed their positions with Carly in bed leaning against the headboard and Julie sitting at the foot of the bed. Shannon returned less than five minutes later with a colorful menu chock full of kid friendly food choices. Carly perused the menu for a few minutes before deciding on a hamburger, french fries and strawberry flavored milk.

"Mommy?" Carly's soft voice asked after they had rung for Shannon and returned the menu with Carly's choices marked.

"What is it, baby?" Julie replied, rubbing Carly's ankle gently through the blanket.

"I wish I could go home." Julie felt like her heart shattered when she heard those five sad words and she moved so she could sit next to Carly, drawing her daughter into her arms and holding her tight.

"I wish you could too, sweetheart. But we're going to have to make the best of this somehow. It won't be easy but we have each other and Aaron. Everything's going to be okay, ladybug."

Mother and daughter held each other for a long time, both of them crying silently, until dinner was brought into Carly's room promptly at six. Julie was pleased to see Carly eat everything on her tray, even the green beans and the applesauce.

"Honey, would you mind if I ask Leighton to come keep you company while I get something to eat and make a phone call?"

Carly chewed the bite of food she had in her mouth and swallowed. "I don't mind, Mommy."

Julie kissed the top of Carly's head and, after finding Leighton and making sure she could keep an eye on Carly, went down to the cafeteria where she bought a tuna sandwich and a chef salad. Feeling a little guilty but knowing she needed the boost of energy and caffeine she also bought a bottle of Coke which she drained a lot more quickly than she'd intended.

After she ate Julie returned to the garden for a third time, opened her phone and pressed the button to speed dial her parents again. The phone rang twice before her mother answered.

"Hey, Mom, it's me again."

"Hi, sweetheart. How's Carly holding up?"

Julie wiped an errant tear from the corner of her eye. "She's scared, but she seems to be bearing up reasonably well considering the rollercoaster ride of the last day and a half. Did you tell Daddy?"

"Yeah, right after I hung up the phone with you earlier. He's going in to work tomorrow and try to arrange some time off so we can come out there. We might not be able to stay long but we want to see you and Carly." As if it were an afterthought Elizabeth Forrester added, "We're also looking forward to meeting that man of yours. Aaron; that's his name, right?"

Julie couldn't help but smile at the idea of her parents and Aaron finally getting to meet each other. "Yes, Mom, his name is Aaron and I already know you're going to be crazy about him."

Elizabeth Forrester laughed, a sound that brought back so many wonderful memories for Julie that it actually caused a physical pain deep in her heart. "I'm sure we will, sweetheart. I love you, honey, and I know Daddy does too."

"Bye, Mom. I love you and Daddy too."

"I'll call you tomorrow afternoon as soon as we find out if your father can take some time off work."

"Thanks, Mom. I can't even begin to tell you how much this means to me."

"Bye, baby. I love you."

Unable to bear it anymore Julie pressed a button to end the call and sat there at the table for a long time, tears silently slipping down her cheeks as she wondered how in the world she was going to survive all that was happening in her life.

CHAPTER 6

"Good morning, my lovely ladies!" Aaron came striding into Carly's hospital room at eight the next morning and Julie was certain she'd never been happier to see anyone in her entire life.

"Hi, Aaron!" Carly cried from where she lay in bed. Aaron gave her a big hug and when he pulled back she noticed the large shopping bag he held in his hand. "What's in the bag, Aaron?"

Julie loved seeing the fascinated curiosity in Carly's face and the mischievous expression in Aaron's eyes. "You can open the bag and see for yourself after I get a proper hello from your mother."

Julie wrapped her arms around Aaron's neck and their lips met in a tender kiss. Aaron had his arms tight around her back, molding her body against him, and for the first time since he'd gone into work the day before Julie felt safe and hopeful once again.

"I missed you last night, Aaron," Julie whispered and Aaron squeezed her again.

"I missed you too, baby." He turned to Carly with a wide grin on his face. "Open the bag, Carly girl."

Carly practically dove for the bag and she squealed with delight as she pulled out her patchwork quilt and one of the pillows from her bed at home.

"Thank you, thank you, thank you!!" she cried and when Aaron came to give her another hug Carly launched herself at him, throwing her arms around his neck in an almost strangling embrace.

The happy mood in the room vanished at the sound of a knock on the door and the appearance of Dr. Marsden dressed in scrubs instead of her good work clothes. Carly's already pale face turned even whiter and Julie felt her own knees begin to tremble.

"Aaron, this is Dr. Marsden. She'll be Carly's oncologist while she's here at the hospital. Dr. Marsden, my boyfriend, Aaron." Julie's voice shook noticeably as she introduced them and she was thoroughly grateful for Aaron coming to stand beside her and taking her hand in his.

The morning nurse, a nice young woman named Allison, came in behind the doctor with a clipboard which she handed to Julie. "We just need you to sign this consent form, Dr. Forrester."

Julie signed the form with shaking hands, barely able to read her own writing. She moved to sit beside Carly on the bed and her daughter immediately leaned into her, the fear in her eyes growing more pronounced when she saw the size of the aspirator for the bone marrow harvest.

"I know this is really scary, Carly, but we're going to try and make it as painless as possible. Do you want Aaron to stay or do you want him to leave the room?"

Carly looked pleadingly at Aaron. "Will you stay, Aaron?"

Aaron was at her side in a second, his arm around her shoulders, and he kissed the top of her head. "Of course, honey, if that's what you want."

Dr. Marsden nodded at Allison and slipped on some surgical gloves. "Now, what I need you to do Carly is roll over onto your stomach and you or your mom can adjust your pants so I can get to your hip bone. You can use the sheet to cover yourself as best you can so you're not too exposed."

Carly was visibly trembling as Julie pulled the waistband of her sweatpants down past her hips and covered her left side with the sheet. Her right hip stayed exposed to give the doctor easy access for the needle insertion. Allison cleaned and sterilized the area with an alcohol swab and then, with a practiced move, injected a small amount of Lidocaine into Carly's hip.

Julie felt tears prick her eyes at the sound of Carly's little whimper when the needle was inserted, knowing that what came next was going to be worse. Kneeling on the floor so she and Carly could be face to face she whispered soothingly to her daughter, hoping it would be enough to distract her from the bone marrow aspiration.

Julie forced herself to focus all her attention on her daughter as the needle was inserted, wincing at Carly's tears when Dr. Marsden began twisting the needle into the bone.

"I need you stay real still, Carly, hon. Try really hard not to move." Dr. Marsden didn't miss a step as she spoke to Carly.

Through her tears Carly managed to whimper, "It hurts really bad."

"We're almost done, sweetie. Just another few minutes, okay."

Aaron stood off to the side, feeling his stomach arguing loudly about whether or not it wanted to keep his breakfast down. The sight of Carly in pain was horrific, but on top of that he had an absurd fear of needles and this particular needle was the biggest one he'd ever seen in his life. Watching this whole process was making him very woozy, but he refused to waffle and risk upsetting Carly.

Finally, after what felt like forever but was really only about ten minutes, Dr. Marsden straightened up and said, "All done, Carly. You did a great job, sweetie. You'll need to lie flat for a few minutes after Allison gets a bandage for your hip and we'll also get you started on some mild pain medication."

Dr. Marsden patted Carly's shoulder gently and winked at her. Carly tried to smile in return but failed rather dismally through her tears. Turning to Julie the doctor began going over the instructions for how to deal with after effects of bone marrow harvest.

"She'll need to lie flat on her back for a while to provide pressure to the procedure sight. After about ten or fifteen minutes, if there's no bleeding, she can resume her normal activities. There will probably be some minor pain so I'll make sure the front desk knows that she can have a mild pain killer if needed. Tylenol or Motrin probably. We should have the results in a few days."

Julie listened intently to Dr. Marsden, though her eyes never lingered far from Carly as she watched Allison applying pressure to the procedure sight and then helping her adjust her pants and roll over onto her back. As soon as she was comfortable Aaron sat down next to her and held her hand. Dr. Marsden didn't seem at all phased by Julie's seeming inattention, just squeezed her shoulder and waved to Carly on her way out the door.

Allison left the room once only to return a few seconds later with a Tylenol and some water. Carly swallowed the pill, still sniffling a little, and Julie ached for her daughter. Allison left again, telling them to call if they needed anything, and as soon as they were alone Julie resumed what was becoming her normal spot at the foot of Carly's bed.

"How are you feeling, ladybug?"

Carly sniffled a little and Julie couldn't help but feel that her daughter's gaze was faintly accusatory. "That hurt really bad, Mommy."

Julie gently squeezed Carly's foot, fighting back tears of her own and looking pleadingly at Aaron. "You were very brave, sweetie," Aaron said, rescuing Julie from having to say anything. "Your mother and I are very proud of you."

"That's right, ladybug," Julie said, trying to calm her roiling emotions. "You did a great job today, baby."

Carly's tears had abated to the occasional sniffle as she leaned into the comforting circle of Aaron's arm around her shoulders. She was just starting to doze off when someone knocked on her door, startling her awake again.

"I'm sorry to interrupt," Dr. Marsden said, softly, stepping part way into the room. She smiled at Carly and then turned to Julie. "Could I speak to you privately for a minute, Julie?"

Unable to speak through the lump in her throat Julie merely nodded and Doctor Marsden stepped back out into the hallway. Julie was overcome with terror, but she kept her face neutral as she went to the head of the bed. Bending over she kissed Carly's cheek and smoothed back the hair on her forehead.

"I'll be right back, honey. I want you to try and get some sleep, OK?"

"I'll try, Mom," Carly said, her voice thick and slurred. She was already almost asleep again.

Julie paused for a moment to look at Aaron and she could see her own fear mirrored in his eyes. She held out her hand and he squeezed it reassuringly. Julie squeezed back once, briefly, then let go and walked out into the hallway outside Carly's room.

She looked around for Dr. Marsden, hands on hips, wondering where they were supposed to talk. As she was looking around, hoping the spot the doctor, a voice spoke up behind her and nearly scared her out of her wits.

"If you're looking for Dr. Marsden, she's out in the garden."

Julie turned, holding a trembling hand over her pounding heart. Shannon, one of Carly's nurses, had come up behind her and Julie hadn't even heard her.

"I'm sorry, Dr. Forrester, I didn't mean to scare you. Dr. Marsden wanted me to let you know where she was. She said she needed to talk to you privately."

Though still feeling the effects of being frightened half to death, Julie managed to smile at Shannon. "Thanks, Shannon."

Julie took the elevator to the rooftop garden and found Dr. Marsden sitting at one of the round tables closest to the door. Hesitating, part of her feeling such overwhelming dread that she wanted to turn tail and run, Julie slowly approached the table. Dr. Marsden heard her, looked up, and smiled at Julie, but Julie could see something hidden behind that smile, something that wasn't good at all.

"Hi, Julie. Please, have a seat."

Julie sat, feeling a nervous sweat beginning to bead on her skin. Dr. Marsden placed a file folder on the table before them, but didn't open it. Julie watched the doctor take a deep breath, gathering her thoughts, and her feeling of terror increased.

"What's wrong with my baby?"

Dr. Marsden took a deep breath, then exhaled with a sigh. "Julie, I've gone over Carly's initial blood test results from the sample taken in the hospital two days ago. I'm certain that this is not Carly's first blast crisis. Judging from the blood samples I'd be willing to bet that she's been having these blast crises for at least three months and probably even longer."

Julie turned away, staring off into space, while her thoughts and emotions churned painfully inside her. She was terrified for her daughter, and suddenly furious with herself as well. A single tear slipped down her cheek and Julie wiped it away angrily.

"So what does this mean for Carly? Did we catch it too late for her?"

Dr. Marsden reached across the table and touched Julie's hand. Julie turned back to look at her and was comforted a fraction by the fiery look of determination in the doctor's eyes.

"We are going to have to treat this very aggressively. But I'm not giving up and neither are you. You're stronger than that and you know it."

"Acute lymphoblastic leukemia is usually fatal within weeks if left untreated. How is it Carly has been otherwise healthy for so long?"

"Every case of ALL is different, Julie. The important thing is not why she's still alive, but the fact that she is and that we have a chance to contain this thing and get rid of it. Right?"

Dr. Marsden gave Julie's hand a brief squeeze as she got up from her chair. As she was leaving the garden she turned back to Julie again.

"Because of the time sensitivity in Carly's treatment and prognosis I've ordered a rush on the bone marrow test results. If the lab is on their toes today we should have the results sometime tomorrow. As soon as I know exactly what I'm dealing with we can attack this thing full force."

Julie managed a small smile for Dr. Marsden. "Thank you."

"You're welcome." Tipping Julie a little wink Dr. Marsden left the garden and left Julie to her own confused and troubled thoughts. She felt lost and alone, something she hadn't felt in a long time, and suddenly she wanted to see Aaron desperately. But when she got up from her chair her weak legs gave out and she sank back down again.

"Oh, God," she moaned, weakly, and the sobs that had been building since she'd first arrived in the garden finally broke free and Julie cried. For the first time in a long, long time Julie cried, wrapping her arms around herself and rocking back and forth in her chair.

Finally, after what felt like forever, the gut wrenching sobs tapered down to sniffles. Julie was left feeling weak and drained as she wiped her eyes on the sleeve of her shirt. The tears were over for the time being, but Julie wasn't ready to face anyone just yet. She was still too confused and scared. Curling up in her chair, tucking her legs beneath her, Julie resumed staring off into space again, waiting and wondering if her life would ever be normal again.

Aaron was beginning to get very worried when Julie hadn't returned after almost three hours. He had just decided to find Leighton and ask her to sit with Carly when Julie came into the room. Aaron was shocked by her appearance; her face was dead pale and her eyes were swollen and rimmed with red and she was shivering as though she had a terrible chill.

"Julie?" Aaron couldn't get his voice to go beyond a whisper. "Julie, honey, what's happened? What's wrong?"

Julie sat down gracelessly in the chair closest to the door, her knees giving way completely, and Aaron watched with growing alarm as she wrapped her arms around herself and began to rock gently back and forth. He knelt in front of her, his hands resting on the arms of the chair.

"Honey, talk to me, please."

Julie finally looked at him, curiously, as though she'd never seen him before. For a long time they just looked at each other, the tension in the room growing painfully thick in the room. When Julie finally spoke Aaron was shocked by the harsh rasp of her voice, but more shocked by what she said.

"Am I a good mother?"

Aaron took Julie's hands in his and kissed them, then looked back up into Julie's pale, watchful face. "You're an amazing mother, Julie. How could you ever doubt that?"

"Dr. Marsden said that this isn't Carly's first blast crisis. She thinks Carly's been sick for months. How could I not have known my baby was sick, Aaron?"

Julie's voice was pleading and her eyes were filling with tears again. Aaron had never seen her quite like this; lost, confused, doubtful, and it scared him.

"Honey, you're not psychic or omniscient. What's happening to Carly doesn't make you a bad mother."

Julie pulled her hands out of his grip. Her voice rose an octave and was filled with a sudden fury that also frightened Aaron. Anger radiated from every pore of Julie's body and he could see the potential for an explosion pretty soon.

"I'm a doctor and a mother. I should have been able to see something like this. If I can't tell when my own daughter is sick, how the hell am I supposed to help my patients?"

Aaron opened his mouth to say something, but Julie cut him off. "I don't want a pep talk, Aaron. I knew she was sick and I didn't do anything about it." Aaron looked at her questioningly and Julie laughed, a harsh and bitter laugh. "She's been complaining of not feeling well for weeks and I just brushed it off. I thought she was either trying to get attention or she just didn't want to go to school or something equally stupid. It's my own stupidity and my own failure that's put her in the hospital."

"That's enough." Aaron's voice was hard with anger and Julie looked at him in surprise. "This pity party you're having isn't helping the situation, it's making it worse. You can feel sorry for yourself if you want, that's fine. If you want to dwell on things that have already happened that can't be changed, that's fine too. But it's not going to help you or your daughter."

Julie got up from her chair, nearly knocking Aaron over in her anger, and went to the window overlooking the city of Phoenix. She was silent for a long time and Aaron was about to apologize when she spoke.

"You're right. What's happened is done, it's over and I have to focus on each day as it comes. Just like I have for damn near twelve years now." Looking away from the window and back to Aaron, Julie smiled ruefully. "I'm sorry, hon. I can't even remember the last time I pitied myself and I hope to God it never happens again."

Aaron went to her, putting his arms around her, and he was relieved when she returned his embrace, resting her cheek against his chest.

"Don't be sorry, Julie. You have a right to be emotional right now. I just couldn't stand to let you doubt yourself as a mother. Not after everything you've already overcome."

Julie rested her chin on Aaron's chest, looking up at him with a small smile playing on her lips. Leaning up on tiptoe she kissed him lightly once, twice, three times. Aaron rested his forehead against hers and began to sway back and forth with her in his arms. They would have stayed that way longer had it not been for the sudden deafening rumble of Aaron's stomach. When he pulled away from her the sheepish expression on his face made Julie laugh. She patted his flat stomach, playfully, and stepped reluctantly out of the warm circle of his arms.

"I'll go get Leighton so we can get lunch," she said, her tone teasing. With another light kiss she breezed out of the room.

Aaron ran his hands through his dark hair, feeling drained and exhausted. He'd never seen Julie such a mess before and it had scared him a great deal. He hoped that she would be able to handle the days and weeks to come because his intuition told him things were going to get worse before they got any better.

CHAPTER 7

Julie woke the next morning with a wretched kink in her neck and back. It felt as though she'd slept the night on a steel slab. Rolling her neck and shoulders Julie stood, stretching her back gingerly and sighing with relief when her spine crackled, the sound reminding her of bubble wrap being squeezed.

Checking on Carly and seeing that her daughter was still asleep Julie slipped into the bathroom. She took a quick shower and dressed in cotton capris and a t-shirt. Pulling her long hair back into a ponytail Julie left the bathroom and smiled when she saw Carly sitting up in bed, looking around blearily.

"Morning, hon. How do you feel?" Carly had woken up the night before long enough to eat something for dinner and had promptly gone back to sleep afterward.

Carly shrugged, still looking half asleep. "OK, I guess." She looked up at her mother, a rather forlorn expression on her face. "Are they doing more tests today, Mommy?"

Julie sat on the edge of the bed beside Carly. "Yeah, they are. I'm sorry, honey. I want this to be over just as much as you do."

Carly wrapped her arms around her mother, squeezing her tight. "Where's Aaron?"

"He had to go to work but he'll be back later this afternoon."

At that moment one of the kitchen staff entered with Carly's breakfast tray. Julie was pleased to see Carly eagerly dive into her french toast and bacon. She was able to eat most of her breakfast and drink all of her milk and orange juice which made Julie happy. Julie ate what Carly wasn't able to and then set the tray aside to be removed at a later time.

"Honey, I need to call Gramma and Grampa. Do you mind if Leighton stays with you for a few minutes?"

"Can I go with you? I want to talk to Gramma."

Carly looked so hopeful that Julie couldn't find it in her heart to deny her. She wasn't sure however if Carly could join her on the rooftop garden where she typically went for some peace and quiet and time to think.

"Let me ask the front desk if you can go to the garden with me."

Julie walked out of the room and up to the front desk where she found Shannon doing some paperwork. When Shannon looked up and saw Julie she smiled brightly.

"Can I help you?"

"I have to go up to the garden to make a phone call. Can Carly come with me?"

"Of course, Dr. Forrester. Just be aware that Dr. Marsden has ordered the creatinine test for today so whenever Carly has to use the restroom let us know. We'll be collecting specimens all day and probably throughout the night until tomorrow morning."

Julie nodded, relieved that Carly would be doing a painless test today. "Not a problem. Thanks, Shannon."

Walking back down the hall to Carly's room Julie poked her head in the door. "Come on, ladybug."

Looking positively delighted Carly jumped out of bed and skipped out the door. She took Julie's hand and together they took the elevator to the third floor and then out to the rooftop garden. Carly took one look at the surrounding view of Phoenix and an expression of awe and wonder spread across her face.

"You can see everything," she said in a tone of wonder.

"Just about all of downtown Phoenix anyway," Julie replied.

They sat at a table and Julie hit the speed dial button to call her parents. The phone rang three times and Julie was growing discouraged when she heard the familiar and comforting sound of her father's voice.

"Hello?"

Feeling tears welling in her eyes Julie willed them away. She was sick and tired of the way she crying at the drop of a hat lately. "Hi, Daddy," she finally said, her voice shaking a little.

"Hi, baby! How are my girls?"

"We're coping. Do you want to talk to your granddaughter for a minute?"

"Honey, I'd love that."

Julie held out the phone and Carly snatched it eagerly. "Hi, Grampa!" she crowed, happily, and Julie smiled at Carly's youthful exuberance.

While Carly chatted with her grandfather Julie carefully studied her appearance. Though outwardly Carly was animated and happy there were telltale signs that something was wrong. She had bruises that looked fresh, she often winced in pain if she moved the wrong way, her face was much too pale and there were faint dark shadows beneath her eyes. Julie knew the cancer was working hard against her and she found herself praying desperately that they had caught it in time to treat it. She knew she wouldn't survive if she lost her baby.

"I love you too, Grampa. Bye!" Carly held the phone out to her mother, startling Julie out of her thoughts. "Here, Mommy. Grampa wants to talk to you."

Julie took the phone. "Hi, Daddy."

"Hi, honey. I just wanted to let you know that I've taken a two week leave of absence from work. I have to finish out the month so we have enough for airfare and everything. We'll be out there the first week of July."

Julie sighed, fighting back tears again. "That's great, Daddy. Thank you. Can I talk to Mom for a minute?"

"She went to do some shopping, honey. Do you want me to have her call when she gets back?"

"No, I have my phone turned off while I'm in the hospital. Tell her I love her and I'll call her soon."

"I will, honey."

"Bye, Daddy. I love you."

"Bye, doll. I love you too."

Julie ended the call and put her phone down on the table. She put her head in her hands, sniffling, and despite her iron will a few tears managed to escape her closed eyes. When she felt a small hand on her shoulder Julie looked up to see Carly staring at her, concern and confusion in her dark eyes.

"Are you alright, Mommy?"

Julie held her arms out and Carly sat down on her lap, resting her cheek against her mother's shoulder. "I'm OK, ladybug. I just miss Grampa and Gramma."

"Me too," Carly sighed.

Julie hugged her tight, rocking her a little bit, and they sat that way for a long, peaceful moment. Julie savored it, wondering how many more moments she had like this. That thought was far too painful and she violently shoved it out of her mind.

"Julie?"

Dr. Marsden's voice interrupted the moment between Julie and her daughter. Julie was in turn irritated and relieved; thinking about losing her daughter hurt worse than any physical pain she'd ever experienced and she welcomed any distraction from those types of thoughts.

"I'm sorry to interrupt."

"It's OK," Julie said, her arms still around her daughter.

Dr. Marsden approached the table. "May I join you?"

"Of course. Is everything alright?"

Sitting down across from Julie the doctor folded her hands in front of her. "I just wanted to let you know in advance that Carly's scheduled for a bone scan this afternoon at 1:00." Dr. Marsden hesitated for a second, then continued with a wary look in Carly's direction. "I'd also like to speak with you privately again, Julie, if that can be arranged."

Julie knew what that was about and the fear hit her again like a blow to the head. She was pleased to hear her voice sound perfectly normal though when she answered. "Let me just take Carly back to her room and get Leighton to keep her company. I'll be right back."

"I'll be in the cafeteria. I haven't had a bite to eat since lunch yesterday."

Julie nodded and, taking Carly's hand, led her out of the garden and onto the elevator. After Carly pushed the button she looked anxiously up at her mother. "Is something wrong, Mom?"

"I don't know, sweetheart. I guess I'll find out." Her voice was distracted, distant almost, and Carly didn't say anything else.

Once Carly was safely in her room Julie searched for Leighton and requested that she stay with Carly while she had a meeting with Dr. Marsden. Julie waited with Carly for ten minutes while Leighton finished up what she had already been doing.

"I'll try not to be too long, Leighton," Julie said when the young woman entered the room.

"Take your time. We'll be just fine."

Julie rose from where she'd been sitting on the bed, kissed Carly's cheek, and headed downstairs to the cafeteria. Dr. Marsden was sitting at a corner table eating a sandwich and drinking a Diet Dr Pepper. When Julie joined her at the table the doctor wiped her lips with a napkin and nodded sheepishly at the bottle of soda.

"That'll give me acid indigestion all day, but I need an energy boost and I hate coffee."

"You got the results from Carly's bone marrow tests."

It was a statement, not a question, and when Julie saw the expression on Dr. Marsden's face she felt her heart sink down to the floor. This was bad, worse than bad, and it looked like things were going downhill fast.

"Carly's body is not producing enough healthy blood cells and the cancer is spreading. We're going to try and contain it, but I don't want you to get your hopes up."

"When will you start actively treating her?"

"We're doing the bone scan today and the rest of Carly's tests will be done tomorrow. I had hoped to spread them out over a few days to limit trauma, but I don't know if we have that much time to waste."

Julie nodded, looking down at the table in a daze. She felt completely numb and the feeling frightened her badly. She wanted to be angry, to feel the old fighting spirit that had kept her going all these years, but instead she felt absolutely nothing.

Dr. Marsden put the cap on her soda bottle and rose from her chair. She patted Julie's shoulder gently as she left the cafeteria but Julie barely even noticed. She simply stared down at the table, willing some sort of emotion to come, but nothing happened, and she remained that way for over an hour before coming to her senses and returning to Carly's room.

Julie kept Carly quiet the rest of the morning until she had to go in for her bone scan at 1:00. They watched a few movies that Aaron had brought from home the day before, both of them curled up against the pillows on Carly's hospital bed. Carly only picked at the sandwich the kitchen staff delivered at noon, despite Julie's almost desperate urging for her to eat more.

At 12:45 they were interrupted from a very short nap by a sharp rap on the door and an orderly entering the room pushing a wheelchair.

"Carly Forrester's escort awaits," he said cheerfully.

Julie felt a terrible ache deep inside when Carly only gave him a token smile. As she was sitting down in the wheelchair Julie saw her wince with pain. It was horrible to see your child in pain and be able to do absolutely nothing about it. Julie wouldn't wish this nightmare on another living soul in the world.

They wheeled their way to radiology where they were greeted cheerfully by Dr. Marsden and a radiology technician.

"Hi, Carly, hon," Dr. Marsden said with a soft smile.

"Hi, Dr. Marsden."

Ignoring everyone else Julie crouched down to Carly's level. "I'll be right here when you come out, ladybug."

Carly looked like she might cry. "OK, Mommy."

Julie watched in agony as Carly was wheeled into the room and helped into a hospital gown. The scan only took about 45 minutes but to Julie it felt like hours. When Carly was finally finished and had changed back into her own clothes Julie felt as though she'd aged about ten years.

When Carly was wheeled out of the room Julie practically pounced on her. "Hey, sweetie. You doing OK?"

Carly nodded, looking a little more chipper and cheerful than she had an hour ago. "I'm fine. That test was easy, Mom."

"Good, sweetheart, I'm glad."

Carly was wheeled back to her room, Julie following along behind, and almost as soon as Carly crawled into bed she was asleep. Julie debated getting something for lunch while Carly was out, but a jaw cracking yawn changed her mind and she curled up as comfortably as she was able to in the torturous sleeper chair, hoping she could at least doze for a few hours before Aaron got there.

When Aaron walked into Carly's room he couldn't help but smile. Both of his girls were sound asleep and looked so wonderfully peaceful. He strode quietly across the room, adjusting Carly's covers, and kissing her forehead, then crouched down next to the sleeper chair where Julie slept.

"Wake up sleeping beauty," he whispered, softly, but Julie merely grunted and shifted a little in her sleep."

Aaron rested his hand on Julie's cheek and brushed a feather light kiss against her lips, but still Julie slept. Aaron had to stifle a little laugh; once Julie was asleep she was out and it took a great deal of effort to wake her.

"I thought sleeping beauty was supposed to awake with her beloved's kiss," he whispered in her ear and finally Julie stirred a little.

Aaron smiled as Julie opened her eyes, blinking blearily. The sweet smile she gave him when she realized he was there warmed his heart in a way nothing ever had before in his life.

"Hey, you're back," she said, her voice a little husky from sleep.

"Yeah, I'm back."

Aaron kissed Julie again and this time was rewarded when she kissed him back, one hand tangled in his dark hair. When he pulled back her eyes were sparkling and Aaron thought she'd never looked quite so beautiful before.

"Why don't I get Leighton to sit with Carly so we can get a bite to eat?"

"That sounds good, babe."

Aaron stood up to let Julie pass, taking her seat on the sleeper chair, and studied Carly's sleeping form while he waited. He found himself noticing the things Julie had already noticed; her too pale complexion, the dark circles under her eyes. This disease was wearing her out fast and it made him angry that there was nothing he could do to help her.

He was still studying Carly intently when Leighton entered the room with Julie following right behind her. After peeking quickly at Carly and seeing she was still sound asleep Julie looked up at Aaron.

"Are you ready to go eat?"

Aaron nodded, a little distractedly. "Yeah, I'm ready whenever you are."

"We'll try not to be too long, Leighton," Julie said softly, taking Aaron's hand and leading him to the door.

"Take your time," Leighton replied, opening a book she'd brought with her.

Aaron and Julie made their way to the elevator and down to the cafeteria. On impulse Aaron stopped Julie and put his hands on her shoulders, turning her to face him.

"Why don't we step out of the hospital for a few minutes and grab some takeout to bring back. We'll get some burgers and fries from Burger King and eat in the garden."

They left the hospital and walked across the parking lot to Aaron's car. Aaron opened the door for Julie before climbing in behind the wheel. He started the car and backed out of the space, navigating carefully through the parking lot and into traffic.

Though they hadn't seen each other all day neither of them said anything as Aaron drove confidently through the streets of Phoenix. Though Aaron tried to banish the thought he couldn't help but wonder if their relationship was going to survive Carly's illness. Since they'd been dating there had never been an awkward silence like this and it was very disconcerting.

Less than ten minutes after leaving the hospital they pulled up to the takeout window of the nearest Burger King. There were two cars ahead of them and Aaron turned to Julie to find out what she wanted.

"What are you getting, honey?"

"Bacon & cheddar burger and fries," she answered, listlessly. "And a strawberry milkshake," she added as an afterthought.

Aaron nodded and inched closer to the speaker as the cars in front of him moved forward. Finally, after what felt like forever but was actually only about two minutes, Aaron rolled up to the speaker.

"Welcome to Burger King. Can I take your order?"

Aaron rolled his eyes at the bored sounding voice coming from the speaker. "I want the bacon cheddar meal with a strawberry milkshake."

"Anything else?"

"Yeah, I also want the mushroom and Swiss meal with a Dr Pepper."

"Is that everything?"

"That's it."

"Your total is $12.57. Please pull up to the first window."

Aaron put the car in gear and drove around to the first window. He handed a twenty dollar bill to the kid working the cash register and waited with growing impatience for the kid to figure out how much change to give back to him. Finally he had his change and pulled up to the second window. He was handed a large bag with their food and the two drinks. Aaron gave Julie the bag which she held on her lap and he placed their drinks in the car's cup holders.

"Sweetheart, are you alright?" Aaron finally asked, desperate to break the silence between them.

"My daughter is dying. No, I am not alright."

The coldness in Julie's voice was like a stab in the heart. "Honey, she's still fighting. We're all still fighting. I haven't given up and you shouldn't either."

"She's been my life for the last ten years. You can't possibly understand what this is like from my perspective."

Forcing himself not to get angry Aaron answered in a soft voice, "You're right. But that doesn't mean that I'm not afraid too. I care about Carly and I hate seeing her so sick and not being able to do anything about it."

Julie didn't respond and the uncomfortable and heavy silence descended over them once again. When they got to the hospital Aaron took their food and his drink up to the garden. Julie took her milkshake and stopped to check on Carly. When she saw her daughter was still sleeping soundly Julie joined Aaron on the rooftop garden.

They ate in silence. Neither of them seemed to know what to say. It was as though some unseen chasm had formed between them and it was terrifying. Aaron loved Julie and he loved Carly. He couldn't imagine losing either one of them.

When she was finished eating Julie tossed her trash in one of the garbage cans. Giving Aaron a token glance and a ghost of a smile she came to where he sat and kissed his cheek.

"I have to get back to Carly."

"Wait a second, Julie," he said, grabbing her wrist. She looked at him expectantly and, after clearing his throat, Aaron said, "I love you, honey. I want to be there for you but I feel like something has come between us. Tell me I'm not losing you."

Julie sat down across from Aaron and took his hands in hers. "Aaron, I love you too. But I have to devote all of myself to Carly right now. Things aren't going to be the way they were a few weeks ago or even a few days ago. Carly is my number one priority and I refuse to apologize for that."

"OK, I can understand that." Aaron hesitated, then, "Do you want me to back off and stop coming around?"

"No, of course not. I love seeing you and it does Carly a world of good to have you by her side. She loves you, Aaron, and so do I. I just need you to understand that I'm a different person than the one you first met. Things have changed, for all of us, and I need to know that you can accept those changes and live with them."

Aaron touched Julie's cheek gently. "Whatever it takes, honey. I'll do anything to keep from losing my girls."

Julie smiled more brightly this time and as she was leaving the garden she stopped to give Aaron a proper and thorough kiss. Aaron stayed on the rooftop garden until well after dark, pondering the things she'd said. He did understand that things were different and that his own fear was nothing compared to what Julie was going through. Feeling a renewed determination to be there for Carly and Julie during this crisis Aaron made a promise to himself that he would only be around when needed and he would take a step back and let Julie focus on her main priority; Carly.

◯ CHAPTER 8 ◯

*T*he following day seemed like a never ending barrage of tests for Carly and it took all of every ounce of Julie's self-control to keep from screaming at the doctors to stop torturing her baby.

The MRI, EKG, and CT scans were easy. No pain and minimal fuss. When the doctor came in for the spinal tap though that was a nightmare. Julie knelt beside the bed at Carly's head, talking softly to her as the needle was carefully inserted between the bones of her spine. Carly was crying by the time they were finished and refused to eat any lunch, saying she wanted to go to sleep.

Dr. Marsden requested another private meeting with Julie after the spinal tap. Julie located Leighton who agreed to stay with Carly for a few minutes. She returned to Carly's room long enough to tuck her in and kiss her cheek. Brushing some of Carly's sweat damp hair away from her face Julie leaned down and rested her forehead against her daughter's for a moment.

"You're such a brave girl, my ladybug. I love you so much."

Carly's sleepy voice answered, "I love you too, Mommy."

Carly was asleep before Julie made it to the hallway. Taking a deep breath just outside Carly's room Julie steeled herself for more bad news before making her way to the rooftop garden where Dr. Marsden was waiting for her.

"So, what's the bad news this time," Julie said as she sat down, not in the mood to beat around the bush.

Dr. Marsden smiled, a wan and tired smile. "As soon as Carly's test results come in I plan to start her on a very aggressive chemotherapy treatment. Probably either tomorrow or the day after at the latest."

"Whatever it takes to save my girl's life, Dr. Marsden."

"I haven't given up and Carly hasn't given up. We still have a shot, Julie, and I intend to take it all the way."

Julie started to say something when the ringing of her cell phone startled them both. Taking the phone out of her jeans pocket Julie frowned at it, thinking that she must have forgotten to shut it off the last time she'd used it.

She flipped the phone open and was flabbergasted at what she saw on the screen. "It's Carly's school," she said, wonderingly.

Dr. Marsden got up from her chair to leave. "If you need me Julie the nurses will be able to find me."

Julie nodded that she had heard and pressed the talk button on the cell phone's keypad. "Hello?" she said, her tone openly curious.

"Hi! Is this Dr. Forrester?"

"Yes it is. Who is this?"

The female voice on the other end of the phone chuckled. "Sorry, I should have introduced myself first. I'm Debra Jerkins."

It took a few seconds for Julie to recognize the name. "You're the teacher who replaced Mrs. Carter a few weeks ago."

"That's right."

"What can I do for you, Mrs. Jerkins? I believe I've already done all the necessary paperwork required for Carly to do her schooling from the hospital."

"That's not why I'm calling, Dr. Forrester." There was a pause on the other end of the line and then, "I've told the students in my class about Carly's condition and that she won't be in class for a while, but they're having a hard time grasping it all. I was hoping to convince you to come talk to them and give them some information from a doctor's perspective."

Julie was stunned. She'd never expected something like this to happen. After a few moment's hesitation Julie said slowly, "I'd like a bit of time to think about that. This is the hardest thing I've ever done, watching my child grow sicker and being able to do nothing about it. Can I get back to you when I've made my decision?"

"That's fine. Just call the front desk and the receptionist will know how to find me. Take your time Dr. Forrester and please don't feel pressured to do this."

"I'll get back to you as soon as I've made my decision, Mrs. Jerkins."

Mrs. Jerkins said goodbye and Julie pressed the end button, feeling a little lightheaded and dizzy. She couldn't believe Carly's teacher actually wanted her to come and explain to the children about Carly's disease. It seemed like a good idea, but Julie needed some time to mull it over before making a decision so she left the garden and returned to Carly's room, relieving Leighton and curling up on the sleeper chair to take a much needed nap.

Julie was confused and disoriented when she woke up, her back aching from being on the sleeper chair for so long. Carly still snored softly from her own bed. Squinting Julie peered at her watch, pressing the button to illuminate the numbers, and was shocked to find that it was almost 5:00. Looking around curiously Julie was surprised to find that Aaron wasn't there.

Throwing the covers back Julie staggered sleepily out of the room and to the front desk. She knew it was Leighton's day to work the morning shift but she needed to make a phone call and she wasn't about to leave Carly all alone. Approaching the desk Julie cleared her throat to get the nurse's attention.

"Can I help you?"

"I hope so. Is there someone here who can keep an eye on my daughter while I go make a phone call?"

"We can check on her periodically," the nurse replied and Julie suddenly felt a little ill.

"Can one of the volunteers sit with her?" Julie asked, desperately.

"I'm sorry, but we don't have any volunteers available tonight." Julie must have looked as stricken as she felt because the doctor continued, her tone soft, "I promise we'll keep a close eye on her. You go do what you need to do."

Though she still felt hesitant Julie went up to the rooftop garden and sat down at her usual table. Taking her phone out of her pocket she hit the speed dial button for Aaron's phone and waited patiently as it began to ring. Finally, on the fifth ring, he answered.

"Hey, hon. Everything OK?

"Yeah, I was just wondering where you were. Usually you're here by now."

"I'm crashing for the night at my place. I'm too tired to drive back to Phoenix tonight." There was silence and then, in a sheepish voice, Aaron added, "You're not mad, are you honey?"

Julie was a little irritated, but she wasn't in the mood to argue. "No, I'm not mad. I just wish you had called to let me know you weren't coming. I was a little worried about you."

Aaron sighed heavily on his end of the phone. "I'm sorry, Jules. You're right, I should have called. It won't happen again."

"Not a big deal. Sleep well tonight, love. Dream about me."

"You are my dream, baby. I love you. Give Carly a kiss for me and tell her I love her too."

"I will, honey. Good night."

"Night, babe."

Julie closed her phone, tucking it back into her pocket. Resting her elbows on the table Julie covered her face with her hands, feeling stressed and tired and wanting more than anything for life to return to the way it had been a week ago when everything had been perfect.

Before she could start pitying herself too much Julie yanked her cell phone out of her pocket again and speed dialed her parent's house in Baltimore. She was beginning to think she wouldn't get through when her mother's familiar, soothing voice finally answered.

"Hello?"

"Hey, Mom."

"Hi, baby!"

The sound of her mother's voice very nearly drove Julie to tears again. Pressing her index finger and thumb against the bridge of her nose Julie took deep steadying breaths, forcing herself not to give in to the tears again. When she felt she had herself under some kind of control she spoke into the phone.

"Daddy said you guys were coming out in early June. Do you know when yet?"

"We've already booked the flight. We're leaving July 8th and we'll be staying until the 22nd."

Julie closed her eyes, feeling a wave of almost unbearable relief flow through her. "I'm so glad, Mom. I can't wait to see you guys."

"How's she doing, honey?"

"Not good, Mom. She's sleeping too much, not eating enough and she's paler than I've ever seen her before." Julie hesitated before adding, "Her oncologist said that this isn't her first blast crisis. She's been sick for three months or more."

"Oh my God, honey."

"I'm so afraid, Mom. I've never been afraid like this before, not even those first few months all alone here when Carly and I first moved."

"I wish there was something I could say or do to make this easier, honey."

Julie let out one harsh, strangled sob. "Just get here as soon as you can, Mommy. I need you."

"A few weeks, baby. Just a few more weeks."

"I love you, Mom. I have to go check on Carly." Julie angrily swiped away the tears that had managed to fall free.

"Bye, baby. Give Carly hugs and kisses for me and Grampa."

"I will, Mom. I love you so much."

"I love you too, baby."

Julie ended the call, tucking her phone back into her pocket, took a few cleansing breaths of the warm night air, and made her way back to Carly's room to wait out the remainder of the evening.

Carly began her first round of chemo treatments the following day. This would be the start of a pattern that lasted over three weeks. Carly would be woken for breakfast, given a chemo treatment in the morning, she would sleep through lunch, have another treatment in the afternoon, pick at her dinner and then sleep the rest of the night.

Aaron was a frequent visitor, coming to the hospital at least five days out of the week, and despite everything that was going on Julie was grateful for his quiet strength.

Julie had called the school to turn down the offer to speak in front of the class. She simply didn't have the heart to do it while Carly was so sick. Mrs. Jerkins had been very understanding; she came to the hospital with a huge teddy bear for Carly and also a stack of get well cards that her classmates had done as a special project.

The chemotherapy was taking a lot out of Carly and they had to change the medication and the dosage half a dozen times before they finally got it right. The first three days of treatment Carly spent more than half the day in the bathroom, vomiting continuously. She grew severely dehydrated and had to be hooked up to an IV saline drip to replenish the lost fluids.

By the end of the second week of treatment the vomiting had slowed down and was limited to an hour or so after treatment. Unfortunately though that was when Carly's hair began to fall out; first in loose strands and then in clumps. Carly sobbed hysterically when the first big handful of hair came out and Julie cried with her, holding Carly and rocking her back and forth. Eventually Carly cried herself to sleep. As soon as Carly was out Julie collapsed, sobbing, in Aaron's arms and he held her, rocking her the way she had rocked Carly.

By the third week of Carly's treatment they seemed to have found a good dosage and a good combination of drugs and Julie began to feel a little hopeful. She suspected some of her good feelings had to do with the imminent arrival of her parents. Even Carly seemed to be perking up a bit the closer it came to their visit. Only Aaron was nervous about meeting her parents and nothing Julie said to him could console him.

On the morning that her parent's plane was scheduled to arrive Julie had arranged for Aaron to stay with Carly. He agreed readily, she knew he loved spending time with Carly, but as she said goodbye to him she sensed that he was growing more and more nervous about meeting her parents.

"Don't worry, honey. They'll love you almost as much as Carly and I do," she said, giving him a kiss on the cheek. Aaron offered her a wan smile and Julie smiled back, squeezing his shoulder gently, before saying goodbye to Carly and leaving the hospital.

Now she was in the insanely crowded Phoenix Sky Harbor International Airport on a Wednesday morning, anxiously trying to spot her parents as passengers departed the planes at Terminal Three. Julie was scanning the crowds, feeling more and more claustrophobic as another half dozen people rammed into her on their way to wherever it was they were going, when she heard the most wonderful voice call her name.

"Julie!"

Grinning broadly at the sight of her mother waving furiously Julie pushed and shoved her way through the crowd and when she finally reached her mother they embraced as though they hadn't seen each other in years. Both of them were crying and when Julie pulled away from her mother to hug her father she was surprised to see tears in his eyes too.

Jeremy Forrester was not normally a crying man, but Julie knew that he had a soft spot where she was concerned and it had been awhile since they'd seen each other last.

"How are you holding up, baby girl?" he whispered in her ear, his raspy voice bringing back a plethora of childhood memories, both good and bad.

Julie hugged her father hard, savoring the odor of pipe smoke that lingered around him combined with the cologne he always wore. When she finally pulled away her father cupped her face in his hands and just studied her face for the longest time, scrutinizing her almost.

"I'm trying to stay strong for Carly, but it's not easy, Daddy. Sometimes all I want to do is go home and crawl into bed and cry." Her mother came to her and looped an arm through hers, the touch soothing in a way she hadn't experienced in years. "I've been spending all my time at the hospital since Carly was admitted. I'm worried about my clinic, about my relationship with Aaron, about everything."

"This is the toughest thing you'll ever do, baby. But you've always been a strong one and you'll see it through. Carly gets that from you and I think she'll be just fine." Her father's words warmed Julie all over and she leaned against him again, inhaling deeply his familiar scent and wishing she could bottle it so it would always be there when she needed to feel his presence.

The three of them chatted about everything under the sun as Julie helped her parents collect their baggage and then escorted them to her car. Julie was more relaxed and happier than she'd been in weeks until her mother said something that made her tense immediately.

"So, have you told Kevin his daughter is sick?"

Julie caught her mother's eye briefly in the rearview mirror. "Kevin is not Carly's father. If he wanted to be her father he shouldn't have disappeared months before she was born and never tried to contact us or anything. I have no intention of telling him anything about her, especially this."

Her mother was quiet for a long time and then she said, so softly that Julie barely heard her, "He has a right to know, Julie. I know you're getting serious with this guy, Aaron, but he's not Carly's father and he never will be. You need to tell Kevin the truth, give him a chance to explain his side of the story and maybe even get to know his child."

Exhaustion and worry had left Julie feeling confused and easily agitated. She pondered her mother's response, wondering if there might be some truth to what she'd said, but her confused brain didn't want to process any more unpleasant information if she could help it so she pushed it aside to deal with later.

"Mom, can we talk about this later. Now isn't the right time or place." When her mother opened her mouth to argue her case some more Julie continued, "I promise I'll consider what you said and then I'll make my own decision. Fair enough?"

Julie could see the reluctant acceptance in her mother's eyes as she glanced in the rearview mirror again and she wondered briefly why her mother was so adamant about Kevin knowing Carly was sick. Her parents had always liked Kevin, until he ran off on her, and it just seemed strange to Julie that her mother would be so interested in whether or not Kevin had the right to know his child was sick.

Traffic was so congested around the airport that the normally ten minute drive ended up taking almost half an hour. Both of Julie's parents were getting very antsy and anxious to see Carly and Julie was growing more and more nervous by the minute about them meeting Aaron for the first time.

Finally, after what felt like forever, Julie managed to find a parking place and she led her parents into the hospital where they boarded the elevator to take them to the seventh floor.

"It's so bright and cheery. It doesn't even really look like a hospital, Julie," her mother exclaimed once they were safely on the elevator.

"I know, that's what I love about it. This is the perfect place for children who are sick. It makes them feel much more comfortable than a regular hospital."

When Julie entered Carly's hospital room she wasn't surprised that her parents had eyes only for Carly. Jeremy and Elizabeth Forrester hadn't seen their granddaughter in over a year and seeing her now, under the current circumstances, was heartbreaking for all of them.

"Oh, Carly, baby!" her mother exclaimed, rushing over to the bed to scoop Carly into a tight hug. Carly hugged her back, burying her face in the warm spot between Elizabeth's neck and shoulder.

"Hi, Gramma," she said, softly enough that Julie barely heard her.

When her mother finally released her Carly was immediately enveloped in another hug, this time by her grandfather. "Hi, princess. How are you feeling?" he asked, kissing her cheek.

"I'm okay, Grampa. I'm really tired a lot and I want to go home, but Mommy and Aaron say I have to stay here to get better."

At the mention of Aaron's name Elizabeth and Jeremy turned their attention away from Carly and openly studied Aaron. Julie was standing slightly in front of him, as though to protect him, as she said, "Mom, Dad, this is Aaron."

Aaron shook hands first with Julie's father and then with her mother. "Pleasure to meet you sir, ma'am."

After the introductions Julie went to locate some extra chairs and they all spent some time together chatting. Things were a little stilted and uncomfortable between Aaron and her parents, something Julie prayed would only be temporary. She didn't think she could handle it if her parents ended up not liking the first man to be part of her life in years.

"I'm heading down to the cafeteria for a cup of coffee," her father said, standing and stretching. Turning to Aaron he added, "Why don't you join me, son. Let the ladies visit alone some."

Aaron shot a quick glance at Julie who smiled encouragingly at him. "I'd be happy to, sir." Standing up from his chair Aaron gave Julie and Carly each a swift kiss on the cheek, then followed Jeremy Forrester out of the room.

As soon as the men were gone Julie turned anxiously to her mother. "So, what do you think of him, Mom?"

Her mother smiled at Julie and patted her knee. "He seems like a charming young man. And it's obvious that he adores you and Carly. What more can a mother ask for?"

Julie didn't say anything else, but she had a horrible feeling her mother wasn't telling her the truth about her feelings towards Aaron. Something was going on with her mother, and possibly her father too, and Julie was almost afraid to think of what it could be.

Aaron sat ramrod straight in his chair, sipping his coffee and wondering why in the world Jeremy wanted to see him alone. After sitting in silence for several long minutes Aaron was startled to hear Jeremy chuckle.

"You can relax a little bit, son. You try and sit any straighter your spine might snap."

Aaron couldn't help but laugh at that. He hadn't realized just how tightly strung he was until Jeremy called him on it.

"So, you and my daughter appear to be getting pretty close. What are your intentions with her and my granddaughter?"

Taking a sip of coffee Aaron considered the question for about half a second. "Mr. Forrester, I love Julie and Carly more than anything in the world and all I want is to make them happy."

Jeremy Forrester didn't answer for a second, but when he did his next question sort of threw Aaron off guard. "What is it you do for a living, Aaron?"

"I'm a sales and operations manager for Wal★Mart."

"What exactly does that mean?" Jeremy asked, taking another sip of coffee.

"Basically I do all the planning for new products and whatnot. I'm the guy that has the responsibility of making sure all the numbers are correct and that things run smoothly. I'm also there as support for the higher up managers."

"Does it pay well?"

Aaron considered the question; it was something he'd never really thought of before. "Not too bad. I'm able to afford payments on my condo and my car with plenty left over to have fun with Julie and Carly. I certainly don't want for anything but there are times when the bills can be daunting, just like they are for everyone in the world right now."

Jeremy nodded thoughtfully, draining the last of his coffee. "That's good, son. You're right down the middle which is what I like." At Aaron's confused expression Jeremy continued. "I was born and raised in a blue-collar family and that's how my Julie was raised as well. Carly's biological father is from a whole different world; came from a family of politicians. I never trusted him even though my wife practically worshiped the ground he walked on. I've always wanted to see my little girl settle down with someone who could consider themselves upper-middle class and I think she's found it with you."

Aaron was silent for a moment, thoughtfully studying the last of the coffee in his cup before he finally drained it and looked up at Jeremy. "Mr. Forrester I promise you that I will do anything and everything to make your girls happy. I love them so much and to have their love in return is the greatest gift I've ever been given."

Jeremy Forrester clapped Aaron on the back in a friendly gesture. "You seem like a good man, son. I hope things work out for you and my daughter."

They left the cafeteria and returned to Carly's hospital room. Aaron felt more than a little relieved that Julie's father seemed to accept him. However he couldn't help but notice the unfriendly way her mother looked at him when he entered the room and he had a feeling it wouldn't be as easy winning her over as it had been with Jeremy.

Jeremy and Elizabeth Forrester spent a fairly uneventful two weeks in Scottsdale with Julie and Carly. The majority of their time was spent at the hospital, though Aaron took them sightseeing a few times and out to dinner. It was obvious that Jeremy heartily approved of Aaron, but Elizabeth remained cold and indifferent towards him. Aaron was hurt by her attitude; he couldn't figure out what he'd done to make her dislike him so strenuously.

Elizabeth spent a great deal of time in private conversation with Julie. Aaron knew that Julie needed her mother's presence, needed to be held and comforted, but Aaron couldn't help but feel a little jealous and insecure that Elizabeth seemed able to provide what Julie needed better than he could.

Though the chemotherapy had stopped inducing horrible bouts of vomiting in Carly, the drugs left her weak and drained and she lost over twenty pounds during the two weeks her grandparents were in Arizona. It hurt everyone to see Carly diminishing before their eyes, helpless to stop it or do anything to make her more comfortable.

They had all developed something of a routine over the last few weeks, even Jeremy and Elizabeth, but the routine was about to be interrupted in more ways than one.

On the morning of July 22nd Julie arranged for Aaron to spend the majority of the day with Carly so she could spend some time with her parents before they left for Baltimore. She took them out to breakfast and they spent a few hours at the hospital visiting with Carly. Julie was thoroughly pleased with how well her father seemed to be getting along with Aaron, but terribly upset that her mother was shunning Aaron like the plague.

The four adults were sitting in chairs near Carly's bed when Elizabeth abruptly said, "Julie, can we speak privately for a few minutes?"

"Sure, Mom," Julie replied, looking more than a little startled.

"We'll be back in a bit," Elizabeth said to her husband, bending to give him a kiss on the cheek.

Julie hugged Carly, who was awake and alert for a change, and then gave Aaron a kiss. Aaron kissed her back, despite being distracted by the look that had passed between Jeremy and Elizabeth. It was as though Jeremy had been warning Elizabeth not to do anything she would later regret and it worried him, especially since Elizabeth didn't seem to like him and had always been so fond of Carly's biological father.

Elizabeth led the way to the elevators, Julie following along behind her, and neither of them spoke as they made their descent to the first floor. They bypassed the cafeteria, heading instead for Starbucks. Julie followed along behind her mother as Elizabeth approached the cashier behind the counter.

"Can I help you, ladies?"

"I'll have an iced coffee with milk. What do you want, Julie?"

"Coconut crème Frappuccino."

The cashier got their drinks and after Elizabeth paid and received her change they weaved in and out among the tables, choosing a spot in the back corner where they could talk privately. Julie took a sip of her drink before she finally asked the question.

"What's this about, Mom?"

Elizabeth hesitated for the briefest second, then said, "We have some things to talk about, Julie."

Julie stiffened, suspecting right away what her mother wanted to talk about. "If this is about Kevin you're wasting your breath," she said, in a clipped and angry tone.

"Well, I'm saying it anyway because it concerns your daughter."

"Nothing about that man concerns Carly, Mother. We've been over this a thousand times. Why do you insist on opening these old wounds?"

"Because I love you, Julie. And I know you love Kevin."

"You're crazy!" Julie hissed, grabbing her coffee and starting to leave the table, more angry than she could ever remember being.

"Sit down, Julie." Elizabeth used the stern tone of voice she'd always used when Julie was a child and it still had the same effect today, despite the fact that Julie was twenty six and a mother herself.

Julie sat back down, but refused to look at her mother. Instead she focused on the table, fuming to herself. When Elizabeth took her hand Julie tried to pull away, but Elizabeth held firm and after a brief struggle Julie gave up and let her mother hold her hand.

"Do you want to know how I know you still love him, Julie?"

Julie shot her mother a scathing look. "Oh, do tell. And by the way; since you seem to have an inside view as to what I'm feeling, why don't tell me what I think of *you* right now?"

Elizabeth smiled, making Julie shake her head in disgust. "You're angry at me, Julie, but you're angrier at yourself. It is impossible to hate someone as much as you hate Kevin if you didn't love him." At Julie's confused and disbelieving expression Elizabeth continued. "It's true. Hate and love are the two most passionate emotions there are. You can't have one without the other."

"This is ridiculous, Mother. I don't understand why you have such an attachment to Kevin." Anger rising to fever pitch Julie added, "I also don't understand what you have against Aaron. He's a wonderful man and he loves Carly as if she were his own. What's so wrong with that?"

"Nothing is wrong with that. But the fact is she isn't his daughter and she never will be."

"Mom, can't we just drop this? Please?"

"Not until I've said what I need to say. Something I should have told you a long time ago."

Julie sighed, running hands through her hair, and finally turned to look at her mother. "Say what you need to say, Mom."

"I've kept in steady contact with Kevin over the last seven years. We talk on the phone a few times a week and every few months he comes to Baltimore so we can have lunch and talk."

Julie just stared at her mother, feeling the anger inside build to a rage that she'd never experienced before. "You have got to be kidding me!?!" Julie spat, wishing for just a second that she could hit someone.

"No, I'm not kidding. I've also given him pictures of Carly; dozens of them."

Julie got up from her chair and tossed her coffee cup, still more than half full, into the trash can. Getting as close to her mother's face as she could Julie said in a low, hissing voice, "You had no right to do that, Mother. You're going back to Maryland today and you better say one hell of a goodbye to Carly because it will be the last time you ever see her. That's a promise."

As Julie turned to leave her mother's voice called after her with infuriating composure, "You do what you need to do, Julie. But you should know that Carly will eventually find out that you've known where her father is for years and haven't told her. Do you think the closeness you two share now will survive that?"

Those words succeeded in stopping Julie in her tracks. As angry as she was she couldn't deny that there was truth to her mother's question. She had always told her daughter that they didn't keep secrets from each other, yet she'd been keeping a huge secret from Carly for nearly a decade.

Julie turned and looked at her mother, fingers tucked into the front pockets of her jeans. Elizabeth's expression was soft, warm, but Julie's persisted.

"You overstepped your bounds, Mother. I don't know if I can forgive you for that."

"Well there's one last thing you need to know. Will you sit down, please?"

After a moment's hesitation Julie sighed and sat down, leaning back in her chair with her arms folded defensively across her chest. "What now?"

"Kevin loves Carly more than you know," her mother began and Julie snorted, quite inelegantly. "You can scoff if you like, but I know that it's true." Elizabeth paused for a moment, and then added, "Did you know that he's bought her a birthday card every year?"

Julie shot a sharp glance at her mother. Elizabeth nodded and continued. "He buys her a birthday present and Christmas presents every year as well. His hall closet is filled with packing cartons filled with presents from the last ten years, all still wrapped with ribbons and bows."

Feeling a sudden softening of her heart Julie forced herself to remember that Kevin had disappeared over eleven years ago, leaving her alone and scared to have her baby and be a single teenage mother. He could pine for his daughter all he wanted; it didn't change anything.

"Next time you talk to him tell him he's wasting his time and his money. Carly's never going to see him and she'll never see any of the crap he buys for her in whatever misguided attempt to gain her favor that he's got going on."

Elizabeth just shook her head, a sad little smile on her face. "I've always thought you were a good mother, Julie. But what you're doing now, what you've been doing for years, isn't to protect Carly. It's to protect yourself and your own heart. You're being selfish, Julie, and someday it will come back and bite you in the ass. Be prepared."

Julie sat in dumbfounded silence in her chair as her mother got up and left the coffee shop. Elizabeth paused to briefly pat Julie's shoulder, but Julie barely felt it. She had so much to think about, things she'd avoided thinking about for years. It wasn't fair of her mother to make things any more complicated than they had to be, and yet that was exactly what Elizabeth had done and now Julie was more confused than she'd ever been in her life.

When Elizabeth returned to Carly's hospital room alone Aaron was immediately alarmed. He had a feeling that whatever Elizabeth had talked to Julie about was unpleasant; both his own instincts and Jeremy's unhappy expression had been enough to tell him that.

"Mrs. Forrester, where's Julie?" he asked, as polite as he could possibly be given the circumstances.

"Don't know," she responded curtly, ignoring the dark look her husband gave her.

Elizabeth sat down in a chair close to Carly, reached out and took her granddaughter's hand in her own. The three adults sat in uncomfortable silence, watching Carly sleep fitfully, for almost an hour before Julie finally appeared. Aaron studied her carefully, looking for any outward sign of distress, and when she caught him looking at her she winked which made him feel a little better.

"Daddy, do you mind if Aaron takes you to the airport? I really want to spend some quiet time with Carly."

"That's fine with me, doll."

Julie turned to Aaron, an almost pleading look in her eyes. "Do you mind, honey? I really want to be alone with Carly for a few minutes."

"I don't mind at all," he replied, knowing that there was more to the situation than Julie was letting on.

Jeremy got up from his chair and Aaron followed suit. While Jeremy went approached Carly's bed and leaned down to kiss her forehead Aaron sidled over to Julie and put his arm around her shoulders. She slipped an arm around his back and leaned against him.

"Is everything OK?" he whispered in her ear, ignoring the black look her mother shot him out of the corner of her eye.

"Not really, but it will be. I'll explain later," she whispered back.

"What are you two talking about over there?" Elizabeth snapped suddenly, looking viciously angry.

Julie's voice was ice cold when she answered. "If I wanted you to know what we were talking about, Mother, I wouldn't be whispering. So mind your own damn business for a change."

"Julie!" Jeremy gaped at his daughter, anger in his eyes, but when Julie stared back at him defiantly he sighed heavily and the anger seemed to deflate like a balloon let out of air. He turned to his wife, who was still looking suspiciously at Julie and Aaron. "We need to go, Elizabeth."

Elizabeth bent over Carly's hospital bed and kissed her forehead. In a loud whisper she said, "Gramma loves you, honey. Someday you'll understand. I promise you that."

Aaron glanced at Julie, stunned by the rage he saw on her face. Her expression softened when Jeremy approached her and Aaron stepped back so Julie could say a proper goodbye to her father.

"Thank you for coming, Daddy. It meant a lot to me."

Jeremy put his arms around her and pulled her against him, his hand resting on the back of her head. "I'm sorry, honey. I'm not sure what's happened between you and your mother, but I have my suspicions and I'm so damn sorry."

Julie looked up at him and he cupped her face in his hands, leaning down to kiss her forehead. "It's not your fault, Daddy."

Jeremy still looked troubled but he didn't say anything, merely hugged Julie once more and then turned to his wife. Elizabeth was sitting on the edge of Carly's bed, holding her granddaughter's hand and talking softly to her.

"We have to go," Jeremy said and Elizabeth sighed, nodded, and got up from the bed.

Julie turned away as her mother walked past her. Jeremy noticed, but chose not to comment on it. He had a feeling enough unfriendly words had passed between his wife and daughter already.

"Ready to go?" Aaron asked, car keys in hand.

"I think so," Jeremy said. They were just outside the door and into the hall when Julie suddenly stopped them.

"Daddy, wait a minute!" When Jeremy turned back to his daughter Julie gave him a hard, fierce hug. "Thank you for accepting Aaron," she whispered in his ear. Jeremy hugged her hard.

They were all silent as they made their way from the hospital to Aaron's car and then from the car to the airport terminal. Aaron helped Jeremy with the bags under Elizabeth's watchful and mistrustful gaze. When they'd checked their luggage Jeremy turned to Aaron.

"It was a real pleasure to have finally met you, Aaron," Jeremy said, holding out his hand.

"Same to you, Jeremy," Aaron replied, shaking the man's hand. Surprising them both Jeremy impulsively pulled Aaron into a quick, tight hug, slapping him on the back before he pulled away.

Elizabeth merely stared at Aaron and he stared back at her, refusing to back down. "It's not necessary for you wait with us, Aaron. I think we can manage all by ourselves."

Aaron nodded, keeping a calm and neutral expression on his face. "Yes, ma'am. It was nice to meet you, Mrs. Forrester." Ignoring Elizabeth's cynical expression Aaron turned to Jeremy and the men shook hands again. "Have a safe flight," he said and left the airport feeling nothing but relief.

When he returned to the hospital and Carly's room he found Julie asleep on the chair. Carly heard him come in and she turned to him with the saddest eyes Aaron had ever seen in his life.

"Aaron?"

Crossing the room Aaron came to sit at the foot of her bed. "What is it, sweetie?" he asked, gently touching her cheek with his finger.

"I don't feel good," she whimpered, a single tear sliding down one pale cheek.

Aaron had to choke back the sob that wanted to escape at the sound of those defeated words. "I know, beautiful, but the medicine should help you get better. You just need to be patient and have faith."

Julie stirred at the sound of his voice and sat up, wincing as she rubbed the back of her neck. "Hey, hon. Did my parents have any trouble at the airport?"

"Not a bit."

Julie smiled at him and came over to sit on the other side of the bed. She leaned over to give him a quick kiss and then gently touched the tip of his nose with her finger. "Thank you, honey. I would have taken them myself but I needed to be with Carly."

They both looked at Carly then and were a bit surprised to see her sound asleep. She had been so fatigued since starting the treatment. Aaron didn't know about Julie, but he certainly felt guilty that there wasn't more he could do. He wanted to ask her what had happened between her and Elizabeth, but decided that it wasn't the right time.

Julie's whispered voice broke into his thoughts. "Aaron, I'm so afraid for her. She's so little and the drugs are taking so much out of her. How much can she stand before it's too much?"

Aaron held out his arm and Julie cuddled against his side, both of them leaning against the foot of Carly's bed. "I don't know, baby, but I do know I'm scared too. I love her so much, like she's my own daughter, and I'd take her place in a second if I thought I could."

They held each other like that for a long time, both of them trapped in the depths of their fear, watching the little girl they loved more than life itself. None of this was fair and Aaron had a horrible feeling deep inside that things were going to get worse before they got better.

CHAPTER 9

In the three weeks after Jeremy and Elizabeth returned to Baltimore Julie, Carly and Aaron developed something of a routine. Carly had chemotherapy treatments twice a day, seven days a week. Twice in a three week period they had to adjust the medication she was taking, once when she had an allergic reaction to one medicine and had a small seizure. Julie spent almost every waking moment with Carly and Aaron came to the hospital almost every day.

Though Carly was weak it didn't keep her from being delighted when Virginia and Evelyn came to visit a few times. It did Julie a world of good to see her friends as well. Having an adult to talk to was a relief and there were no words to describe how grateful she was to them for being there.

Julie spoke to her father several times during those three weeks, though she refused to talk to her mother. Elizabeth had told Jeremy what she said to Julie and Jeremy had been outraged. Aaron had tried to find out what had transpired between Julie and her mother, but Julie refused to discuss it and after a few days Aaron chose to drop the subject. If she wanted to talk about it she would come to him.

Unfortunately the hard times weren't over yet. In fact, they were just beginning.

On a stifling hot summer day in mid-August, about six weeks after Carly began her chemotherapy treatment, Julie and Aaron were seated in yet another doctor's office awaiting the results of Carly's most recent bone marrow biopsy. They both knew that Dr. Marsden was concerned that Carly wasn't responding as well to the treatment as they had expected, but neither of them was willing to admit what that might mean for Carly.

Julie was wound so tightly that she nearly jumped out of her chair when the office door opened and Dr. Marsden entered the room. Aaron squeezed her hand gently and felt Julie relax a fraction.

"I'm not going to waste your time with a lot of small talk and pleasantries," the doctor began, sitting in the chair and folding her hands on the desk. "Carly's not responding well to any of the drug combinations we've tried. There are two options that I can see at this point; we keep trying to find a cocktail that works for her or we start considering a bone marrow transplant."

Both Aaron and Julie shrank back in their seats as though they'd been slapped. Hearing it put so bluntly was physically painful, but Aaron couldn't deny that he was grateful to Dr. Marsden for being totally straight and honest with them.

Now Dr. Marsden looked intently at Julie. "I know that you understand what all of this really means, Julie. More than almost any of the parents who have sat across from me and heard this kind of news. That's why I feel I can give you straight information, because you have the knowledge to make an informed decision." Dr. Marsden let those words sink in before continuing. "Carly's strength is waning and her body is becoming too tired to fight the cancer. In my opinion a bone marrow transplant is the option with the fewest question marks available.

Julie got up from her chair and went to the window in Dr. Marsden's office. Aaron didn't go to her, sensing her need to be alone. After staring silently out the window for a few minutes Julie turned back to Dr. Marsden.

"I say let's do it."

"We'll add her to the donor list right away," Dr. Marsden said, making a note on the sheet of paper in front of her.

"I want to be tested. As soon as possible," Julie said and Aaron was absurdly pleased to see the old fighting spirit he'd fallen in love with coming out of her again.

Dr. Marsden nodded; she would have expected nothing less from Julie. "We'll do a biopsy tomorrow morning."

"Make it two," Aaron spoke up from where he sat. Julie shot him a look and started to say something but Aaron stared back fiercely. "Don't bother, Julie. I love her too and if I have something that can save her life then it's hers."

Julie sighed resignedly, but she was smiling at the same time. "Thank you," she said, her voice barely above a whisper.

There was a brief silence in the room, but the moment was broken when Dr. Marsden cleared her throat. "I'll schedule you both for a biopsy tomorrow morning."

"Thank you, Dr. Marsden. For everything you're doing and for being straight with me."

Dr. Marsden came around the desk and took Julie's hands, squeezing them gently, and then releasing them. "Carly's a brave little girl and I haven't given up hope yet. We're not done fighting, not by a long shot."

Julie smiled, blinking back tears. Dr. Marsden shook Aaron's hand and escorted them out of her office. As soon as they were alone Aaron put his arms around Julie and hugged her tightly. She wrapped her arms around his waist, hugging him back, clinging to him like a drowning person would cling to a life preserver.

"She's right, honey. We're not done fighting yet," Aaron said, squeezing Julie even tighter.

"I know. It's just so hard to see this happening to my baby. She's so weak and fragile already; I don't know how much more she can take before her body just gives up." She looked up at Aaron pleadingly. "I can't live without her, Aaron."

"We're going to do everything we can to make sure you don't have to, Julie. Whatever it takes."

After sharing another quick kiss they returned, hand in hand, to Carly's room. Carly was awake and alert when they entered the room so they were able to explain to her what was happening. Sitting at the foot of Carly's bed Julie gave Carly the facts as best she could, choosing her words carefully so she wouldn't overwhelm her daughter with too much technical information.

"Carly, the doctor says that the chemotherapy drugs aren't working as well as she'd like them to. So I've decided . . ." She stopped there to glance at Aaron and when he nodded ever so slightly she continued. "We've decided that the best treatment option is a bone marrow transplant."

"What does that mean, Mommy?"

"Well, first you'll have to go through some pretty aggressive radiation treatment and then you'll have an operation to exchange your bone marrow for someone else's."

"Someone else? Like who, Mommy?"

"Aaron and I will be tested to see if we're a match for you, but if we're not then we might have to put you on what's called a donor list. It means we have to wait until we find just the right person to do the transplant with."

"Will I get to go home after the operation?"

Julie glanced at Aaron again before she answered. "Not right away, sweetie. It'll probably be another few weeks, maybe even a month or longer, before you'll be well enough to go home. Do you understand?"

Carly sighed heavily and then nodded. "I just want to get better, Mommy."

Julie reached out to hug her daughter. "I want that too, baby. I want that more than anything else in the world." Julie held her daughter for a long moment, then pulled back to look seriously at her. "Would you mind if Aaron stays with you for a while? I have a few things I need to do."

Carly nodded, yawning widely, and Julie kissed her cheek. Turning to Aaron she noticed the concerned expression on his face and hastened to reassure him. "I just need a few minutes alone to think. I'll be in the garden."

"OK," Aaron said, leaning down to give Julie a light kiss. She kissed him back, her hand on his neck.

Feeling overwhelmed and with a tension headache building up behind her eyes Julie went up to the rooftop garden. This had become her safe place since Carly's admittance to the hospital. It was a place where she could go to get some peace and quiet and do some thinking. And right now she had something very important to think about.

Though she would never admit it to her mother, Elizabeth had made some valid points the day they had their argument. Julie was angry at Kevin and the fact that she kept Kevin such a close secret from Carly haunted her every minute of every day. Julie would be perfectly happy to never see Kevin again, but as of now he had something important working in his favor: as Carly's biological father, he had the potential to be a bone marrow donor for her.

For over an hour Julie mulled over the situation, first deciding that she should tell him and then deciding against it. Back and forth this went on until a voice behind her startled her out of her wits.

"Julie, is everything okay?"

Aaron's voice startled Julie, but before she could get angry at him for leaving Carly he raised his hands in a placating gesture and said, "Don't worry, honey, she's playing a game with Leighton. I just needed some fresh air and I saw you looked agitated. What happened?"

Julie looked at him, her heart overflowing with love for him, and she hated herself for the hurt she knew her words were going to cause him. But when it came to Carly she had no choice; any option to save her daughter, no matter how difficult, was all that mattered to Julie at this point.

"I'm going to tell Kevin that Carly's sick. He might be a viable donor for her since he is biologically related to her."

Julie watched Aaron carefully and braced herself when she saw the hurt and rage fill his face. Aaron's voice was deadly quiet as he said, "Did I hear you right? You're telling the bastard that ran off on you and Carly before she was even born. What makes you think he'll even care, Julie?"

The words struck a nerve deep down inside, a nerve that Julie had thought was buried too deep to notice anymore, but it made itself known now as she automatically defended Kevin. "I know Kevin; he'll want to help Carly."

Aaron started pacing the garden, his hands in his hair, and he gave a mirthless laugh before turning back to her. "I can't believe this is actually happening, Julie. I've been there for you and Carly every step through this whole mess. Doesn't that mean anything to you? Do you even care that this hurts me?"

Julie was angry now too and she stood so that she was face to face with Aaron. "Of course I care, but she's my daughter, Aaron. If there's even the slightest chance that Kevin can help save her life I'm taking it and running with it. If you can't understand that then maybe I don't know you as well as I thought."

Aaron gave Julie such a cold, angry look that it frightened her for a brief second. Then the look passed and Aaron stalked away, slamming through the door to the garden. She heard him hit the button for the elevator, but made no move to stop him.

Taking her phone out of her jeans pocket Julie dialed the number on Kevin's business card from memory. Over the years since her mother had given her the card Julie had looked at it so frequently that she had the number memorized. Dialing it now Julie held the phone to her ear, listening to it ring. She was about to give up when a familiar voice finally picked up.

"ADA Meyers."

Julie hesitated for a brief second, a wave of emotion crashing over her at the sound of Kevin's voice. Then, in a voice barely above a whisper, she finally spoke. "Hello, Kevin. It's Julie."

CHAPTER 10

Kevin Meyers was sitting at his desk working on a deposition when the phone rang. Distracted he picked up the receiver and brought it to his ear.

"ADA Meyers." When the voice on the other end of the phone spoke Kevin felt his heart literally stop beating for a split second.

"Hello, Kevin. It's Julie."

Kevin closed his eyes, praying silently that it wasn't a dream, that he was really hearing Julie's angelic voice. He gripped the phone tightly as a thousand different emotions slammed into him from all directions. He'd dreamed of this moment for eleven years and now that it was here he didn't want it to ever end.

For a long moment Kevin was completely unsure what to say, until finally it came to him.

"Julie, I'm so sorry."

Her voice was tinged with anger and bitterness when she answered him. "Don't bother, Kevin, that's not why I'm calling. Carly's sick and I need your help. Can you come to Arizona?"

Kevin suddenly felt sick and his voice was barely a whisper as he asked, "What do you mean she's sick, Julie?"

Julie sighed heavily and he knew she didn't want to go into detail. He was relieved however when she finally said, "Carly has leukemia and she needs a bone marrow transplant. Because you're biologically related to her you could be a viable match."

"Where in Arizona? I'll be on the first available flight I can get," Kevin answered, digging for his appointment book and trying to figure out how he was going to juggle his schedule so he could take some time off.

Julie's voice registered surprise when she said, "Really? I didn't think you'd agree so easily. We're staying at the Phoenix Children's Hospital and the airport it only about ten minutes away."

"Like I said, I'll be there. Just give me your number so I can give you the flight information."

Julie recited her cell phone number which Kevin jotted on a scrap of paper. Just before he hung up he said, in a pleading voice, "Julie, please don't write me off completely before you see me. There are so many things I want to tell you. Whether you believe me or not is up to you but I really need to get this off my chest."

After a slight hesitation Julie sighed and said, "We'll see. I'm not making any promises, about anything right now. All I want is to know if you can save my daughter's life."

"I'll see you soon, Julie. Bye."

Julie didn't even bother to say goodbye before ending the call, but Kevin didn't care. At that moment he had much more important issues to think about and deal with.

For the next hour and a half Kevin made over a dozen phone calls to reschedule appointments and meetings. His secretary could have handled it but Kevin felt it was important for people to hear from him why he was cancelling. He was relieved when nobody gave him a hard time and most of the people he spoke to offered prayers for everything to work out. His two best friends, Nate Prescott and Rodney Ashton, were incredibly sympathetic and even offered to accompany him when he went to Arizona for company, an offer he appreciated but declined.

By the time he wrapped up the last of the business calls Kevin was drained and he still wasn't finished yet. Deciding to make the rest of his phone calls from home Kevin picked up some Greek take-out for dinner and collapsed on the couch in his comfortably air conditioned living room. While he was eating Kevin started up his laptop computer and accessed a travel website where he made his flight reservations. He had hoped to be able to get a few hours' sleep before leaving but the earliest flight left at five A.M. and he wanted to get there as soon as possible. Shaking his head as he booked the flight as well as a hotel room nearby Kevin figured he could just sleep on the plane if he got tired enough.

After booking the flight, hotel and rental car Kevin called Julie with the information and then called his sister Katie. Kevin and his sister had always been close and their bond had only grown stronger when she was disowned by their father. Kevin respected her so much for choosing her own path in life and not caring about the family name or fortune. He and his sister talked for twenty minutes and for Kevin that time was cathartic. He was able to really express his feelings in a way he hadn't with anyone else and it made what he had to do next a tiny bit easier.

After he finished talking to his sister Kevin dialed one last number. He knew this phone call was going to be the most difficult and he prepared himself for a fight as the phone rang. After several rings Kevin found himself hoping that nobody would answer, but unfortunately those hopes were soon dashed.

"Hello?"

Kevin had to bite back a laugh at the ultra-refined way his father insisted on talking. He knew this wasn't going to be an easy conversation and it was likely that he'd be picked off the family tree for what he was doing, but he found he no longer cared.

"Hi, Dad," he finally said.

"Hello, Kevin. Is something wrong, son?"

Snorting inwardly at his father's fake sounding concern Kevin said, "I'm afraid I'm going to have to cancel on the dinner party next week. I have an emergency that needs to be dealt with in a timely manner."

Thomas Meyers was silent for a second. "An emergency? What could possibly be more important than this dinner party? You know I arranged this specifically to establish the fact that you're interested in entering politics," he finally said, his voice tinged with disbelief.

"I got a phone call from Julie today. Carly is very sick; she has leukemia and she needs a bone marrow transplant. Julie's not a match nor is anyone else in her family. We're hoping that I can be a donor match for her."

Kevin's father sighed and Kevin could picture him rubbing his eyes with a terribly put upon expression on his face. "I thought I had dealt adequately with that problem. I thought you'd finally begun to understand that I did what was best for you."

"No Dad," Kevin interrupted," you did what was best for you. I loved Julie eleven years ago and I still love her today. Carly is a sick little girl and if I can help her I will."

Thomas Meyers sighed again and Kevin braced himself for the guilt trips and the threats that he assumed were coming. "What about your future, Kevin?" he finally asked.

"You mean the future you've mapped out for me with no consideration for what I want?" Kevin responded, unable to keep the bitterness from his tone.

"Kevin, I've tried my best to explain to you that I know what's best for you. I tried to help your sister and look what happened to her."

Kevin was angry now as he snapped, "Yeah, Dad, look at her now. She's working at a job she loves, she's married to a man she loves and she has three amazing kids. She has a life of her own because she was brave enough to step away from the family influence. I wish I'd had that kind of courage."

"Kevin, don't do this," his father said, the stern tone of his voice plainly saying that he knew his orders would be obeyed, just as they had always been before. "That child is nothing to you. She probably isn't even yours, but if she is it doesn't matter. You're not obligated to get involved. Those people aren't good enough to mingle with people like us, Kevin. They're nothing more than low class trailer trash."

"Stop saying that!!" Kevin screamed into the phone, suddenly feeling his blood pressure skyrocketing. He began pacing the living room of his apartment as he continued, "I am so sick and tired of hearing you say that all the time. We are no better than anyone else just because we have money and influence. If I were smart I'd be using that influence to help make the world a better place, but no. I got sucked into your world and I was stuck for a long time. Not anymore, Dad. I'm going to Arizona to help save my daughter's life and there's nothing you can do about it."

Thomas Meyers voice was cold, emotionless as he said, "Kevin if you don't attend this dinner party you're cut off. For good. I won't tolerate this disobedience any longer."

"This is easily the best thing you've ever done for me, Dad. I couldn't care less about the family name or the money anymore. When a little girl's life is at stake it sort of puts things into perspective for a man."

"Goodbye, Kevin. Good luck trying to maintain the lifestyle you've grown accustomed to."

"I have a good job with a good paycheck. I'm not worried about myself anymore. The only thing that matters right now is helping Carly. Goodbye, Dad. I hope you enjoy the rest of your life."

Before his father could say another word Kevin pushed the button to end the call, closing the phone and tossing it onto the coffee table. He leaned back against the couch, scrubbing his hands tiredly against his face, and tried to catch hold of his raging emotions. He hated having to do that, but his only other option would be to cave in and let a little girl die. He simply couldn't do that; even he wasn't that much of a coward.

Surprisingly Kevin wasn't all that upset about cutting himself from his father's life. In many ways it was a relief, like having a huge burden lifted from his shoulders. He just hoped he'd have a chance to explain things to his mother before his father twisted things around to make Kevin look like the bad guy. Thomas Meyers was really good at doing that.

Rising from the couch Kevin stretched, his spine crackling loudly, and headed into the bedroom to pack. Figuring he'd be in Arizona for a week at least Kevin decided to use the largest of his suitcases and he spent the next hour getting ready for the trip. When his suitcase was all ready to go he seriously considered taking a quick nap, but a glance at his watch suggested that it wouldn't be a good idea. Kevin didn't want to take any chances on missing his flight and he knew that if he went to bed now he'd never get up in time.

After pacing the condo for several long, tense hours Kevin finally hauled his luggage downstairs and hailed a cab. Once at Logan Airport he was able to check his luggage fairly quickly and was one of the first to board the flight. Since he was traveling first class he had his pick of seats. Once situated Kevin requested a pillow and blanket and was asleep even before the plane was finished filling up.

Kevin slept soundly during the four and a half hour flight from Boston to Phoenix and when he woke to the sound of people preparing for the landing he felt surprisingly refreshed. As he exited the plane in the Phoenix Airport Kevin couldn't help but feel excited at the idea of seeing Julie again. He knew he wouldn't be welcomed with open arms, but he was determined to convince her to give him a second chance. He wanted to be a family with Julie and Carly and he was going to do everything in his power to make that happen.

Julie was reluctant to leave Carly long enough to go to the airport and pick up Kevin, but Aaron assured her that Carly was in good hands with him. She took so long saying goodbye to Carly that she was very nearly late getting to the airport.

When she entered the appropriate terminal Julie found a bench and sat down where she could see the passengers when they departed the plane. Checking her watch Julie saw that she still had almost ten minutes to wait so she sat back, crossing her arms across her chest and attempting to get comfortable.

Julie hated the idea of bringing Kevin back into her life, but she had to put aside her own feelings if she wanted to see her daughter get better. Kevin might not be good for anything else but if he could save Carly's life Julie might just find it in her heart to not hate him so much.

The sudden stream of people passing her made Julie look up and she was abruptly jerked from her thoughts when she spotted Kevin. He was even better looking than he had been when he was seventeen and Julie felt an uncomfortable tug deep inside her.

Standing up Julie waved at Kevin and when he spotted her a big smile spread across his face and he began striding quickly towards her. It seemed like no time before he was standing right in front of her and for a long moment Julie didn't know what to do, what to say, how to act.

"Hi, Jules," Kevin said, breaking the uncomfortable silence between them.

"Hello, Kevin." Julie winced at the coldness in her own voice, but there was nothing she could do about it. "You ready to go?"

"Let me just grab my other bag," Kevin said brightly, shifting his carry-on bag on his shoulder.

Julie followed Kevin to the baggage claim and waited while he retrieved his suitcase. The sudden extra space between them gave Julie a chance to catch her breath and check her thoughts. This was what she'd been afraid of; Kevin had always had this effect on her and sometimes she really hated him for it. More than that though she hated herself for letting him do this to her.

"I'm all set. I have a rental car waiting so if you want to take me there that'd be great," Kevin said, breaking into Julie's thoughts.

"Yeah, I can do that. The rental office is right across the road."

Julie led the way out of the crowded airport and across the parking lot to her car. Unlocking the driver's side door Julie pushed the button to unlock Kevin's door and slid behind the wheel. Sitting in the car together was an unpleasant experience and Julie had to force herself to focus and not let Kevin's inherent charms get to her.

Backing carefully out of her parking space Julie navigated slowly out of the airport lot and across the street to the rental office where she parked in the nearest spot she could find. Julie put the car in gear and chanced a quick glance over at Kevin.

"I'll wait here for you. You can follow me to your hotel and then to the hospital."

"Thanks, Jules. I'll leave my stuff here until I get my keys."

Julie didn't respond as Kevin climbed out of the car, but she couldn't stop herself from admiring his physique as he walked into the office. Shaking her head to clear it Julie thought about Aaron and that steadied her a little bit. Less than five minutes later Kevin returned with a set of car keys in his hand. Opening the back door of Julie's car he leaned in and grabbed his luggage.

"We're going to the hotel first, right?" he asked Julie.

"It's probably easier to do that. You can drop your stuff off and then we can go to the hospital and talk to Dr. Marsden about the biopsy."

"Sounds good to me."

Kevin closed the car door and took his luggage to a rental car that was parked near the office. Julie waited until she saw him signal to her that he was ready before starting her car and putting it in gear. Thankfully traffic was fairly light and they made it the hotel in good time. Julie waited again while Kevin went inside and got the key to his room where he stashed his luggage before returning to the lot. Julie was surprised when Kevin approached her car door instead of heading for his rental.

"Is there someplace nearby we can stop so I can grab a bite to eat?" he asked, leaning in her window. "I haven't had anything since last night."

Julie leaned away from him, feeling incredibly uncomfortable having him in her personal space that way. She was also a little irritated; she wanted to get back to Carly and he wanted to stop and eat.

"There's a cafeteria in the hospital," she said, a little coldly.

Kevin winced away from her and Julie felt a little guilty, but she had to get back to Carly before she went crazy. This was the longest she'd been away from her daughter since Carly got sick and it was starting to bother her badly.

"I guess that'll have to do," Kevin said and strode across the lot to his car. Judging from his posture Julie could tell he was angry but at that point she didn't care. Carly was more important.

It took longer to reach the hospital than Julie had anticipated and she was developing a serious case of road rage by the time she parked in her usual space in the hospital parking lot. Kevin parked beside her and they both climbed out of their cars at the same time.

"Lead the way," Kevin said.

Julie slung her purse over her shoulder and made her way into the hospital. She saw a few people she recognized and waved at them. Julie was in such a hurry to see Carly that Kevin had to take extra strides to keep up with her. Julie was relieved to see the elevator nearly full when she and Kevin got on. This made it easier to keep her distance from Kevin and get some sort of perspective on this whole crazy situation.

When they reached the door to Carly's room Kevin started to follow Julie inside but Julie put a firm hand on his chest and pushed him back.

"What?" Kevin asked, an angry expression on his face.

"You're not going in there, Kevin," Julie said, also getting angry.

"Then what the hell did you bring me here for if I don't even get to see my daughter?"

Kevin's tone frightened Julie a little bit but she was determined to stand her ground. It didn't hurt knowing that Aaron wasn't far away if she needed him.

"The only reason you're here is because you might be a bone marrow match for Carly."

Kevin clenched his fists tightly, looking ready to punch something and Julie steadied herself, prepared to yell for Aaron if it became necessary.

"This isn't fair, Julie! I have a right to see my daughter, damnit!"

"You gave up your rights when you disappeared eleven years ago, Kevin. Now stay here."

They glared at each other for a long moment. Then, cursing to himself, Kevin turned away from Julie and began pacing back and forth. Julie was pretty certain that Kevin would stay put so she entered Carly's room and found Aaron standing near the door with his hands clenched into fists and a fighting expression on his face.

"It's okay, honey. He's waiting out in the hall."

"He damn well better stay there or I'll tear him into little pieces," Aaron said, an edge in his voice that Julie had never heard before.

Glancing over at the bed Julie saw that Carly was asleep so she turned back to Aaron. Sidling up to him Julie pressed against him, wrapping her arms around his waist.

"You know I kind of like seeing this side of you. It's very sexy."

Aaron's face softened and, chuckling, he bent to kiss the tip of her nose. "Well in that case I'll have to get angry more often."

Julie leaned into him, breathing deeply the scent of his cologne, letting his warmth seep into her and comfort her.

"How was Carly?" she asked.

Aaron sighed a little sadly and hugged Julie closer to him. "She fell asleep shortly after you left," he said.

Closing her eyes to stave off the tears that were beginning to form Julie whispered, "I'm so scared, Aaron. I hate this whole mess. I hate having Kevin here." Her voice broke and Aaron gently rocked her in his arms.

"I don't like it either, honey. But if he can save her life then maybe he's not entirely useless."

Reluctantly Julie pulled away from the safety of Aaron's arms and brushed away the tears that had trickled down her cheeks.

"I have to take Kevin to see Dr. Marsden about the biopsy. You'll be okay with Carly, right?"

Aaron touched Julie's cheek gently. "Of course I will."

Leaning up on her tiptoes Julie kissed Aaron's cheek and squeezed his hand tightly, feeling his love give her strength. When she left Carly's room she found Kevin crouched on the floor leaning against the wall with his head in his hands.

"Are you ready to go talk to the doctor?" Julie asked a little hesitantly.

When Kevin looked up his eyes were red rimmed and raw looking. When he answered his voice was thick and raspy with emotion.

"Yeah, I'm ready."

Julie led the way to Dr. Marsden's office. Kevin sat down in one of the waiting room chairs while Julie approached the receptionist window. Dr. Marsden's receptionist was very familiar with Julie by now and greeted her with a friendly smile.

"Hi, Dr. Forrester. How can I help you today?"

"I have my daughter's biological father here to schedule a bone marrow biopsy. Dr. Marsden said to let her know as soon as he arrived."

The receptionist held up a finger, signaling Julie to wait, and picked up the phone. After punching in a few numbers there was silence for a moment until someone on the other end picked up.

"Dr. Marsden, I have Julie Forrester here. She needs to schedule someone for a bone marrow biopsy." The receptionist listened for a moment and then, "Yes, Doctor. I'll send them right back."

"You know where to go," the receptionist said as she hung up the telephone.

"Thanks," Julie said, trying and failing to smile.

Julie motioned to Kevin who followed her obediently through the door and down the hall to a door marked with a plaque that read Dr. Rebecca Marsden/Oncologist. Julie knocked once before opening the office door and poking her head inside. The doctor was seated behind a large desk and when she looked up and saw Julie she smiled brightly.

"Hi, Julie."

"Hi, Dr. Marsden," Julie said. "This is Carly's biological father, Kevin."

"It's a pleasure to meet you, Kevin," Dr. Marsden said, shaking Kevin's hand.

"Kevin's here to have a bone marrow biopsy done to see if he's a match for Carly," Julie said.

Dr. Marsden's face lit up and her smile grew even wider. "That's excellent!" she exclaimed. "Let me check my schedule and see when we can have it done. The sooner the better."

Julie waited anxiously as the doctor perused her schedule. Finally Dr. Marsden looked up and said, "How does first thing tomorrow morning sound?"

"Are you serious? That soon?" Julie couldn't believe it had been that easy. "Is that okay for you, Kevin?" she asked.

"That's fine. What time should I be here?"

"We'll do the test at seven thirty so be here about fifteen minutes early to get the paperwork done."

Julie shook Dr. Marsden's hand, feeling more hopeful than she had in a very long time. "Thank you for getting us in so early."

"It's my pleasure, Julie. I'll see you in the morning."

Dr. Marsden showed them out of her office and they wordlessly returned to the seventh floor. It was Kevin who eventually broke the silence.

"Since I have to be up so early I'm going to head out and get some food and some sleep. Will I see you tomorrow morning?"

Julie hesitated for a second, and then said, "Yeah, I'll be there."

Kevin simply nodded and turned to leave. He was halfway down the hall when Julie called out to him. "Hey, Kevin?" He turned to look at her, an inquisitive expression on his face. After a pause Julie said simply, "Thank you."

Without a word Kevin simply smiled and continued down the corridor to the elevator. Julie watched with warring emotions as he got in and the doors closed. With a sigh Julie turned and headed back into Carly's room, anxious to be alone with her daughter and Aaron.

Lying on his hotel bed with his hands laced behind his head Kevin pondered the events of the day. He felt a little better since getting some food in him. Outside the hospital he had asked a man for directions to the nearest fast food place which turned out to be Arby's and had grabbed a to-go order which he took back to the room.

Though he was no longer hungry Kevin was definitely still angry at Julie for the way she'd acted and the way she had treated him. He firmly believed that he had every right to see his daughter. If she kept up with her current attitude he was going to have to seek professional help in securing the right to see Carly. After all, it wasn't his fault he hadn't been around the last ten years.

Sighing Kevin had to admit that he couldn't blame the situation entirely on his father. If he'd been brave, like Katie, and not so dependent on the family money he might have been able to be a part of Julie and Carly's lives. But he'd been a coward and he was willing to admit that. It wasn't an easy thing to admit, especially for a man, but he had learned to accept the fact of his cowardice.

With a huge yawn Kevin rolled over on his side and shut off the lamp. He'd already called the front desk and set up an alarm for six thirty the following morning. And as exhausted as he was at the moment Kevin knew he would have no trouble sleeping that night.

Julie was sitting in the waiting room the following morning when Kevin walked in looking bleary eyed and half asleep. He waved in her general direction before approaching the receptionist desk. Julie was idly flipping through a magazine she'd picked up, occasionally reading an article and then promptly forgetting every word of it. When Kevin sat down in a chair across from her she was almost grateful for his presence for at least it distracted her from everything else that was going on.

"Did you sleep last night?" Julie asked after a moment of silence.

"Like a rock. The desk clerk had to call twice before I finally got out of bed."

"I miss sleeping in a bed," Julie said a little wistfully. When Kevin looked at her curiously she continued, "I've been using a sleeper chair since Carly was admitted to the hospital. It's the only way I can stay with her and there's no way I'm leaving her for an entire night."

They lapsed into an uncomfortable silence again while Kevin filled out the required paperwork and returned it to the receptionist. A few seconds later a nurse appeared looking, in Julie's opinion, way too chipper for so early in the morning.

"Kevin Meyers?" the nurse asked brightly.

Kevin stood and started to follow the nurse, then looked back and asked Julie, "Aren't you coming with me?"

"No, but don't worry. You're in the best hands possible."

Looking nervous but resolute Kevin followed the nurse through the swinging door and out of sight. Julie leaned her head back against the wall and closed her eyes as she waited for him to come back.

Kevin was taken to a small exam room off of Dr. Marsden's office where he was given a hospital gown and told to strip down naked. He did so, feeling more than a little exposed with the paper thin gown open in the back. That feeling of exposure only got worse as the doctor came in and instructed him to lie down on the table, face down, and the next thing he knew the gown had been flipped up to completely expose his buttocks.

Trying to steady his breathing and keep his composure Kevin let his mind wander, thinking about Julie and Carly. He kept his eyes closed the entire time the biopsy was taking place, feeling a horrible grinding pain when the needle went through his bone, but it was over within a few minutes.

"You did great, Kevin," Dr. Marsden said, smiling at him. Kevin managed a small smile in return, though his stomach was rolling queasily. "You'll have to stay here for another fifteen or twenty minutes, but after that you can go about your day as usual. We should have the results in about a week."

The doctor left the room while the nurses bustled about, taking his vital signs and periodically checking the site of the procedure to see if it was still bleeding. Once the bleeding stopped the nurses informed him he could get dressed again which he did, moving a bit more slowly than usual. His hip ached and he was suddenly exhausted. Even seeing Julie waiting for him didn't perk him up that much.

"Dr. Marsden said you did great and everything went well. Now all we have to do is wait and see."

Kevin nodded, stifling a yawn with the back of his hand. "I'm sorry, Jules, but I'm exhausted. Do you mind if I head back to the hotel to get some sleep?"

"Of course I don't mind. Go and get some rest; you can call me later to let me know how you're feeling."

Julie walked Kevin to his car, waving at him until she could no longer see him in the distance, and then made her way back up to Carly's room to spend the rest of the day with her daughter and prepare to wait for the results that had the potential to change their lives.

Kevin pulled into the parking lot of the hotel and parked as close to his unit as possible. Getting out of the car he winced at the ache in his hip. Limping a little Kevin made his way into the hotel and to his room, the pain growing increasingly worse, and he couldn't wait to take a few of the Tylenol the nurse had given him before he left the hospital.

When he entered his room he headed straight for the bed where he sat down, gingerly, unsure if putting pressure on his hip would hurt. Actually, it was a relief to be on a soft surface and he leaned back against the pillows, stretching his legs out in front of him.

For a few minutes he simply sat there, thinking about the craziness of the last two days and wondering where it would all lead. He was just about to doze off when he remembered that he'd promised Katie he'd call when he arrived. He reached for the phone on the nightstand, hoping that she hadn't been too worried.

Leaning against the pillows again Kevin dialed Katie's number and waited as the phone began to ring. It was on the fifth ring and he was about to give up when Katie finally answered.

"Hello?"

"Hey, Kat, it's me."

"Kevin! It's about time!" The indignation and scolding in his older sister's voice made Kevin smile.

"I'm sorry, Kat. I was so distracted when I first got here that I completely forgot to call."

"No worries. Have you seen Julie?"

Kevin felt his heart skip a little beat. "Yeah, I saw her. She's even more beautiful now than she was when we were kids."

Katie's voice was softer now, almost hesitant. "What about Carly? Have you seen her?"

Tears stung Kevin's eyes and he had to take a deep breath to compose himself. "No, Julie won't let me see her."

"I'm so sorry, Kev," Katie whispered.

"So am I. It's my own fault though." Kevin hesitated a second before he continued. "She has a boyfriend. It seems pretty serious. I

186

think I've really lost her, Kat." His last words were choked as a sob threatened to tear loose from his chest.

"Kevin, you can't give up on her!" Katie's voice was stern, forceful, and Kevin was a little taken aback.

"I can't push her either, Katie."

"I didn't say to push her, Kevin. But let her know why you did what you did. If you don't you'll be miserable for the rest of your life."

There was silence between them for a long moment. "Katie? How did you do it? Get away from him?"

Katie sighed heavily. "Kev, it's different for a woman. I had a good man I knew I could depend on when I was disinherited." After a hesitant pause Katie added, "I also wasn't afraid of the old bastard."

"And I've always been afraid of him," Kevin said, more to himself than to his sister.

"Since you were a baby," Katie answered and Kevin could hear the sadness in her tone.

Kevin laughed, a little bitterly. "Well, he's not a problem anymore. He disowned me when I told him I was coming to Arizona for Carly."

"Kevin, that's a good thing!" Katie cried, excitedly. "You're smart, you're successful and you can do this on your own without Thomas' help. I know you can."

Kevin smiled, feeling a sudden powerful love for his sister. "Thanks, Kat. I think I need a nap now. I just had a needle the size of a corkscrew inserted in my hip and I'm feeling pretty sore."

"Take care of yourself, Kev. And don't give up. Promise me?"

"I promise. Give the kids hugs for me."

"I will. And you give Julie my best, for her and for Carly."

"I will. Bye, Kat."

"Bye, Kev."

Kevin hung up the phone and then leaned back on the bed, closing his eyes and letting the exhaustion overtake him. He fell asleep within seconds and slept soundly for fifteen hours, getting up only to use the bathroom when necessary.

Aaron had to leave early the following morning to go into work for a few hours and within minutes Julie missed his quiet, strong presence. The breakfast trays came in promptly at 7:30 and Julie was almost finished with hers and encouraging Carly to eat more of hers when they were interrupted by a knock on the door. One of the morning nurses poked her head inside.

"Excuse me, Dr. Forrester? Dr. Marsden has asked to speak to you and to Mr. Meyers as soon as possible."

Julie nodded to show that she had heard and understood, not trusting her voice. Suddenly she felt cold with terror and she wished desperately that Aaron were there to offer reassurance.

"Why do you have to see the doctor again, Mom?" Carly asked from her bed, making Julie jump in surprise.

"She probably wants to talk to me about your treatment, honey. That's all."

Julie went to the front desk and located someone who could sit with Carly for a few minutes. Before heading to Dr. Marsden's office Julie doubled back to Carly's room to give her a quick kiss on the cheek. She then headed to the rooftop garden and to her usual table where she pulled her cell phone out of her pocket and called Kevin. Kevin answered on the second ring.

"Julie? Is everything OK?"

"Dr. Marsden needs to speak to both of us. How fast can you get here?"

"Ten minutes," he said.

Julie didn't even have a chance to thank him before he ended the call. She waited outside on a bench, her foot tapping the ground incessantly, until finally Kevin pulled into the lot. He parked rather haphazardly and jumped out of the car. When he reached Julie she immediately turned and led him to the elevator. Neither of them said a word until Julie reached the welcome desk.

"We're here to see Dr. Marsden. She should be expecting us."

The receptionist smiled at her and said, "Go on back. She's waiting for you."

Julie didn't even bother to knock on the door, just pushed it open and stood there uncertainly for a long moment. "Well?" she finally choked out and when Dr. Marsden smiled the tension in the room seemed to evaporate.

"He's a match," Dr. Marsden said, calmly, but with a twinkle of excitement in her eyes.

Julie hid her face in her hands for a moment and Kevin suspected she was crying. But when she turned to him her eyes were dry and they were both surprise when she threw her arms around his neck. Kevin put his arms around her back, hugging her so tightly he lifted her off the floor, and then for good measure he spun her around a few times, both of them laughing joyfully.

When he set her on her feet again Julie surprised him by kissing his cheek. "Thank you, Kevin. I'll never forget this gift for as long as I live."

Kevin cupped her face in his hands and leaned down to kiss her forehead. "You're welcome."

"How soon can we do the transplant, Rebecca?" Julie asked, turning to the doctor.

"Well we have to do some high intensity radiation treatments first, that'll take a few days, but as soon as that's over with we do the transplant and go from there."

Julie and Dr. Marsden hugged, both of them laughing, while Kevin stayed silent in the background. The excitement and the hope in the air was palpable, but it came with an air of lingering uncertainty. Even a bone marrow transplant wasn't a certain thing. It was their best option, but it might not do the job and they all knew that they had to prepare for the worst case scenario.

After leaving the doctor's office Julie and Kevin went back to the seventh floor to tell Aaron. He let out a roar of excitement and swept Julie into a hug. Kevin tried not to be jealous, but it was blatantly obvious how deeply Julie and Aaron loved each other. He was leaning against the wall outside Carly's room when Julie appeared holding hands with Aaron. Kevin hadn't been expecting this and he tried to keep the shock from his expression as Julie introduced them.

"Kevin, this is my boyfriend, Aaron. Aaron, Carly's biological father, Kevin."

Kevin shook Aaron's hand, forcing himself not to try breaking the man's hand. "It's a pleasure to meet you, Aaron"

"Same here, Kevin. I just want to thank you for what you're doing. It's very noble of you and we really appreciate it."

Kevin fought back his jealousy as he watched Aaron slip his arm around Julie's waist and the way she leaned into him. Julie's eyes were shining and she radiated happiness and relief. Kevin watched as Julie tugged on Aaron's arm and said, "Let's go talk to Carly. She'll be thrilled to hear the news."

"Nice meeting you, Kevin," Aaron said, dismissively, as he and Julie headed back into Carly's room to talk to her.

Kevin waited in the corridor while Julie and Aaron talked to Carly. He couldn't keep from smiling at the sound of Carly's excited voice asking her mother when she'd be able to go home again. Julie stayed with Carly for almost twenty minutes before returning to the corridor and when she saw Kevin she approached him, an air of caution surrounding her.

"I talked to Aaron and he's agreed to watch Carly for a few hours. I want to take you out to dinner, to celebrate. Is that okay with you?"

Kevin hesitated for a second; he wasn't sure if Julie was doing this because she wanted to or as a detached way to thank him for just happening to be a bone marrow match for Carly. Even though he knew he might regret it later Kevin had to be certain that this was what she wanted.

"Are you sure, Julie? You don't have to do this, you know."

"I know that. I want to; I think it would be good for us to talk about some stuff, clear the air between us. How many opportunities like this are we going to get again?"

Kevin understood the meaning behind her words, knew that she was ready to hear his version of the truth behind his disappearance all those years ago and he couldn't put into words how grateful and relieved he felt. So he said, simply, "Thank you, Julie."

"You're welcome." Julie smiled softly at him.

"Should I pick you up or do you want to meet somewhere?" Kevin finally asked, proud of himself for keeping his voice steady.

"I want to spend some time with Carly so how about I meet you outside your hotel around five. Is that good for you?"

"I can't wait. I'll see you later, Jules." Kevin hesitated for just a second, then, taking a huge risk, he leaned over and kissed Julie's cheek.

Hoping that he hadn't pushed too hard Kevin walked away without another word. He probably shouldn't have kissed her, but at the time he'd felt compelled and there was nothing he could do to stop it from happening.

Sighing Julie watched Kevin walk away and when she could no longer see him she returned to Carly's room, trying and failing to not think about the fact that she was still attracted to him and would have to make a very difficult decision down the road.

"So, what did you want to talk about?"

They were sitting in a corner booth at an Outback Steakhouse in Phoenix. Kevin had been wrestling with growing anxiety all afternoon while waiting to see Julie and he had decided he was done playing games; he wanted to get all the cards out on the table once and for all.

Julie paused as she was reaching for her drink. She hesitated before taking a sip and then said, carefully, "What do you mean?"

Kevin simply looked at her, studying her, and Julie looked away under the intensity of his gaze. "I don't want to go on like this anymore, Julie. I know it's too late, but I want you to know the truth."

Julie gazed at him and he could tell she was struggling with her thoughts. On the one hand she could go on the way she had, believing he was a horrible and evil person, or she could listen to his side of the story and then have to decide if she believed him or not. Finally she sighed and said, "Go ahead."

Kevin took a deep breath to steady himself, and then began the story that had haunted him for years. "You know how I grew up; I had everything I ever wanted and it was the only way of life I ever knew. My old man used that against me from the time I was old enough to contradict him. I know I shouldn't have let him dictate my life for so long but I was afraid of being cut off from the family; for a long time I felt like I needed the name and the money. I've only just begun to realize that I don't need all that as much as I thought I did.

The night you told me you were pregnant I went home and told my parents. My mother didn't say much, she was well trained by my father, but he had a lot to say about it and we ended up having a huge fight. It was bad enough that it almost came to blows. He didn't say anything to me for over a week and I started to think that maybe he was just being a blowhard. I found out differently less than a week after I told them about the pregnancy.

I left school that afternoon and found my father leaning against my car. When I asked him what he was doing there he told me we were moving to Connecticut. I knew why he was doing it and I threatened to run away. My father just laughed and told me it would be a waste of time because he could have me tracked and brought home within hours. I was a coward; I went with him.

By the time I was able to get away from him you had already left Baltimore. After I finished high school I went to see your parents and I begged them to tell me where you were. Your mother took pity on me and gave me one of Carly's baby pictures, but she refused to tell me anything about you or Carly. I've tried to get on with my life since then, but you and Carly are my life. I love you Julie and I want us to have another chance."

Julie had tears in her eyes by the time Kevin finished his story. Deep down she had to admit she'd always suspected that Kevin's father had something to do with why he'd disappeared. Hearing him say it with such earnest emotion in his voice made it more real and the reality of the situation left Julie in a terrible bind. She loved Aaron, but she was still in love with Kevin too, she couldn't deny it any longer.

Reaching across the table Julie grasped Kevin's hand. "I hate your father for doing this to us. He robbed you of the chance to know your daughter, robbed a little girl of knowing her father. All because I didn't come from a rich and powerful family."

Julie knew she sounded bitter, but she didn't care. She had a right to be bitter and she noticed that Kevin didn't argue with her about the way she felt. Julie was lost in thought until Kevin squeezed her hand to get her attention.

"Can we get out of here?" he asked and Julie knew what he had in mind.

Throwing some bills on the table, more than enough to cover their meals and the tip, Julie stood and reached for her purse. Slinging it over her shoulder she followed Kevin out into the parking lot and she didn't argue when he climbed into the driver's seat of the car. Julie was quiet as Kevin navigated the car through the streets of Phoenix until they reached his hotel.

Kevin parked the car and climbed out, going around to the passenger door to open Julie's door for her. Taking her hand he led her into the hotel. When they reached his room Kevin unlocked the door, then stopped and turned to Julie, his hands on her shoulders, wanting to be sure this was what she wanted.

"Are you sure, Jules?"

Julie didn't answer. Instead she closed the gap between them, her hands on his waist, and she lifted her face to his, her lips barely brushing his in a tantalizing invitation. With a guttural groan Kevin drew Julie into his arms and pressed his lips to hers, kissing her with a passion that left them both breathless.

Reaching behind him Kevin found the doorknob and turned, pushing the door open. They stumble stepped their way into the room, slamming the door shut behind them. The sense of urgency and desperation was intense as they pulled and tugged at clothing, leaving a trail behind them on the way to the bed.

Julie felt a moment's guilt as they tumbled onto the bed, but she was soon lost in Kevin's kisses and his hands on her skin.

Their lovemaking was fiery and passionate, like nothing Julie had ever experienced before, and afterward they lay together in a breathless, sweaty tangle.

When she caught her breath Julie rolled over onto her side to look at Kevin and when she saw the concern and worry in his eyes she smiled, reaching out to gently touch his face.

"Don't look so guilty; I'm a big girl and I knew what I was getting into. I can't stay long though. Carly's probably wondering where I am." Julie kissed Kevin deeply and when she pulled back his eyes were sparkling like jewels. "Dream about me tonight," she said, coyly.

"I've dreamt about you every night for the last eleven years," Kevin said and Julie smiled.

After locating all of her clothing Julie dressed and, with one last kiss goodbye, left the hotel and drove the short distance to the hospital. Aaron was asleep in the chair and Carly was drifting in and out of sleep, but she opened her eyes when Julie kissed her forehead.

"Hi, Mommy," Carly said, her voice weak and strained.

"Hi, baby."

It broke Julie's heart seeing how diminished her daughter looked lying there in that hospital bed. She suddenly hated herself for spending so much time thinking about the men in her life and the choice she was going to be forced to make when she should have been focusing on her sick little girl, spending as much time as possible with Carly just in case the unthinkable happened.

Reaching out to gently touch Carly's cheek Julie marveled at the softness of her daughter's skin. Fighting back tears Julie whispered, "I love you so much, baby."

"I love you too, Mommy."

Carly stretched her hand out and Julie took it, squeezing very gently to avoid bruising her daughter. Julie watched as Carly drifted back to sleep, a small smile on her lips, and when she was sure Carly was asleep Julie gave in to the tears that had been threatening to fall since she walked into the room.

Aaron heard Julie crying and got up from the chair, crossing the room to put his arms around her. Though she was torn by guilt and uncertainty Julie leaned against Aaron, needing to be held and comforted, and she suddenly hated herself for betraying Aaron's trust in her.

That night Julie watched Carly sleep for a long time, determined to focus entirely on her daughter's health and the upcoming procedures she would have to endure. Now was not the time to be torn between two men she loved who loved her deeply in return. She'd figure out what she was going to do after Carly's transplant, when she was sure that she wasn't going to lose her little girl. Only then could Julie really concentrate on the decision that she knew she was going to have to make.

For the two days following the news that Kevin was a donor match Carly was moved to a sterile, germ free room to prevent infection and given extremely high doses of chemotherapy and radiation. While Carly was kept in the sterile room only Julie was allowed in to see her and she had to wear protective, germ proof clothes.

On the third day Carly had to be awake much earlier than usual. Though Julie argued against it Dr. Marsden insisted that she leave the room while they did the transplant. Carly looked terrified and Julie was heartbroken, reduced to watching the procedure through a window in the door to Carly's room.

The bone marrow transplant was similar in many ways to a basic blood transfusion except Carly's vital signs had to be monitored at all times for signs of distress. The procedure itself took almost five hours; five of the longest and most agonizing hours of Julie's life. When the door to Carly's room opened and Dr. Marsden came out Julie was trembling with anxiety.

"Well?" she asked, desperately.

"She did great, Julie. Now all we can do is wait and see what happens. She'll be kept here, in this room, for about two to four weeks and she'll be in the hospital for another two months, but I'm confident that she's going to pull through."

Julie let out a breath she hadn't even realized she was holding. "Thank you, God!" she cried, not caring that tears were streaming down her cheeks.

Dr. Marsden laughed and took Julie's hand, squeezing it hard. "She's a brave girl, like her mother." She gave Julie's hand another tight squeeze. "I'll be back to check on you both a little later." She started to walk away when Julie called after her.

"Can I go in and see Carly?"

Dr. Marsden hesitated for a second and Julie felt her heart sink. Then, after thinking about it for a few seconds, Dr. Marsden responded. "You can, but I'd advise you to go tell your men what you know first. Going in and out of Carly's room too often threatens the germ free protection that she needs right now."

"Thank you, Dr. Marsden," Julie said. Dr. Marsden tipped her a wink and then walked away.

Julie watched Carly through the window for a few more minutes before heading to the waiting room. Aaron was sitting in a chair reading a magazine and Kevin sat on the couch on the other side of the room. Julie had been touched when Kevin insisted on waiting to see how Carly made out, though it bothered her that they were sitting so far apart from each other.

Kevin saw Julie first and quickly got up from the couch, crossing the room in three long strides. This got Aaron's attention and he stood too, both of them facing Julie with expectant looks on their faces. Julie smiled at them and both men relaxed a fraction.

"She did great. She'll be in the hospital for another couple months, but she did beautifully and Dr. Marsden is confident that she'll pull through."

Aaron laughed and grabbed Julie in his arms. Julie hugged him hard, laughing along with him when he lifted her off her feet and spun her around. When he set her down she turned to look at Kevin. His eyes were shining and he seemed torn between a myriad of emotions. Julie hesitated for just a second before she put her arms around Kevin, hugging him hard.

"Thank you, Kevin. You helped save my baby's life. I can't thank you enough for this gift."

Kevin hugged her back, trying to burn the feeling of her body close to him permanently into his memory. He had a horrible, sinking suspicion that this was Julie's way of telling him goodbye.

When Julie released him she reached up and lightly touched his cheek, her eyes sparkling with unshed tears. Looking from Kevin to Aaron and back again she smiled softly, looking happier and more radiant than she had in countless weeks.

"I have to get back to Carly."

Julie turned to head back to Carly's room, but stopped and turned around again, facing the two men. She blew them both a kiss, her vision blurred with tears, and then continued on her way to see her daughter. No matter what choice she made concerning Aaron and Kevin people were going to get hurt; it was inevitable. But that didn't change the fact that she had a gut wrenching decision to make and she needed to make it soon.

CHAPTER 11

*T*hree weeks after Carly's bone marrow transplant she was moved back to her regular hospital room. In those three short weeks she had perked up considerably and was chomping at the bit to go home, driving both Julie and Aaron crazy.

Kevin had remained in Arizona during those three weeks, afraid of not being kept up to date once he returned to Boston. Julie was struggling with the idea of letting Kevin see Carly. Julie had let go of a lot of the bitterness she'd held onto for years, had let go of the past in a way and was ready to look toward the future without the jaded attitude she'd held for years. But she still had something important to tell Carly and she knew it wouldn't be easy.

One day after breakfast Julie went up to the rooftop garden and sat at her usual table to think. She was there for over an hour before returning to Carly's room. Aaron was sitting in a chair in the corner reading a book and Carly was sitting on her bed watching television. When Julie came into the room she switched the TV off, ignoring Carly's indignant protests.

"Mom!?! I was watching that!"

"I know sweetheart, but we need to talk." Julie turned to Aaron who had looked up from his book. "Carly and I need some private time. Is that OK, hon?"

"Of course. I'll be nearby if you need me." Aaron placed a marker in his book and left the room, kissing both Julie and Carly on the way out.

Julie sat down at the foot of Carly's bed, her legs crossed comfortably, facing her daughter. Carly was looking at her curiously, expectantly, and Julie felt her heart break with the knowledge that Carly's trust in her might never be the same after this conversation.

"Carly, I love you so much. You know that, right?"

Carly looked surprised. "Of course, Mommy. I love you too."

Julie smiled, reaching out to gently touch the top of Carly's head, feeling the new growth of hair that was just beginning to emerge. "My sweet little ladybug," she whispered, softly.

"Mommy, what's wrong?" Carly asked. She looked like she might cry so Julie forced herself to continue.

"Carly, I haven't been telling you the truth about your father," she said, her voice even. Carly looked like she'd been slapped. "I've known where he is for the last seven years or so."

Julie was unsurprised to see a look of anger come over Carly's face. "I thought we didn't keep secrets from each other, Mom!" she cried, her voice rising with each word. "You lied to me!"

"I know, sweetheart. And if I could take it back and do it over again I would do it differently. But what's done is done and it can't be changed."

"Why didn't you tell me the truth?" Carly demanded, arms folded angrily across her chest.

Julie took a deep breath and let it out on a long sigh. "I could sit here and say that it was for your own good, but it would be another lie and I'm through lying to you. I did it because of my own selfish pride, because I was angry at your father, and because I felt like I had to prove to everyone that I didn't need help raising you. All those reasons were wrong and you can never know how sorry I am for what I did. Even Mom's make mistakes sometimes and I can admit that I made a big mistake."

Carly glared at her mother. "I'm still mad at you, Mom. You told me we were a team and that we didn't keep secrets."

Julie hesitated a second before reaching out and taking Carly's hand. Carly tried to pull it away but Julie held firm and finally Carly relented.

"I know you're angry with me and you have every right to be. But I think I might have something that can help make up for what I did."

"What?" Carly asked, suspiciously.

Julie smiled at her, her eyes dancing with mirth. She went to the door of Carly's hospital room and peeked around the corner. Kevin was standing just outside the door. Julie had already spoken to him about what she was planning to do and he had been waiting impatiently since Aaron left the room, glaring at him on the way out. When he saw Julie he felt his heart begin to race and his hands trembled.

Julie smiled at him, a joyous expression on her face. "Kevin, come say hello to your daughter."

A broad grin spread across Kevin's face. He reminded Julie of a little boy on Christmas morning discovering that Santa had brought him everything on his list. Julie beckoned him into the room and he followed obediently. When he saw Carly sitting on the bed, looking at him in shocked disbelief, he knew he would remember the moment forever.

Julie stepped back a little bit as Kevin slowly approached the bed. She watched with tears in her eyes as Carly and Kevin studied each other carefully. When Kevin finally reached the bed he sat down gingerly on the edge, facing Carly. The two of them just looked at each other for the longest moment. Then Kevin held out his hand and Carly took it.

"I'm so glad to finally meet you, Carly," Kevin said, his voice barely above a whisper. Julie saw that he was crying a little and she knew she'd done the right thing.

"I'm glad to meet you too," Carly said, softly.

The next thing Julie knew Carly was up on her knees with her arms around Kevin's neck and the two of them were hugging like drowning people clinging to a life preserver. Julie managed to smile through her own tears. She knew Aaron would be angry, but she would deal with that when it came. For the time being the only thing that mattered was Carly, Kevin and this amazing moment when they were united as a family for the first time.

Kevin sat with Carly for most of that afternoon, the two of them talking like long lost friends. When Aaron returned and saw Kevin he had been irate and Julie had been forced to follow him out of the room, catching up with him just before he got to the elevator as she tried her best to explain her reasoning. Their argument still lingered in her mind that night as she was trying to sleep.

"How could you let him in there?" Aaron asked angrily when Julie grabbed his arm.

"He's her father." Kevin snorted derisively which Julie chose to ignore. "And for your information I did it for Carly, not for Kevin." She thought about that and realized it wasn't entirely true. "Mostly for Carly anyway," she amended.

Aaron looked away from Julie, trying to control his anger, and Julie understood that he was more hurt than angry. This was confirmed by the look in his eyes when he finally turned back to face her.

"The least you could have done was talk to me first. I think I deserved that much." He shook his head, looking near tears. "Although lately I'm not sure where I stand with you. Maybe my time here is done."

With that he got onto the elevator and pushed a button. Julie was speechless as the elevator doors closed and was unable to respond to the last thing he'd said. All she knew was that she'd made one of her men happy and the other one miserable which only made the decision she had to make that much more difficult.

Trying to find a comfortable position Julie sighed in exasperation, longing for a good night's sleep in a comfortable bed. Her back was never going to be the same again after all this time spent sleeping in the rack of torture that the hospital called a sleeper chair.

Staring up at the ceiling Julie knew that the time had come for a decision to be made. Kevin was leaving for Boston in two days and she had to choose. But that was easier said than done. She loved both of her men and so did Carly. It was all a matter of which decision could she make that she wouldn't look back on and wonder if she'd done the right thing.

Julie lay awake for a long time that night, not falling asleep until the early morning hours, and even then her sleep was restless at best as even in sleep her mind was turning over everything in her head, trying to make an impossible decision between the two men who loved her and her daughter.

CHAPTER 12

K evin sat on a bench outside the hospital as he waited for Julie to emerge. It had been almost three weeks since Carly's bone marrow transplant and she was growing stronger and healthier by the day. Kevin had wanted to stay in Arizona longer, but if he wanted to keep his job he had to return to Boston and soon.

Sitting there on the bench Kevin leaned back and closed his eyes, trying to remember in detail every single moment he'd spent with Julie since arriving in Phoenix. The thought of returning to Boston and never seeing the woman he loved again was almost too much to bear. He didn't know how he was going to survive when he couldn't see Julie every day as he had for the last few weeks.

"Hey, there. You ready to go?"

Julie's lilting voice broke startled Kevin out of his thoughts. Looking up at her Kevin forced a smile to his lips, having to fight back the urge to beg her to let him stay with her and Carly. She hadn't specifically said that she'd chosen Aaron, but Kevin knew from her body language and the tense way she held herself around him that she'd made her choice.

"Ready as I'll ever be," he finally answered, standing up and grabbing the handle of his suitcase. "How's Carly handling everything?"

Julie looked sad and worried. "She's upset. She wants you to stay longer." Julie was quiet for a moment before she continued. "But she's tough and now that she knows you and knows that you're part of her life I think she'll be OK."

Kevin nodded, but stayed silent. Saying goodbye to Carly had been the most gut wrenching experience of his life and afterward he'd had to go the men's restroom to cry. He'd stayed in there nearly ten minutes, long enough for Julie to get worried enough to go in after him.

They crossed the parking lot and climbed into their separate cars. Julie intended to follow Kevin to the airport so they could say goodbye in relative privacy. Kevin was grateful that the airport wasn't far away because his vision was impaired by the tears that were threatening to fall.

They arrived at the airport with more than an hour to spare before Kevin had to board his plane. He returned the rental car and rode with Julie to the terminal where he was able to check his baggage quickly and without any trouble.

Julie had found a seat near the baggage claim and Kevin joined her, both of them sitting stiffly and not saying anything. Kevin suspected it wouldn't do any good, but he had to say the words or he'd regret it for the rest of his life.

"I love you, Julie. I don't want to leave."

"Please, don't say that, Kevin. Don't make this any harder than it already is, please."

Kevin could hear the teary quality of Julie's voice and for a moment he wondered if he were getting through to her. Kevin touched Julie's face, coaxing her to look at him, and when their eyes met he said the words again. "I love you. I've never stopped loving you and I want us to have a chance."

Julie began shaking her head as though trying to ward off what Kevin was saying, but he persisted. "We could be a family; you, me and Carly. Can you honestly say that you won't live with regrets, be haunted by never ending 'what if's' after I'm gone?"

Julie looked down at her hands folding and unfolding in her lap. "I do love you, Kevin. Seeing you again and knowing why you really left back then has been such a wonderful gift. But I love Aaron too and I made a commitment to him. I can't go back on that. Too many people will be hurt if I leave him"

"But it's OK to hurt me? It could still work between us, just like we always said it would. Do you really want to go all the way with this guy if you're not completely sure he's the one? Julie, this isn't about what's right for other people or what'll make others happy. This is about you and what you want and what you want for Carly."

Kevin was growing desperate now, though he knew deep down his words would have no effect on Julie's decision. He couldn't leave without trying though, not if he ever wanted to sleep at night again. Kevin felt his heart break though when Julie stood and swung her purse over one shoulder.

"I have to go back, Kevin. I'm so sorry. I hate hurting you like this"

Kevin stood too and faced her, taking her hand in his. Julie pulled her hand free and touched his face, tears slipping unheeded down her cheeks as she caressed his face. Kevin closed his eyes and savored her touch, wishing with everything he had that this wasn't the last time he'd ever see her. Julie lightly traced Kevin's lips with her fingers, then turned and began walking away.

"Julie, please don't do this! I love you!" Kevin called after her, ignoring the looks he was receiving from the people around him.

Julie stopped for a second and Kevin could tell her shoulders were shaking with the effort of controlling her sobs. But to Kevin's dismay she began walking again and soon she had been swallowed up by the crowded terminal. Kevin's knees gave way and if the seat hadn't been behind him he would have ended up on the floor. Putting his head in his hands Kevin let the tears fall, not fully aware of just how much pain he was in until a strangled sob ripped from his chest. After that there was no stopping it and he simply sat there and cried.

Julie made it from the airport to the hospital simply by force of will. Her vision was completely obscured by a film of tears and her chest was beginning to ache with the force of her sobs. Pulling into the hospital parking lot Julie parked the car and leaned her head against the steering wheel, giving in to the gut wrenching sobs.

When the sobs tapered down to hitches and hiccups Julie opened her visor mirror and winced at the sight of her blotchy, tear stained face. She did the best she could do with her appearance then, taking a deep breath, climbed out of the car and headed into the hospital.

She was able to keep her composure until she reached the door to Carly's room and saw Aaron sitting in the chair watching Carly sleep. Seeing Aaron suddenly brought everything into clearer focus and she knew then exactly what she wanted, what she had to do.

Aaron looked up and when he saw her standing there in the doorway an unreadable expression came over his face. "Did Kevin leave yet?" he asked, trying his best to keep his voice casual.

Julie met Aaron's gaze and held it, "His plane leaves in an hour."

Aaron looked intently at Julie, studying her almost, and then simply nodded his head. "Are you OK with that?" he finally asked and Julie winced at the uncertainty in his voice.

"Let me go get Leighton to watch Carly. We need to talk and I'd rather do it somewhere private."

Aaron didn't answer as Julie turned and left the room. She got lucky in her search for Leighton who immediately agreed to sit with Carly for a little while. Julie returned to her daughter's room and said to Aaron, "Will you come with me to the garden, Aaron?"

He hesitated for a second before rising from the chair and joining Julie. Julie turned to Leighton. "We'll try not to be too long, Leighton."

"Take your time," she replied and Julie smiled at her before leading the way up to the rooftop garden. Neither of them spoke for a few long moments; they simply sat at Julie's usual table, both deep in thought.

"Did you sleep with him, Julie?" Aaron finally asked.

The abruptness of his question left Julie feeling off balance and she was unable to meet his eyes. Her silence was all Aaron needed to confirm what he'd been suspecting for a while.

"You don't want him to leave, do you?"

Julie reached for Aaron's hand and, after a moment's hesitation, Aaron reluctantly allowed her to intertwine her fingers with his.

"Aaron, you need to understand something. Kevin and I will always have a connection, a unique bond, because we share a child together. There's a part of me that will always love Kevin. I've let go of the pain and bitterness from my past that I've carried around for years and it feels amazing. I feel light and free again, more like my old self than I've been in years. Can you understand that?"

"What does that mean for us?" Aaron asked, his voice barely audible.

Julie touched Aaron's chin with her finger, coaxing him to look at her. He looked up and their eyes met and held for a long moment.

"It means that I love you, Aaron. I'm sorry for hurting you and I know that what I did with Kevin hurts you. But it was something I had to do. It put paid to my past in a way that I don't thing else could have. Can you forgive me?"

Aaron couldn't help but feel suddenly hopeful. "Does that mean you're choosing me?" he asked, slowly.

Julie smiled at him, leaned over and kissed his cheek. "I chose you months ago. It just took me a little while to realize it." She kissed him again. "I love you, Aaron," she repeated, her voice husky with emotion.

Aaron put his arms around Julie, pulling her close, as a wide smile spread across his face. Julie hugged him back, her arms tight around his neck, and she closed her eyes, savoring everything about this amazing man that she loved. The scent of his cologne, the way his beard stubble scratched at her skin, the feel of his hard body against hers. At that moment she knew in her heart, without a doubt, she had made the right decision.

CHAPTER 13

fter over three grueling months, on the first day of October, Carly was released from the hospital and on her way home. Carly was absolutely giddy with excitement as she crawled into the backseat of Aaron's car. She was still going to have to do outpatient therapy for the next year and would be cooped up in the house for another few months, but they all agreed it was better than the hospital.

The three of them kept up a steady stream of chatter during the thirty minute drive from Phoenix to Scottsdale. When they pulled into the townhouse complex parking lot Julie saw what was waiting for them and her jaw dropped in shock.

Standing in front of their unit stood a small crowd of people beneath a huge banner that said 'Welcome Home, Carly!' painted on it in rainbow colors. It seemed like everyone she and Carly knew and loved was there. Evelyn, Virginia, and Nancy were there, beaming broadly. Julie was touched to see that Leighton had come to welcome Carly home and she could tell that it made Carly happy to see her friend as well. Julie's best friends were there as were Carly's friends and their parents.

After parking the car Aaron went around to the passenger side and helped Carly out of the car. Julie held her hand as they made their slow way up the walk and Carly was immediately engulfed in hugs from everyone. Julie had tears slipping down her cheeks as her friends hugged her and told her how glad they were that Carly was better. Aaron stayed a safe distance away and Julie turned to him, wondering if he had been expecting this.

"Did you know they were planning this?"

Aaron shrugged, a sheepish expression on his face. "I might have heard something," he said, evasively, and Julie laughed.

"We're not staying long. Carly needs her rest; we just had to come and welcome you guys home," Julie's friend Sanya said and Julie hugged her again.

"Thank you all so much. This means more than you can possibly imagine."

The joy Julie felt at the wonderful welcome home surprise was indescribable. She'd always known that she and her daughter had a lot of friends, but this had shown them just how wonderful those friends really were. It truly was a wonderful homecoming for all of them.

Julie woke from a sound sleep late that night. Turning over she looked at Aaron who was sprawled on his back, sound asleep. Looking at the clock she squinted, bringing the digital numbers into focus. It was only 2:30. She couldn't figure out what had woken her.

Softly, so she wouldn't wake Aaron, Julie crawled out of bed and crept cautiously out of the bedroom and down the hall to Carly's room. Carly's door was only partly shut and Julie eased it open slowly, not wanting to wake her sleeping daughter. Slipping quietly into the room Julie sat on the edge of Carly's bed.

Carly was half on her side and half on her belly, the covers tangled around her. Julie straightened the sheets and blanket, pulling them up around Carly. After a moment's hesitation Julie reached out a hand and gently touched Carly's face, amazed as she always was at how beautiful her daughter was. She seemed even more beautiful now than ever before, now that she was going to live.

For a long time Julie sat there, watching her daughter sleep, before finally standing up from the bed. She bent and kissed Carly's cheek, smiling when her daughter snorted softly in her sleep, and went back to bed. When she crawled into bed and pulled the covers up she was startled at the sound of Aaron's voice beside her.

"Where did you go?" he asked, softly.

Julie rolled over to face him. "I went to check on Carly. I'm sorry if I woke you, honey."

Aaron sidled closer to Julie, putting his arms around her, and she snuggled against him. "It's alright. Is Carly OK"

"She's sound asleep," Julie said.

"Is something wrong, honey?" Aaron asked, his fingers running lightly up and down her arm. His touch made Julie's skin tingle deliciously.

"Nothing's wrong. In fact, for the first time in months, everything is just right. Carly's healthy, you and I are together and happy and I've put paid to my past with Kevin." Julie lifted her head from where it rested on Aaron's chest and looked at him, a soft expression in her eyes. "Everything is perfect," she whispered softly.

She lay her head back down on Aaron's chest, savoring his arms around her, the steady rise and fall of his chest as he breathed. Just before drifting back to sleep in Aaron's arms Julie's last thought was that it couldn't possibly get any better than this.

EPILOGUE

October 2011

*A*mazingly, it did get better. The literal definition of the word "gift" reads something like this: something given voluntarily without payment in return, as to show favor toward someone, honor an occasion, or make a gesture of assistance; present. That definition summed up in just a few words what Kevin had given to Carly six years ago. By giving Carly the gift of life he was also giving Julie the gift of a life more wonderful than anything she'd ever dared to hope for.

Now at the age of thirty two Julie was a wife, a mother and still a doctor. It was the wife and mother that defined most aspects of her life. Julie was living the life she'd once dreamed of, the life she'd given up believing she could ever have, and there were still days when she almost couldn't believe it was real.

Aaron proposed to Julie on Christmas day in 2005. They were married in a small church ceremony three months later in March of 2006. Carly was her mother's maid of honor and the church was packed with family and friends. After the wedding Julie and Aaron left for their honeymoon to Bermuda where they spent ten glorious days. Carly was left in the care of Evelyn while her mother and Aaron were gone.

After a year of outpatient therapy Carly was declared cancer free in late summer of 2006. Her relationship with her father over the last six years grew in leaps and bounds. Julie and Kevin had worked out a tentative visitation arrangement that satisfied both of them. Now at the age of sixteen Carly was testing the boundaries of her mother's patience more and more often. When Carly asked to go to Boston this past summer Julie had agreed, knowing that she and her daughter needed some space from each other.

Without being under the thumb of his father Kevin had been able to move on with his own life as well. It had taken him a few years to accept that his relationship with Julie was truly over. Meeting Candace, the woman who would become his wife in 2008, helped as well. Candace was as different from Julie as it was possible to be and Kevin was deeply in love with her. Kevin became a father for the second time just last year when Candace gave birth to a daughter; McKenna.

On their first anniversary Aaron told Julie he wanted to start a family of their own. Julie threw out her birth control the following day and was pregnant within weeks. Their son, Daniel Jeremy, was born in December of 2007. Audrey Virginia followed in 2010, completing their little family.

Along with all the happiness and joy of the past six years there was sadness as well. Julie's dear friend and Carly's longtime babysitter, Virginia, passed away of a massive coronary in 2006. In addition Julie and her mother were still not on speaking terms. Neither Julie nor Carly had spoken to or seen Elizabeth since July of 2005. Jeremy called frequently and visited when he could. He admitted to Julie that her mother had been furious when Julie married Aaron. The tension between Jeremy and Elizabeth eventually became too much and they divorced in 2009 after over thirty years of marriage.

For many months Julie blamed herself for the divorce, but after a lot of long talks with her father she realized that there had been tension in the marriage for years and that a split had seemed inevitable at some point. After the divorce Jeremy moved to Arizona to be closer to Julie and her family which delighted them all to no end. It hurt Julie that she and her mother had grown so far apart. Julie had been close to her mother as a child, but as long as Elizabeth refused to accept Aaron as part of the family there could be no hope for reconciliation.

The amazing life Julie led now was a precious gift. She was even more deeply in love with her husband than she had been the day they exchanged their vows and rings. She had three gorgeous children. Carly was cancer free, a senior in high school and preparing for college and a bright future the following year. Daniel and Audrey were growing up fast and were the absolute joy of Julie's life.

If anyone had told Julie six years ago that she would be this happy someday she would have said they were crazy. But now, watching her husband and children playing outside on the back patio, Julie knew she'd received an extraordinary gift, one that she would cherish and protect always.

With a content smile playing on her lips Julie slipped out onto the patio to join her family as they played together under the bright Arizona sunshine.

ABOUT THE AUTHOR

*W*riting a novel shouldn't be about making money or becoming famous. It should be about touching the readers' lives and that is what I hope to accomplish with my work. Being a published author has been a lifelong goal of mine. To see my work published would ultimately fulfill something inside me. As a full time college student I recently completed a Writing class in which I learned a great deal about how to hone my craft and make it better. I am 28 years old, single and I've lived the majority of my life in Hawley, Pennsylvania.